I0656680

Andrew Lang, Francesco Colonna

The Strife of Love in a Dream

being the Elizabethan version of the first book of the Hypnerotomachia

Andrew Lang, Francesco Colonna

The Strife of Love in a Dream
being the Elizabethan version of the first book of the Hypnerotomachia

ISBN/EAN: 9783337438852

Printed in Europe, USA, Canada, Australia, Japan

Cover: Foto ©Andreas Hilbeck / pixelio.de

More available books at **www.hansebooks.com**

The Tudor Library.

THE STRIFE OF LOVE IN A DREAM.

*** *Five hundred copies of this Edition are printed.*

THE

STRIFE OF LOVE IN A DREAM

BEING

THE ELIZABETHAN VERSION

OF

THE FIRST BOOK OF THE

HYPNEROTOMACHIA

OF

FRANCESCO COLONNA

A NEW EDITION

BY

ANDREW LANG, M.A.

LONDON

PUBLISHED BY DAVID NUTT IN THE STRAND

MDCCCXC

INTRODUCTION.

EIGHT or nine years ago I chanced to go into the shop of Mr. Toovey, in Piccadilly, and began turning over the cheaper and less considered of his books. Among them I found "*Hypnerotomachia.* The strife of Loue in a Dreame. At London, Printed for Simon Waterson, and are to be sold at his shop, in S. Paules Churchyard, at Cheape-gate, 1592." This is the usual title, my specimen, as will be seen, varied slightly. The Bodleian copy also contains this (the 2nd) title. The book was a small thin quarto, not in good condition. It contained no name of author or translator, and the initials, R. D., of the dedication (the most interesting part of the work), tell us nothing. Mr. Douce conjectures that they may stand for Robert Dallyngton, the translator of "The Mirrour of Mirth, etc., from the French of Bonaventure des Periers," London, 1583, 4to. The woodcuts were excessively debased reminiscences of those famous examples in the Aldine edition of 1499. The little book seemed an oddity, and I purchased it from Mr. Toovey for the sum of twenty shillings. I was then but an ignorant collector of the Cheap and the Odd in books, and Mr. Toovey's own attention had been given to more beautiful things than this shabby quarto. I took it home, read it, wrote a little article on it in the *St. James's Gazette*, and found out that the volume was imperfect. Having exhausted my interest in it, I carried it back to Mr. Toovey, pointed out the absence of the last five pages, and returned it, in exchange for "*Les Memoires de la Reyne Marguerite*, à Paris, chez Claude Barbin, dans la Grand' Salle du Pallais, au Signe de la Croix. M.D.C.LXI," in yellow morocco. I never made a worse bargain. The *Hypnerotomachia*, imperfect as my copy was, is among the very rarest of books, and therefore among the most desirable. This particular copy, by the way, was "printed for Iohn Busbie, and to be sold at his Schoppe, at the west doore of Paules." Meanwhile M. Claude Popelin had long been lying in wait for the English version of Francesco Colonna's book. He was engaged on his excellent version of the original, to which this preface owes a boundless debt for information.[1] The English version was not to be found in the British Museum, nor in the Bibliothèque Nationale, nor in the libraries of Berlin, Amsterdam, the Hague, Leyden, Utrecht, Vienna, or Munich, nor have I heard of it even in America. In short this despised and rejected tract is among the extreme rarities of the world. And I had swopped it for *La Reyne Marguérite* in a new edition! One man's loss is another's gain, and M. Popelin, hunting the sale rooms in London, bought my castaway copy "à un de ces prix qu'on n'avoue pas à sa ménagère." M. Popelin deserved to get it for his learned edition, and I deserved to lose it for my carelessness. I am only sorry

[1] Liseux, Paris, 1883.

I did not know he wanted it, when it would have been much at his service, for love, and the *ménagère* would not have been justly vexed by extravagance *Vile damnum*, after all, the loss of the book, if we look only at the literary merits of the *Hypnerotomachia* in Elizabethan English. The translation is ignorant and unintelligible: a meaning cannot be made out of much of it, and the sense, when the translator does "deviate into sense," is not always that of his original. We have reprinted it with absolute fidelity. The idea of altering the punctuation was mooted, but where the translator's meaning was obscure, the original text cast no light on it whatever; so any alteration would have been conjectural. Thus the volume reappears with all its sins on its head, except the horrors of its barbarous illustrations. For these miseries, a few examples copied from the original have been substituted. Obvious misprints alone have been corrected, and the text is reproduced from the example in the Bodleian Library at Oxford.

About the original *Hypnerotomachia*, and its author, and illustrator, and meaning, all that is ever likely to be known has been set forth by M. Popelin. As is usual in antiquarian subjects, where almost everything is uncertain, there is a great deal of learning about Francesco Colonna, the author, his mistress Polia, his purpose, and his book. The *Hypnerotomachia Poliphili*, "Loves strife in a dream with the Loves of Pollia," as we may paraphrase the title, was published, in folio, by Aldus Manutius in 1499. It contains an hundred and seventy-two woodcuts, which have been attributed, wildly, to Raphael, to either Bellini, to Andrea Mantegna, to the two Montagnas, to Carpaccio, to the author himself, to the anonymous Master of the Dolphins, to the Bolognese engraver Peregrini, and probably to other people.[1] M. Eugène Piot introduced the belief in the Master of the Dolphins, who illustrated many other books for the Aldi. M. Popelin is inclined to agree with M. Piot, especially as the animals in an *Æsop* illustrated by the Master of the Dolphins closely resemble those in the *Hypnerotomachia*. Mr. W. B. Scott (*Athenæum*, March 27, April 10, 1880) votes for Stephanus Caesenus Peregrinus. This opinion rests on certain initials, subscribed to the frontispieces of certain other works of the period. But nothing can certainly be known, and internal evidence is notoriously untrustworthy. As Mr. Carlyle says about the poet of the Nibelungenlied, to be certain about the letters that make up his name would be of very little benefit to us. It is probable that many an artist of his date, inspired by the old art and the new learning, could do all that he did.

Francesco Colonna, too, the author of the *Hypnerotomachia*, is little more than the shadow of a name. Benoît de Court, writing in 1533 on the *Arresta Amorum* of Martial de Paris, calls Colonna *multiscius*, "full of knowledge." That he knew a great deal about ancient architecture, rather late Greek and Roman essayists, and obscure mythology, is clear enough from his book, whereof the object is to make a parade of learning. Rabelais cites him in *Gargantua* (i. ix.).

In the seventeenth and eighteenth centuries authors on architecture speak highly of Colonna, and offer guesses about his biography. He was said to have belonged to a family of Lucca, and to have been born in Venice about 1433. If his book was finished, as the colophon says, in 1467, when he would have been thirty-four, it may contain

[1] Popelin, i. cxcviii.

all the lore and the learning of his youth, a sacrifice of them to the goddess of Pedantry,

Une chapelle de parfums
Et de cierges mélancholiques.

The biography, however, is made up, like many classical biographies, out of hints in the author's work. Polia, the beloved of Francesco, would be, on this showing, Ippolita, niece of Teodoro Lelio, bishop of Treviso, in whose household Colonna had a place. The authority cited is a MS. note on a copy of the book in the library of the Dominicans delle Zatere. The note points out that the first letters of each chapter in the book, when placed together in order, produce—

Poliam frater Franciscus Colonna peramavit. Ad huc vivit Venetiis in S. Iohannæ et Paulo.

The biography, or romance, goes on to say that Polia and Francesco were betrothed; that, in terror of the plague, the lady vowed to take the veil if she escaped with life; that she kept her word, and that Colonna also went into religion, and became a monk in 1464. But all this is pure fiction. Colonna was a monk as early as 1455. From a Venetian MS. in the convent of St. John and St. Paul, we gather that Colonna died, at a great old age, in 1527. M. Popelin's personal researches in Italy have added nothing to the few scattered notices of a long and quiet life. As to Polia, we must guess for ourselves whether she was once a living girl, whether she was a mere ideal, or whether she is an allegory of antique beauty and learning. The prettiest and most human passage in the book contains, at least, a picture of life, and tells how Polia was sitting at her window, sunning her long yellow locks, when Poliphile passed by, and was caught in that golden net, as Lucius was by the hair of Fotis.

Every day he wandered by the palace windows, every night he would sing beneath them, and all to no avail. Then Polia, in fear of a pestilence, "vowed herself to Diana." In vain he implored her to be his, with abundance of reference to the Fates, Atys, Agave, Pentheus, Scylla, and Charybdis, and that African lake which is cold by day under the sun, and boiling hot at night. Perhaps no woman was ever in this manner wooed; Poliphile, we may be certain, never urged his suit in this absurd way; more probably there was no suit to urge, no Polia, no love affair, nothing but the inexperienced day-dream of a young monk who is sorry for his lost youth, and feigns in fancy the kisses that never were real. Polia beholds, in a dream, the punishments that love inflicts on his rebels and renegades (as in Boccaccio), and betakes herself to consult Venus in her temple. Here she is told a good deal about the two shafts of Love, the leaden and the golden, and learns the sad fate of a lady who scorned desire till she was twenty-eight, and at that advanced age was smitten by passion, and given to a hideous old man in marriage. The second state of this lady was therefore worse than the first, and the nauseous descriptions prove that "realism" is no new thing in literature. The lady determined to slay herself, but, classical to the last, she crowned herself with fatal smylax, and the leaves of ostry, appropriate vegetables, before dealing the fatal stroke. Venus then points out to Polia that if she wastes her time in youth, she will vainly dye her hair, and rouge in her longing later years.

It is an inordinately long sermon, rich in pedantry, and with a Greek epigram or two for text. Polia repents, and thinks of all the classic stories about hard-hearted and despairing lovers. She seeks Poliphile, finds him fainting, she upbraids Lucina (who has presided over her own birth), and finally, rouses Poliphile, sits on his knee, and kisses him in a hearty fashion, sympathetically rendered by the artist. He was tired, no doubt, of nymphs, cupids, pyramids, fountains, altars, tombs, and was happy to design persons who loved " in a more human sort of way." But presently the priestesses of Diana, in the exercise of their duty, turned poor Polia and her lover out of the temple. After the reconciled lovers have told their stories with immense learning and at enormous length, Poliphile is wakened, as Rufinus was kept awake, by the song of the nightingale, singing,

Τηρεὺς, Τηρεὺς ἐμὲ ἐβιάσατο.

And he rises, and behold it is all a dream, and none of it probably was ever anything but a dream. Perhaps Polia was Πολία;—hoar antiquity. Perhaps she was but a pale imitation of the Lauras and Beatrices of Italian poetry. We may believe that the author had seen fair ladies bathing their locks in the sunlight to steal its golden dye, but it is hard to believe that he ever ventured to woo any one of them, with his examples out of Pliny, Ptolemy, Hyginus, and Ovid. He was fond of antiquity no doubt, but in an almost barbaric fashion. He carried to absurd lengths the uncritical fanaticism of the Renaissance. He did, indeed, love what was beautiful in art, and in architecture and sculpture especially. But he loved it all with a pedantic lack of discrimination. His learning is late, and sometimes mediæval. Pliny supplies him with the marvellous natural history of plants and animals, with their wonderful virtues, which was so dear to Lilly and the Euphuists. Nature herself he has never observed at all, and he reads into her all the fables that folklore or folly devised, and false learning and false taste perpetrated. As Pliny, Ælian, and mediæval works as credulous as theirs supply Colonna with a work of ideal grotesques; as he lives, so to speak, on an earth peopled by monsters out of missals, so Vitruvius inspires that delight in architecture which is, perhaps, the real motive of his long romance. Using the common mediæval formula of a dream, in that dream he sees palaces, pyramids, fountains, statues, and is far less in love with Polia than with the Roman art of buildings; with altars, pillars, marbles of Paros, or of Syene. An amphitheatre intoxicates him; he waxes enthusiastic over baths and tombs, and long classical pageants, masques of gods, with all their appropriate symbolism. He is "an art-intoxicated man," bemused and almost maddened by a vision of æsthetic triumphs. When he speaks of the intoxication of the senses, as he does more than need be, the nymphs who allure him are ghosts risen from old marbles, or figures from the frescoes of his sympathetic contemporaries. Such frescoes of triumphant pagan processions were frequently painted by an artist of Treviso, Donatello, on the walls of the Bishop's palace. We may easily fancy Colonna watching these as they grew beneath the painter's hand, revelling in them, releasing the nymphs and goddesses from them in a book which is itself the revel of the sensuous Renaissance. His landscape is usually a garden landscape, artificial enough, artificial as the odd pedantic medley of his language, a mixture of styles, tongues, and idioms, which has been compared to the jargon of Rabelais's Limousin. From the dedicatory epistle it seems that Colonna wrote his book in another language first, perhaps in Latin, and then translated it into what could hardly be called the vernacular. He uses many words from the Greek, as *philopono*, laborious, *chrysocari*, with golden head (of Polia), *gampsounycha*, with crooked talons, and so forth. Greek was so new, then, and so delightful was their learning to the learned, as later to Ronsard and the French Pleiad, that they thought it could never be out of place. Such Greek as Colonna's is rather like the Baboo English, which often makes us laugh. Perhaps most of our Greek is little better, and Colonna's queer words are not odder than *Panmixia*, a new invention of scientific men. His extreme indulgence in allusions to obscure myths is another trait of his manner which becomes excessively fatiguing. His whole work, in fact, is a specimen of the Renaissance in its fever of paganism. He is a Christian monk, vowed to poverty and chastity, and nothing is dear to him but heathenism and luxury in all its forms. Beautiful naked bodies, beautiful faces, beautiful buildings, fountains, temples, triumphs of dead gods, a Venus of onyx and sardonyx, nursing a Cupid above the sepulchre of Adonis, these things and such as these are his sole delight. The book is, indeed, a dream, and the dream of a monk, insatiate of material loveliness, and the pride of life ; revelling in a fancied feast of knowledge, art, language, and love. M. Popelin has shown how much Colonna owes to the *Fiametta* of Boccaccio, how, especially, Boccaccio and our author paint the beauty of women in similar terms, but these pictures were, in fact, the commonplace of the new age, touched by the classics, just as red lips, curled locks, and eyes of vair, are the commonplace in mediæval romances, such as *Aucassin et Nicolete*. Indeed the *Hypnerotomachia* holds as much of the Middle Ages as of the Renaissance. There is the old machinery, the dream on May Day, the wandering in woods, the terrible monsters, the meetings with nymphs, and with the beloved, the strain of allegory. All this was familiar to Chaucer, and before Chaucer. The mythological allusions, too, had long been favourites, the real novelty is in the pell-mell of multifarious knowledge, the lack of humanity and knightly love, the odd mixed style, the superabundant details about works of art. It is as if the spirit of the Renaissance, pedantry and all, had entered violently into a monkish reader of the "Romance of the Rose," driving out a few affectations, and bringing with it many others and worse.

It would not turn to the credit of human taste, had a work in which the wrong kind of learning is the inspiration, proved popular at any time. And at no time was the *Hypnerotomachia* popular. Like a French author of the last century, who was copiously illustrated, Dorat, Colonna has not been merged in the sea of time, but *se sauve sur les planches*. The number and beauty of the designs in his pages has caused many to turn them over, who dream of nothing less than reading him. The first edition, by Aldus, at Venice, in 1499, is a splendid folio. It was put forth at the expense of Leonardo Crasso, who says he was loath that so admirable a book should lie longer in darkness. Of this Crasso, except that he was master of arts, and a doctor in Canon Law, very little is known. He came of a Milanese house, and dwelt in Verona. The date of the book is given in a note at the end of the *errata*, which in most examples have been torn out, perhaps because the owners preferred the much earlier date (1466) of the Colophon. This edition did not sell well. In the years 1507-1511, Leonardo Crasso, who paid the expenses of publication, asked for a ten years' extension of his privilege. The work had cost him hundreds of ducats, and the disturbed times had made it a drug in the market. The unlucky Crasso found out (what is true though a hundred Mr. Besants deny it) that there is considerable risk in the business of publishing. Only rich people with splendid libraries could afford to buy such a costly and cumbrous volume, the taste of the day preferred the little Aldine octavoes. Probably Crasso was left with many examples of the *Hypnerotomachia* on his shelves. A second edition was published at the press of the Aldines in 1545, with woodcuts inferior, in a few instances, to the original illustrations. In the following year, 1546, Loys Cyaneus put forth, for Jacques Kerver, the first French translation, a folio of 326 pages. The translation is by Jean Martin, or was edited by him. The woodcuts have been characteristically reproduced by a French artist. They are more graceful and elegant than the older work. Many will agree with M. Popelin in preferring the French to the Italian designs. The artist is unknown, Jean Cousin, Geoffrey Tory, and Jean Gonjon have been named. In France there have been six editions of the book between 1540 and 1811. None of these versions was faithful to the original, though none perhaps deserts it so readily as our English paraphrase. Mr. Richard Copley Christie, author of the Life of Etienne Dolet, possesses a French MS. rendering of 1703, the author whereof, Elie Richard, has taken singular liberties with the text. As M. Popelin quotes the old proverb, *Traduttore, travitore.* Imperfect and reckless as is our English version, it is not likely that any one will find it worth while to translate into English the *Hypnerotomachia* once more. The style might have pleased Leigh Hunt, or the unripe youth of Keats. They would have enjoyed the florid quaintnesses, as when the sun "crysped up his irradient heyres," or where we read of "the christalline teares of the sweete morning." "By reason of the milde and gentle ayre ther was a still quyet whisht," is another pretty phrase; indeed, Keats, when at work on *Endymion*, might have ransacked this old book for Elizabethan dainties. The dictionary maker and word-hunter will find rare sport in such terms as "mustulent," "fertlesse," "quadranguled plaints," "gracilament," "terrible eyes cavernate," "a wrympled forehead" (*wrymple* is good), "silver crolley," "cleare appact," "incalcerate light," and "gulaterie," the "vypered caduce," "remigiall bones." There are pretty odd names of flowers, as "Venus Navill," "Erogennet," "mouse-ear," "Lady hayre," "Prickmaddam," "goulden locks," and so forth, and wild spellings, as Pscyphes for Psyche, reminding one of Spsiche, in Lagrange's register of Moliere's theatre. There is now and then in the struggling and tormented style a little oasis, refreshed with "the sweet chirpings and quiet singing of Birds, and the temperate and healthful ayre," or where "under this auncient, sure, and fair bridge did run a most cleare swift water, deviding itself into two currents, which ran most colde, making a soft continual still noyse in their freesed, broken, and *nibbled* channels." One is reminded of Horace and his

> *rura, quae Liris quieta*
> *Mordet aqua taciturnus amnis,*

or Lucretius with his

> *ripas radentia flumina rodunt.*

There are pleasing groups too in the old translations: the three damsels with an ewer of gold, a bason, and a towell of white silk, recall the nymphs in Circe's hall, or a singularly charming scene in the *Mabinogion*, or a beautiful fresco of Botticelli's once in the Villa Lemmi. The white dress of the girls "leaving to be seen the pleasant valley between their fair breasts," proves the monkish author to have had a taste for other than architectural beauties; evidence of this is more copious in the original text, though, in the translation too, the monk finds the maids "flamigerous." But on the whole, he prefers that modest nymph "whose sweet proportioned body needed no pinching in with French wastes," which he calls "unwholesome weare," but which have survived all preachings of moralists and remonstrances of artists. Indeed Poliphile, for an ecclesiastic, has a very pretty taste in female attire, which he describes not less lovingly than his arches and tombs, fountains and altars. He has, as he says, "greedy eyes," "greedy eyes and unsatiable desire to look and overlook the exquisite perfection of ancient work." This is all his care, the delight of the eye, and all his book is a laborious revel of æsthetic enjoyment. He has a kind of gluttony beauty, his work is the overladen banquet of an artistic Barmecide. Thus it is, in its way, a true example and illustration of the Italian Renaissance, a compendium of its pleasures and pedantries, a fantastic effort to satisfy its desire of things impossible. *Impossibilium cupitor* is the author, and one may blame or praise the change of mood which makes him almost impossible to read. However, Colonna had a theory of life, a vision of his own of what life should be, to be desirable. It is as impossible, and almost as uninviting, as any other ideal, social or political. For life, as it is, may not be perfect, but it is more endurable than life as visionaries would remake it, and, at least, we can taste and moderately enjoy all ideals "in this world, the isle of dreams."

HYPNEROTOMACHIA

THE STRIFE OF LOUE IN A DREAME

AT LONDON

PRINTED FOR WILLIAM HOLME, AND ARE TO BE SOLD AT HIS SHOPPE, NEERE THE GREAT NORTH DOORE OF PAULES.

MDXCII.

TO THE THRISE

HONOVRABLE AND EVER LYVING VERTVES OF

SYR PHILLIP SYDNEY KNIGHT;

AND TO THE

RIGHT HONORABLE AND OTHERS WHATSOEVER,

WHO LIVING LOVED HIM, AND

BEING DEAD GIVE HIM

HIS DVE.

To the Right Honourable ROBERT DEUORAX, Earle of Effex and Ewe, Vifcount Hereford, and Bourghchier, Lorde Ferrers of Chartley, Bourghchier and Louaine, Maifter of the Queenes Maieftics Horfe, and Knight of the moft noble order of the Garter, is wifhed, the perfection of all happineffe, and tryumphant felicitie in his life, and in the worlde to come.

Hen I had determined (Right honorable) to dedicate this Booke, to the euerlyuing vertues of that matchleffe Knight *Syr Phillip Sydney;* me thought that I could not finde out a more Noble perfonage then your felfe, and more fit, to patronize, fhield, and defende my dutie to the deade, then your Honour, whofe greatnes is fuch, and vertues of that power, as who fo commendeth them, deferueth not to be accounted a flatterer, but he that doth not the fame, may be thought an euill willer. Hovv your Honor vvill accept hereof, I make no doubt, becauſe that curteſie attendeth vpon true nobilitie; but my humble requeſt is, that your Honor may not thinke of me (by the tytle of the Booke, and ſome part of the diſcourſe) as if I vvere amorous, and did ſpeake according to my ovvne paſſions, for I beeing reſtrained of my liberty, and helde in the graue of obliuion, where I ſtill as yet remaine; oppreſſed with Melancholie, and wearied vvith deeper ſtudies, I vvas glad to beguile the time with theſe conceits, anothomiſing in them, the vanitie of this life, and vncertaintie of the delights therof, in the Dreame of *Poliphilus;* which if it ſhall pleaſe your Honor at conuenient leyſure to looke ouer, pardoning what you finde amiſſe, and weighing my good will, I ſhall thinke my ſelfe moſt happy.

And thus I humbly take my leaue, vntill that I may preſent your Honour, with a matter more fitting the ſame.

Your Honors deuoted,

R. D.

ANONYMI ELEGIA AD LECTOREM.

C*Andide* Poliphilum *narrentem somnia* Lector
auſcultus, ſummo ſomnia meſſa polo,
Non operam perdes; non hæc audiſſe pigebit,
Tam variis mirum rebus abundant opus.
Si grauis & tetricus contemnis erotica, rerum
noſce precor ſeriem tam bene diſpoſitam,
Abnuis? ac ſaltem ſtylus & noua lingua novuſq;
ſermo grauis, ſophia, ſi rogat aſpicias.
Id quoq; ſi renuis; geometrica cerne vetuſta
plurima millicis diſce referta notis.
Hic ſunt Pyramides, thermæ, ingentiſq; coloſſi,
ac Obeliſcorum forma vetusta patet.
Hic diuerſa baſis fulget, variæque columnæ
illarumq; arcus; Zophora, epistilia,
Et capita atq; trabes, et cum quadrante coronæ
ſymmetriæ, & quicquid tecta ſuperba facit.
Hic regnim cernes exculta palatia, cultus
Nympharum, fontes, egregraſque epulus.
Hinc bicolor chorea eſt latronum, expreſſaque tota
in Laberintheis vita hominem tenebris.
Hinc lege de triplici quæ maieſtate tonantis
Dicat; & in portis egerit ipſe tribus.
Polia qua fuerit forma quam culta; tryumphos
inde louis ſpecta quatuor ætherios.
Haec præter uarios effectus narrut amoris,
atque opera & quantum ſæuiat ille Deus.

·D· DITI ET PROXER· S
.V. .F.
TREBIAE .Q.
.L.S.TREBII FILIAE A
moris monument.& pietatis aul.
sibustius uir cum .Q. summo cum
desiderio deliciose uix .men.i.d.iii·
Hæc.m.ux .quam amantiss. mihi in-
fœliciss. lachrymas & æternos luctus
reliq . extremo perturbata zelome
cum suspicaret alia em fœmi.ia-
cuiss. in furorem dulciss.conuer
so amore semet ferr.pectus per med.
transuecto necauit.hei ux.cur hoc?
mi care con.nec factũ tãt.sed et suspe
ctum amanti demere debueras.uale
lib. at ego incerta ĩfœli. &
trepida uita soluta
quiesco.
NATV RAE NOVER CAE INEVITA BILE STATV TVM
NATV RAE MATRIS BENI GNVM EDI CTV M

POLIPHILI HYPNEROTOMACHIA,

Wherein he sheweth, that all humaine and worldlie things are but a dreame, and but as vanitie it *selfe, In the setting foorth whereof many things* are figured worthie of remembrance. *The Author beginneth his* Hypnerotomachia, *to set downe the hower and time when in his sleepe it seemed to him that hee was in a quiet solitarie desart, and uninhabited plaine, and from thence afterward how he entered vnaduisedly before he was aware, with great feare, into a darke obscure and vnfrequented wood.*

The Discription of the Morning.

HAT HOURE AS PHŒBUS[1] issuing foorth, did bewtifie with brightnesse the forhead of *Leucothea*,[2] and appearing out of the Occean waues, not fully shewing his turning wheeles, that had beene hung vp, but speedily with his swift horses *Pyrous* & *Eous*,[3] hastning his course, and giuing a tincture to the Spiders webbes, among the greene leaues and tender prickles of the Vermilion Roses, in the pursuite whereof he shewed himselfe most swift & glistering, now vpon the neuer resting and still-moouing waues, he crysped vp his irradient heyres.

[1] Phœbus the Sunne.

[2] Leucothea the morning.

[3] Pyr & Eo, the horses of the Sunne.

Vppon whose vprising, euen at that instant, the vnhorned Moone dismounted hir selfe, losing from hir Chariot hir two horses, the one white and the other browne, and drewe to the Horrison[1] different from the Hemisphere[2] from whence she came.

And when as the mountaines and hilles were beautifull, and the northeast winds had left of to make barraine with the sharpnesse of their blasts the tender sprigs, to disquiet the moouing reedes, the fenny Bulrush, and weake Cyprus; to torment the foulding Vines; to trouble the bending Willowe, and to breake downe the brittle Firre bowghes, vnder the hornes of the lasciuious Bull, as they do in winter.

At that very houre, as the diuers coulered flowers and greene meades at the comming of the sunne of *Hypperion*[3] feare not his burning heate, being bedued and sprinkled with the Christalline teares of the sweete morning, when as the Halcyons[4] vpon the leuell waues of the stil, calme, and quiet flowing seas, do build their nests in sight of the sandie shore, whereas the sorrowfull *Ero* with scalding sighes did behold the dolorous and vngrate departure of hir swimming *Leander*.[5]

I lying vpon my bed, an oportune and meet freend to a wearie body, no creature accompaning me in my chamber, besides the attender vppon my body, and vsuall night lights, who after that she had vsed diuers speeches, to the end shee might comfort me, hauing vnderstood before of me, the originall cause of my hollow and deepe sighes, she indeuored hir best to moderate, if at least she might, that, my perturbed and pittifull estate. But when she sawe that I was desirous of sleepe, she tooke leaue to depart.

Then I being left alone to the high cogitations of loue, hauing passed ouer a long and tedious night without sleepe, through my barren fortune, and aduerse constellation, altogether vncomforted and sorrowfull, by means of

[1] Horison, a circle deuiding the halfe speare of the firmament from the other halfe which we doe not see.

[2] Hemispere is halfe the compasse of the visible heauen.

[3] Hyperion the Sunne.

[4] Halcyons are certaine byrds which building nere the shore vpon the waues, there will be no storme vntill the young be hatched.

[5] Leander, a young man of Abydos, who in swimming ouer Hellespont (a narow sea by Byzantium, which parteth Europ from Asia) to Sestus, was in the sight of his louer Ero of Sestus drowned, which she seeing, threw hir self down into the sea and died with him.

my vntimely and not prosperous loue, weeping, I recounted from point to point, what a thing vnequall loue is: and how fitly one may loue that dooth not loue; and what defence there may bee made against the vnaccustomed, yet dayly assaults of loue: for a naked soule altogether vnarmed, the seditious strife, especially being intestine: a fresh still sitting vpon with vnstable and new thoughts.

In this sort brought to so miserable an estate, and for a long while plunged in a deepe poole of bitter sorrowes, at length my wandring sences being wearie to feede still vpon vnsauorie and fayned pleasure, but directly and without deceit, vppon the rare diuine obiect: whose reuerende *Idea* is deeply imprinted within me, and liueth ingrauen in the secret of my heart, from which proceedeth this so great and vncessant a strife, continually renuing my cruell torments without intermission. I began the conditions of those miserable louers, who for their mistresses pleasures desire their owne deaths, and in their best delights do think themselues most vnhappie, feeding their framed passions not otherwise then with fithfull imaginations, and then as a weary bodye after a sore labour, so I, somewhat in outward shew qualified, in the payne of my sorrowfull thoughts, and hauing incloystered and shut vp the course of my distilling teares; whose drops had watered my pale cheekes, thorow amorous griefe, desired some needfull rest.

At length my moyst eyes being closed within their bloudshotten and reddish liddes, presently betwixt a bitter life and a sweet death, I was in them inuaded and ouercome, with a heauie sleepe, who with my minde and watchfull spirits, were no pertakers of so high an operation.

Methought that I was in a large, plaine, and champion

place, all greene and diuersly spotted with many sorted flowers, wherby it seemed passingly adorned. In which by reason of the milde and gentle ayre, there was a still quyet whisht: Insomuch that my attentiue eares did heare no noyse, neither did any framed speech peirce into them, but with the gratious beames of the sunne, the sliding time passed.

In which place with a fearefull admiration, looking about me, I sayd thus to my selfe. Heere appeareth no humaine creature to my sight, nor syluã beast, flying bird, coũtrey house, field tent, or shepheards cote: neyther vpon the gras could I perceiue feeding eyther flock of sheep, or heard of cattell, or rustike herdman with Oten pipe making pastorall melodie, but onely taking the benefit of the place, and quietnesse of the plaine, which assured mee to be without feare, I directed my course still forward, regarding on eyther side the tender leues and thick grasse which rested vnstirred, without the beholding of any motion.

At length my ignorant steepes brought me into a thick wood, wherinto being a pritty way entred, I could not tell how to get out of it. Wherevpon a soddaine feare inuaded my hart, and diffused itselfe into euery ioynt, so that my couler began to waxe pale, and the rather by reason that I was alone and vnarmed, and could not finde any track or path, eyther to direct me forward or lead me back againe. But a darke wood of thick bushes, sharpe thornes, tall ashes haled of the Viper, towgh Elmes beloued of the fruitfull vines, harde Ebony, strong Okes, soft Beeche and browne Hasils, who intertuining one anothers branches with a natural goodwill opposed themselues, to resist the entrance of the gratious sunne shine, with the greene couerture of their innumerable leaues. And in this sort I found myselfe in a fresh shadowe, a coole ayre, and a solytarie thicket.

Wherevpon my reason perswaded me to beleeue, that this vast wood, was onely a receptacle for sauage and hurtfull beasts, as the tusked Bore, the furious and bloudthirstie Beare, the hissing serpent, and inuading Woolfe, against which I was vnprouided to make resistance but rayther as a praye sent amongst them, miserablie to haue my flesh and bones rent and gnawne in peeces.

And thus forecasting the woorst that might follow I was resolued not to abide there, but to seeke to get out, that I might the better eschew such suspected occurrents, and taking my selfe to my feete, I wandred now this way, now that way, sometime to the right hand, sometime to the left : nowe forwarde, then backe againe, not knowing how to goe among the thicke bowghes and tearing thornes, bearing vpon my face: rending my clothes, and houlding me sometimes hanging in them, whereby my hast in getting foorth was much hyndered. In this vnaccustomed labour: and without any helpe but onely the keeping of the sunne still vpon one side, to direct mee streight forwarde: I grewe extreamely hoate and faynte, not knowing what to doe, but onely in a wearye body to conteine a minde distraught through troublesome thoughts, breathing out hollow and deepe sighes, desiring helpe of the pittifull *Cretensian Ariadne*, who for the destroying of hir monstrous brother the *Mynotaur*[1]: gaue vnto the deceitfull *Theseus* a clew of thred to conduct him foorth of the intricate laborinth, that I also by some such meanes might be deliuered out of this obscure wood.

[1] Minotaurus, a monster in Creete, born of Pasiphae, which being inclosed in the laborinth fed on mans flesh, whome Theseus slew and got out of the laborinth by a clew of thred giuen by Ariadne King Minoes daughter, after wife to Theseus, who did forsake hir, and left hir in a disinhabited Ile, notwithstanding that she had saued his life.

THE SECOND CHAPTER.

Poliphilus thus distempered in this daungerous and obscure wood, at length getteth foorth, and being come to a faire Riuer, indeuoring to rest himselfe and coole his heate, he heard a most delightful harmonie, which made him forget to drinke, and followe after the voice, whiche brought him to a woorse perplexitie.

FEARE AND DESIRE OF FREEdome thus occupying my sences, my vnderstanding was blinded, neyther did I knowe whether it were better for mee eyther to wishe for hated death, or in so dreadfull a place to hope for desired life. Thus euery way discontent, I did indeuour, with all force and diligence to get foorth, wherin the more I did striue the more I found my selfe intangled, and so infeebled with wearinesse that euery side I feared, when some cruell beast should come and deuoure me, or els vnawares to tumble downe into some deepe pit or hollow place.

Wherefore more trembling then in mustulent *Autume* be the yealow coulored leaues, hauing left their moisture, being thorowlye searched with the furious northwinde I lifted vp my hart to God, desiring as *Achemenides* being afraide of the horrible *Cyclops* rather to be slaine by the hands of *Aeneas* his enemie, rather then to suffer so odious a death.

And my deuoute prayer, sincerely vnited to a contrite heart, powring out a fountaine of teares with a stedfast beliefe to be deliuered I found myselfe in a short space gotten at libertie, like a new day crept out of a darke and tempestuous night. My eyes before vsed to such obumbrated darkenes could scarse abide to behould the light, thorow watery sadnes. Neuerthelesse glad I was to see the light: as one set at libertie, that had beene chayned vp in a deepe dungeon and obscure darkenesse. Verye thirstie I was, my clothes torne, my face and hands scratched and netteled, and withall so extreamely set on heate, as the fresh ayre seemed to doe me more hurt then good, neither did it any waye ease my body, desirous to keepe his new recouered scope and libertie.

And after that I had a little rowsed vp my mynde, and sommoned together my sences in some better sort, I sought a meanes to quench my inordinate thyrst, procured and increased through innumerable sighes, and extreame labour of body. Thus casting my eyes with a diligent regarde about the plaine, to find some Fountaine whereat I might refresh myselfe: a pleasant spring or head of water did offer itselfe vnto me with a great vayne boyling vp, about the which did growe diuers sweet hearbes and water flowers, and from the same did flowe a cleare and chrystalline current streame, which deuided into diuers branches ran thorow the desart wood, with a turning and winding body, receyuing into it other little channels vnlading themselues.

In whose courses the stones lift vp by nature, and trunkes of trees denyed any longer by their roots to be vpholden, did cause a stopping hinderance to their current and whuzing fall, which still augmented by other vndissonant torrents, from high and fertlesse mountaines in the plaine, shewed a beautifull brightnes and soft passing course, to the which short windedly comming, by meanes of my fearefull flight, I dld see a little obscure light, thorow the tops of the high trees, somewhat deuiding themselues ouer the water, and with the rest of their bodyes and branches, as it were seperating the heauens from my lifted vp eyes. A horrible place to be in, vnaccompanyed of any creature.

And suddainly hearing the fall of trees, through the force of a whyrle winde, & noise of the broken bowghes, with a redoubled and hoarse sound a farre of, and yet brought to the eccho of the water thorow the thick wood, I grew into a new astonishment.

And at this instant thus terrified and afflycted, and yet without any receiued hurt, being vpon my knees bowed downe, and inclosing the hollownesse of my hand, therewith determined to make me a necessary drinking vessel : I had no sooner put the same into the water, offring to my mouth the long desired moysture thereby to refrygerate and coole the extreame heate of my burning heart, which at that time would haue beene more acceptable vnto me, then eyther *Hypanis* and *Ganges* be to the *Indians*, *Tygris* or *Euphrates* to the *Armenians*, or *Xeylus* to the *Aethiopian* nation, or to the *Egyptians* his innundation, inbybing theyr burnt and rosted mould, or yet the riuer *Po* to the *Ligurians*.

Euen then also it fell so out, that I had no sooner taken into the palme of my hand, offering the same to my open mouth ready to receiue it : [then] I heard a doricall songe, wherewith I was as greatly delighted, as if I had heard the Thracian *Thamiras*, which thorough my eares presented it selfe to my vnquiet heart with so sweete and delectable a deliuerie, with a voyce not terrestriall, with so great a harmonie and incredible a fayning shrilnesse, and vnusuall proportion, as is possible to bee imagined by [by no man's minde, nor of] no toungc sufficiently to be commended. The sweetnes whereof so greatly delighted me, as thereby I was rauished of my remembrance, and my vnderstanding so taken from me, as I let fall my desired water thorough the loosned ioynts of my feeble hands.

And then euen as a birde, which through the sweetnes of the call forgetteth to remember the Fowlers deceit, so I letting slip that which nature stood in need of, hastened my selfe back with all speed, towarde that attractiue melodie, which the more I coasted, the further it seemed still from me, sometime heere, sometimes there, and still as I shifted places, so the same also chaunged with a delectable voyce and heauenly consent. Thus vainly running vp and downe, I knew not after what, I grew wearie, faint, and drye, and so feeble, that my legges could but with great paine, vphould my distempered body. And my grieu d spirits vnabled long to support the same, what with the feare that I had bin in, what with extreame thirst, what with long and wilesome trauell, and what with doubting the worst that might insue, Thus hote, faint, and drye: I knew not what to do but euen to procure rest for my weary member[s]. I marueled first at this straunge accedent, and was amazed at this inhumane harmonye, but most of all in that I was in a straunge contry, and vninhabited, being onelye fertill and beawtyfull to behould, besydes that I greatly sorrowed for the losse of the fayer ryuer which I had so greatly labored to finde out, and now so lightly carlesly to haue lost the benifit thereof. In this sort I was houlden in an intrycate minde of doubts, at length ouercome with all kinde of greefes, my whole bodye trembling and languish-inge vnder a broade and mightye Oke full of Acornes, standing in the middest of a spatious and large green meade, extending forth in thicke and leauie armes to make a coole shadowe, vnder whose bodye breathing I rested my selfe vppon the deawye hearbes, and lying vppon my left syde I drewe my breath in the freshe ayre more shortly betwixt my drye and wrinckled lips, then

the weary running heart, pinched in the haunche and struck in the brest, not able any longer to beare vp his weighty head, or sustaine his body vpon his bowing knees, but dying prostrates himselfe. And lying thus in such an agonie, I thought vpon the strifes of weake fortune, and the inchauntments of the malicious *Cyrces*, as if I had by hir charmes and quadranguled plaints, been bereaued of my sences. In these such so great & exceeding doubts : O *hi me* when might I there among so

many dyuerse and sundry sorts of hearbes finde the *Mercurial Moli*[1] with his blacke roote, for my helpe and remedie. Againe me thought that it was not so with me. What then ? euen a hard appoyntment to delay my desired death. And thus remayning in these pernitious thoughts, my strength debylitated : I looked for no other helpe, but to drawe and receiue fresh ayre into that brest, which panted with a small remainder of vytall warmnesse, taking into my hands halfe aliue, as my last refuge, the moyst and bedewed leaues, preserued in coole shadow of the greene Oke : putting the same to my pale and drye lippes, with a greedy desire in licking of them to satisfie f. 5.
my distempred mouth with theyr moisture, wishing for such a wel as *Hypsipyle*[2] shewed the Grecians : Fearing least that vnawares as I had ruffled in the wood I were bitten with the serpent *Dipsa*[3] my thirst was so vnsupportable. Then renuing my oulde cogitations : as I lay under this mightie Oke : I was oppressed with \ emynent sleepe ouer all my members : when againe I dreamed in this sorte.

[1] Moly an herb greatly commended of Homer, and thought to be souereigne against inchauntments of moderne authors altogether vnknowne.

[2] Hypsipile was daughter to Thaos king of Lemnos, who alone when all women of that Iland had slaine their husbands & kinsmen, saued hir father : she also shewed the Grecians the fountaine Langia in the wood of Nemea in Achaia where Hercules slue a lion.

[3] Dipsa a kind of snakes that Lucan mentioneth, whose byting procureth extreame drynes or thirste.

THE THIRD CHAPTER.

Poliphilus sheweth, that he thought he did sleep againe, and in his dreame that he was in a Vallie, inuironed with mountaines and hilles, the end whereof was shut vp in a maruellous sort, with a mightie pyramides worthie of admiration: vpon the top whereof was a high obeliske, which with great pleasure hee beheld, and diligently discribeth.

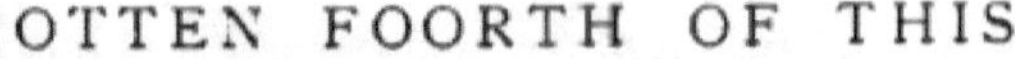
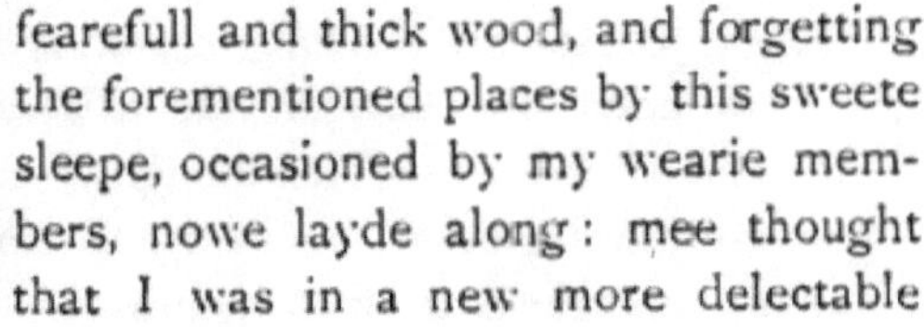

GOTTEN FOORTH OF THIS fearefull and thick wood, and forgetting the forementioned places by this sweete sleepe, occasioned by my wearie members, nowe layde along: mee thought that I was in a new more delectable place, far excelling the former, which consisted not of fertles mountaine and craggie winding rockes, contayning wide caues, but being a delicate valley, in the which did rise a small mounting of no great height, sprinkled heare and there with young Okes, Ashes, Palme trees broad leaued, *Aesculies*,[1] Holme, Chestnut, Sugerchist, Poplars, wilde Oliue, and Oppies disposed some hyer then other, according to the mounting or fall of the place, in the plaine whereof was an other kinde of thicket of medicinable simples like little young trees, as the flowering *Genista*[2] enuironed with diuers green hearbs, Tetrifolie, Sheere grasse, hunnisuckle, the musked Angelica, Crowfoot, Elapium and Rugwoort, with other profitable and vnknowne hearbes and flowers heare and there diuerslie

[1] Aesculus is a tree bearing both greater fruite and broder leaues then the Oke.

[2] Genista beareth a cod and yellowe flower, vines are bound therewith. Elaphium is like to Angelica, but not in smell, the hart thereon rubbeth his head when it is veluet.

disposed. A little beyond in the same valley, I founde a sandie or grauelly plaine, yet bespotted with greene tuffes, in which place grew a faire Palme tree with his leaues like the Culter of a plowe, and abounding with sweet and pleasant fruite, some set high, some lowe, some in a meane, some in the very top, an elect and f. 5b.
chosen signe of victorie. Neither in this place was there any habitation or creature whatsoeuer. Thus walking solitarily betwixt the trees, growing distantly one from another, I perswaded my selfe, that to this no earthly situation was comparable : in which thought, I soddainely espied vpon my left hand, an hungrie and carniuorous Woolfe, gaping vpon me with open mouthe.

At the sight whereof immediatly, my hayre stood right vp, and I would haue cryed out, but could not : and presently the Woolfe ranne awaye : wherevpon returning to my selfe, and casting my eyes towards the wooddie mountaines, which seemed to ioyne themselues together, beeing looked vnto a farre off, I sawe the forme of a tower of an incredible heygth, with a spyre vnperfectlie appearing, all being of very auncient forme and workemanship.

And drawing neare vnto this building, I beheld the gratious mountaines before a farre of seeming small, by comming neerer and neerer, by little and little, to lift vp themselues more and more, at the first seeming to mee that they had ioyned together with the building which was an inclosure or end of the valley betwixt mountaine and mountaine : which thing I thought worthy the noting, and without further delay I addressed my selfe more neerer therevnto. And by how much the more I approximated the same, by so much the more the excellencie of the woorke shewed it selfe, increasing my desire to behould the same. For there appeared no longer a substance of vnknowne forme, but a rare Obelisk vpon a vast frame and stonie foundation, the heigth whereof without comparison did exceed the toppes of the sidelying mountaynes, although I thought that they had beene the renowned *Olympus*,[1] the famous *Caucasus*,[2] and not inferior to *Cyllenus*.[3]

To this sollitarie place thus desiredlye comming, with vnspeakeable delight, at pleasure I behelde the straunge manner of the arte, the hugenesse of the frame, and the woonderfull excellencie of the woorkmanship. Maruelling and considering the compasse and largenesse of this broken and decayed obiect, made of the pure glistering marble of *Paros*.[4] The squared stones ioyned togither without anye cement, and the pointed quadrangulate corner stones streightlye fitted and smoothlye pullished, the edges whereof were of an exquisite vermillion coulour, as is possible to bee deuised: and so iust set, as betwixt the ioynts, euen the enemie to the woorke (if euer there were anye) could not deuise to hide the point of the smallest Spanish needle vsed of the best workewomen. And there in this so noble a piece of worke, I found a proportioned substance to euery shape and likenesse that can be thought vpon and called to remembrance, partly decayed, and some still whole remaining, with pillers small vpon great, with their excellent heads of an exact and most perfect closing, crowned battelments, embost caruings, bearing forth like embroderie, arched beames, mightie mettaline images, ouerthrowne and broken in sunder, the tronke of their exact and perfect members, appearing hollow of brasse. Skyffes, small boates and vessels of *Numidian* stone and *Porphyr*, and diuers couloured marble. Great lauers, condites, and other infinite fragments of notable woorkmanship, far different

[1] Olimpus a hil in Greece between Macedonie and Thesalie, so high, that of the Poets it is sometime taken for heauen.

[2] Caucasus a mightie hill in Asia which parteth India from Scythia.

[3] Cillenus a hill of Arcadia, where Iupiter begat Mercurie vpon Maia.

[4] Paros is one of the 35. Isles called Cyclades and Sporades, in the sea Aegeum which deuideth Europ from Asia.

and inferiour from that they were, in their perfection, but now brought back as it were to their first vnshapelines, being fallen and cast downe, some heere, some there, vpon the earth from the which they were taken. Among the broken and decayed places wherof great sundrie wall weeds and hearbes, especially the vnshaking Anagyre, the Lentise of both kindes, beares foote, Dogges head, Gladen greene, spotted Iuie, Centarie, and diuers such like. And in the myldered places of broken walles grew Howslike, and the hanging Cymbalaria, bryers, and pricking brambles, among the which crept Swifts and Lyzarts which I sawe crawling among the ouergrowne stones, which at the first sight in this silent and solitarie place, made me to be warily afraid of them. On euery side there lay fallen downe smoothe round pieces of serpent spotted Marble, purple and red diuerse couloured. Fragments of strange histories, *Panglyphic* and *Hemygliphic* compendiously caracterized, shewing the excellencie thereof, vndoubtedly accusing our age, that the perfection of such an art is forgotten.

Panglyphic be wholy carued from the head to the foote in all members, Hemigliphic apeare but halfe.

Then comming to the myddle fronture of the great and excellent woorke, I sawe an sole large and maruey-lous porche worthy of great estimation, proportioned according to the huge quantitie of the rest of the whole work, which was placed betwixt and continued in building from the one and the other of the mountaines hare lipped,
and aboue arched, whose space betwixt as I doe coniecture f. 6b.
was in measure sixe furlongs, and twelue paces. The top of which mountaines were perpendicularly equall eyther of them touching the azured skey. At the sight whereof I imagined with my selfe and deuised to thinke with what yron instruments, with what labour of mens hands, and number of workmen, such a piece of woorke could bee by great strength framed, with much paine layde together,

and a long time in finishing. There then this woonder full frame willingly as it were ioyned hands and vnited it selfe with the one and the other mightie mountaines, by meanes whereof the foresaid valley there had an end, that no man could go further forward or backe againe but to enter in by this broade, large, and wide open porche.

Vpon this massie frame and mightie woorkmanship, which I take to be in heigth from the roofe or top to the foote, fiue parts of a furlong, was placed a high and woonderfull Pyramides, after the fashion of a square poynted Diamond, and such incredible workemanship that could neuer be deuised and erected, without inestimable charge, great helpe, and long time. So that I thought the excellencie thereof vnthought vpon, to bee a myrrour, the sight whereof was able to dasell any humaine eyes, and quaile the rest of the spirituall sences. What shall I say more? for so far as the reache of my capacitie will afoorde me leaue, in this sort I briefely describe the same.

Euery side or quarter of this foure squared frame, whervpon the foote of the Pyramides did stand, did extend themselues in length six furlongs,[1] which in compasse about euery side æquilatered of like bredth, dooth multiplie to 24 furlongs. Then lifting vp the lynes on high from the foure corners, so much as eueryе corner is distant in length from an other, meeting in the top, so as the Perpendicular line may fall iust vpon the center of the Dyagon, stretching from both corners of the plynts or square foote, iust and conueniently ioyned together doe make a perfect pyramidall figure. Which immence and woonderfull forme, with a maruelous and exquise Symmetrie and due proportion mounting vp laboursomly foote

[1] A furlong is 16. pole euery pole being 16 foote.

by foote, conteyned 1410 degrees or steppes, taking away 10 degrees to make vp the head and gracilament of the Pyramides in whose place was set a huge Cube or foure square stone of forme like a dye, sound and firme of a monstrous thicknesse and incredible weight to bee carryed so high. And of the same stone of *Paros* as f. 7.
were the steps: which cube and square stone was the Basis and foote set under the Obilisk, which I haue in hand to describe.

This mightie big stone sharpe topt, sliding downe the extream part from corner to corner, flat sided by the Diameter, was fower paces, at euery equall distant corner, whereof was the foote of a harpie of moulten mettall, their steales and clawes armed. Firmlye and stronglie set in with led, in euery corner of the Cube, or foure square head of the Pyramides, meeting together ouer the Diagonike line. Of proportioned thicknesse in heigth two paces. Which thus closing and mette together, made the socket of the great Obelisk: which Socket was beautified with leaues, fruites and flowers, of shining cast mettall, and of conuenient bignesse. Wherevpon the weight of the Obelisk was borne. The breadth whereof was two paces, and seauen in heigth, artificiously sharping of the stone of *Thebais* called *Pyrus*. Vpon the smooth plains whereof, pure and bright shining as a looking glasse, were moste excellently cut *Aegiptian Hyerogliphs.*

Vpon the pointe of which Obelisk, with great arte and diligence, was fastned a copper base, in the which also there was a turning deuise infixed: whervpon did stand the shape of a beautifull nimph framed of the aforesayd matter, able to amaze the continuall diligent behoulder. Of such a proportion as the common stature might be considered and perfectly seene, notwithstanding the exceeding heigth thereof in the ayre. Besides the greatnesse of the figure or image: it was a woonder to thinke how such a weight should bee carryed and set in such a place and so high. Couered with a habite blowne abroad with the winde, and shewing parte of the naked substance of the legges and thighes: with two wings growing out from the shoulder blades, and spred abroad as if shee were readye to flye, turning hir fayre face and sweete regarding countenance towardes hir wings. The tresses of hir haire flying abroade the vpper part or crowne naked and bare. In hir right hand she held from hir sight a copie or horne stuft full of many good things, stopped vp, and the mouth downewarde, hir left hand fastned and harde holden to hir naked brest. This Image and stature was with euery blast of wind turned, and mooued about with such a noyse and tinkling in the hollownes of the metaline deuise: as if the mynte of the Queene of England had bin going there. And when the foote of the phane or Image in turning about, did rub and grinde vpon the copper base, fixed vpon the pointe of the Obeliske, it gaue such a sound, as if the tower bell of Saint Iohns Colledge in the famous Vniuersitie of Cambridge had beene rung: or that in the pompeous Batches of the mightie *Hadrian:* or that in the fift Pyramides standing vpon foure. This Obeliske in my iudgement was such, as neyther that in the *Vaticane* in *Alexandria* or Babilon, may bee equally compared vnto it, but rather esteemed far inferiour. It conteined in it such a heape of woonders, as I could not without great astonishment looke vpon it. As also consider the hugenesse of the worke, the excessiue sumptuousnesse, the straunge inuention, the rare performance, and exquisite diligence of the woorkeman. With what art inuented? with what power, humaine force, and incredible meanes, enuying (if I may speake it) the workmanship of the heauens, such and so mightie weights should be transported and carryed into the skyes? with what Cranes, winding beames, Trocles, round pullies, Capres bearing out deuices, and Poliplasies, and drawing frames, and roped tryces, therein being vnskilfull, I slip it ouer with silence.

Let vs returne then to the huge Pyramides, standing vpon a strong and sound plynth or foure square foote, fourteene paces in heigth, and in length sixe furlongs, which was the foundation and bottom of the weightie pyramides, which I perswaded my selfe was not brought from any other place, but euen with plaine labour and workemanship hewen out of the selfe same mountaines, and reduced to this figure and proportion in his owne proper place.

Which great quadrant and square woorke, ioyned not fast to the collaterate and sidelying rockes, but was betwixt spaced and seperated on eyther sides tenne paces. Vpon the right hand as I went of the aforesaid plynth or square sheame, there was most perfectly carued the vyperous head of the fearefull *Medusa*, in a most furious and rigorous forme to looke vpon, and as it were yelling out: with terrible eyes cauernate and hollow skowling vnder ther ouerhanging browes with a wrympled and forrowed forehead and gaping wide open mouth, which being hollowed with a dyrect waye from the Catill, and vppon stone by a mediane lyne perpendicular to the center of the far shewing Pyramides, made a large enterance and cōming vnto it, at which opening mouth, compassed with fowlded haires of unrepartable curiousnes, artificiall cunning and costly woorkmanshyppe the assending the turning stayers shewed them selues, and in stead of tresses of haire platted with laces I saw fearefull vypers and winding serpents growing out from the scalpe of the monstrous head confusedly twysting together and hissing, so liuely portrayed and set foorth, that they made me afrayde to behould them, In their eyes were placed most shining stones, in such sort, as if I had not beene perswaded and knowne that they were stones indeed, I durst not haue drawne neere them.

And the aforesayde entrie cut out of the firme stone, led to the scale and compassing passage in the center, with winding steps tending to the highest parte of the stately Pyramides, and opening vpon the out side of the catill or cube: vpon the which the shining obeliske was founded. And among the rest of such notable partes that I beheld, me thought that this deuise was woorth the noting, because the artifitious and most cunning architect with an exquisite and perspicuous inuention, had made to the stayres certaine loopes or small windowes,
9. imbracing the bountifull beames of the sunne correspondently on three parts, the lower, the middle, and supreame: The lower taking light from the higher, and the higher from the catabasse or lower with their opposite reflexions shewing a maruellous faire light, they were so fitly disposed by the calculate rule of the artificious Mathematrician, to the Orientall Meridionall and Occidentall partes of the ayre, that euery houre of the day the sunne shined in, and gaue light to the whole scale, the same loopes or windolets in diuerse places symmetrially and definitely dispersed and set.

To the aforesaid entrance thorow the open mouth of *Medusa*, I came by a long gallorie to a salying scale or downe going staire opening at the foot and pauement of the building vpon my right hand against one of the collaterall and side-lying mountaines, betwixt which there was out of the stone and open space cut out of tenne paces vp, into the which I ascended boldely without resistance, and being come to the beginning of the staire in the aforesaid mouth by innumerable steppes and degrees, not without great wearines and disinesse of head, by often turning about, I came to so incredible a height, that my eies would not suffer me to looke downe to the ground, insomuch, that me thought that euery thing below vpon the plaine had lost his shape, and seemed vnperfect. In the opening and comming out of this circulate and turning assence many pillars of fused and molten mettall were aptly disposed and surely fixed: the inter-space betwixt euery one and other one foote, and in height halfe a pase, railed and ioyned togither aboue with a battelled coronet al along the said pillar and of the same metall compassing about the opening of the staire, lest that any comming foorth vnawares should fall downe headlong, For the immesurable height thereof woulde cause a giddines in the head, and bring a staggering to the feete: vpon the plaine of the obeliske there was infixed a table of brasse fastened and soldered in about the height of a man, with an ancient inscription in Latine, Greeke, and Arabike, by the which I plainely vnderstoode that the same was dedicated to the Sunne, and the measure of the work wholy set downe and described, the name of the Architector noted on the obeliske in Greek letters.

ΛΙΧΑΣ Ο ΛΙΒΙΚΟΣ ΛΙΘΟΔΟΜΟΣ ΩΡΘΟΣΕΝ ΜΕ.

Lichas Libucus architectus me erexit.

Lichas a Libian architector set me vp.

Let vs returne and come backe to the consideration of f. 9b
the But and tessell or square, subiect and vphoulder of the

Pyramides in the fronte and foreside whereof I beheld ingrauen a *Gigantomachie* and combate betwixt Giauntes, the onely enemie to vitall breath, surpassinglie well cut, with the quick motions and liuelie agilities of their large and tall bodyes, vnpossible to be rightlye described, the artificiall handling thereof, as it were enuying the woorke of nature it selfe, as if theyr eyes and feete had mooued together, and coasted from one part to an other, with an expedite passage and swift course. In such sorte seemed they vpon theyr strong and mightie horsses, some being cast downe, other stumbling and falling: many wounded and hurt, yeelding vp their desired liues; some troden downe and mischieued vnder the feete of the fierce and vnrestrained horsses. Other casting off their armour wrastling and togging one with an other: some headlong with their heeles vpwarde, falling and not come to the ground from off their horsses. Other some lying vpon the earth, houlding vp their sheilds and Targets, offended with the one hand, and defended with the other. Many with their shimitaries and curtilaxes, some with long swordes two handed after the auncient Persian manner, others with diuers deadly and strange fashioned mortall weapons: some wearing habergions and helmets, with diuers deuises vpon their crests: other naked and vnarmed, leaping and rushing in among the thickest, thereby shewing theyr haughtie, inuincible, and vndaunted courages, resolute for death. Some with fearefull countenances crying out, other shewing obstinate and furious visages, although they were assured to dye, strongly abiding the proofe of their paine, and the cutting in sunder of their fatall thread, others slaine before them, with diuers vncothe and straunge warlike and deadly instruments. Shewing their strong members, their swelling muskels standing out, offering to the sight and eyes of the behoulder, the dutie of theyr bones, and the hollownesse in the places, where theyr strong sinewes be strayned. Their conflict and combate seemed so fearefull, bloudie, deadly, cruell, and horrible: as if *Mars* himselfe had beene fighting with *Porphirion* and *Alcion*, who made a noyse lyke the braying of Asses.

This catagliphic imagerie, did exceed a naturall and
common stature and proportion of men, carued in priuie
white marble, the ground thereof as black as iet, a perfect f. 10.
foile to beautifie and set foorth with pale Christaline and
siluer crolley of innumerable huge bodyes, their last indeuours, their present actions, the fashion of their armor,
the diuersitie of their deaths, & vncertaine & doubtful
victorie. The discharge of my vndertaken discription
whereof, prooueth maymed and lame, by reason that my
vnderstanding is wearie, my memorie confused with
varietie, and my sight dimmed with continuall gasing,
that my senses will not aford me rightly, and as their
dewe, fitly to manifest part, much lesse to describe at large
the whole manner of their curious *Lythoglyphi.*

After this I became to cast with my selfe, what should mooue and cause such a pride & burning desire in any man, to fetch from far, and gather together so mightie stones with so great trauell: With what carriage, who were the conueyers and porters, with what manner of wheeles, and rowling deuises, and vpholding supporters, so great, large and innumerable a sort of stones should be brought thither, and of what matter theyr cement that ioyned and held them together, was made the heygth of the Obelisk and statelinesse of the Pyramides, exceeding the imagined conceit of *Dimocrates* proposed to *Alexander* the great, about a worke to be performed vpon the hill *Athos.*

For the strangenes of the Egiptian building might giue place to this. The famous laborinth were far inferior, *Lemnos* is not to be rehearsed, the Theaters of old time were in comparison but warriners lodges, neyther did the famous *Mausoley* come any thing neere. Which certainly maketh me absolutely perswaded, that he which wrote the seauen woonders of the world, neuer hard of this: neyther in any age hath there been seene or imagined the like, no not the sepulcher of *Ninus*.

Lastly I woondered what foundation and arches were able to vphold so monstrous a weight, whether the pyllars were hexagons or tetragons, and what varietie of columnes, and what number might serue, and after what sorte proportionately disposed and set. For the better vnderstanding and more perfect knowledge wherof, I conueyghed my selfe in at the open & spacious porche and enterance, within the which was an obscure and vast hollownes; which porche, together with the proud and stately buylding (things worthy of memorie) shall in some sorte be descrybed as followeth.

THE FOURTH CHAPTER.

Poliphilus, after the discription of the huge Pyramides and Obeliske, discourseth of maruelous woorkes in this chapter, namely of a horsse of Colos. of an Oliphant, but especially of a most rare and straunge Porche.

IGHTLYE AND LAWFULLYE may I haue leaue to write, that in the whole world there was neuer such an other, so pompeous, glorious, and magnificent a peece of worke, by mans eyes scene or crediblie reported. The woonderfull excellencie and rare straungenesse whereof, as I beheld what with delight, and what with admiration, my sences were so cuptiuated and tyed therevnto, that no other solace or pleasure, did eyther occurre or take place in my swift flying thought.

But that when I applyed my sences to consider, and addressed my eyes with diligent obseruation, curiouslie to ouerlooke euerie perticular part of this sweete composed obiect, and most rare and goodly imagerie and virgin like bodyes, without cracke or flawe, with a long drawne breath, and somewhat opening my mouth, I set a deepe sighe. In so much as my amorous and sounding breathing, by reason of the thicknesse of the ayre in this solytarie and lone place, gaue an eccho and did put me in minde of my Angelike and extreame desired *Polia*.

O hi me that so small or anye intermission should cause that hir louely and celestiall Idea and shape was not still imprinted in my minde, and continued a dayly companion, in whose brest my life is resolued to abide, and rest as vnder the protection of a most sure and approoued shield and safe defence.

And by this way I was brought to a place where were diuers and sundrie excellent sorts of auncient deuises and woorkemanships: first of all, I beheld a most fayre porche, past all sence to describe (for the incredible curiousness thereof, as euer was built or deuised) and the rather for that our mother toung and vulgar speeche, may not affoord apt and peculiar words, for such a piece of artificiall worke.

Before this gorgeous and glorious porche, you shall
11. vnderstand that in the open ayre there was a fowre square court of thirtie paces by his Diameter, paued with pure fine marble, poynted foote square, wrought checkerwise of diuers fashions, and sundrie best fitting coulours: but in many places, by meanes of the ruine of the auncient walke, and olde pillers, broken in peeces and ouergrowne.

And in the vtmost partes of the aforesaide court, to the right hand, and the left, towards the mountaines, there was two straight rowes of pillars, with a space betwixt for the interiect *Arcostile*, as the quantities of both columnes required, the first course or order of setting the pyllars, beginning on both sides equall to the Lymbus or extreame part of the fronte of the porche, the space betwixt pyllars and pillars xv. paces. Of which collumnes or great pillars, some and the greatest parte or number were whole. With their capitels or heads, wrought with a waued shell worke,

A columne consisteth of his Capitell that is the head. Astragalus, that is the subiect of the capitell next the columne. Hypotrachelie the shaft of the columne. And Hypothesis, that is the foote whereon the columne standeth, exceeding the bignes of the columne.

and cyllerie or draperie, their corners bearing out and inanulated or turned in like a curled locke of hayre, or the vpper head of a base Viall aboue the pinnes, which straine the stringes of the instrument to a musicall concord; with their subiect Astragals, writhing and hanging heere and there, making the capitall thrise so big as the bottom thereof of the columne, wherevpon was placed the Epistile or streight beame, the greatest part decayed and many columnes widowed and depriued of their Capitels, buryed in ruine both Astragals and shafts of the columnes and their bases or feete.

Fast ioyning to which order or set rowes of pillars, there grew ould plaine trees, wylde Oliues, Pine apple, and pricking brambles. I coniectured that it was made for to ride horses in, to trot and gallop, the ring, to manage, carreie, and coruet in, or els some open gallerie, couered close ouer head, vnder propt with pillers, and of a large widenesse to walke drie in, and to take a temperate ayre in, not too subtile.

Aboue in this great Court paued as aforesayd, in the passage towardes the Porche, somme tenne paces, I beheld a prodigious winged vaughting horse, of moulten brasse, of an exceeding bignesse, his wings fanning out. His hooues standing vpon a smooth plaine base or frame, fiue foote brode, and nine feete in length, in heigth proportionable to the bredth and length: with his head at libertie and vnbrideled: hauing his two small eares, the one standing forward, and the other drawne back, with a f. 11b.
long waued maine, falling from his crest on the contrarye side; vpon whose backes diuers young youthes assayed to ride, but not one was able to sit stedfast by reason of his swiftnesse and high bounding, from whom some were fallen downe, lying wide open to the ayre, some groueling,

other falling headlong, betwixt the horsse and the earth, the rest in vaine houlding by the hayre of his maine, some forceing to get vp vpon him, and others indeuoring to recouer themselues from vnder his feete.

Vpon the vpper part of the frame and base, there was infixed and fastned with lead, a footing or thick crust, of the same mettall that the horse was, and vpon the which he stoode, and those that were ouerthrowne did lye, somewhat shorter and narrower then the base or subiect frame; the whole masse or composition cast of a peece and
12. of the same mettall, maruelouslie founded. Lastlye you could not perceiue that any were contented with his rowghnes, as appeared by their framed countenances, shewing a discontent which they could not vtter being sencelesse images, not differing otherwayes thorough the excellent conning of the craftisman from liuing creatures, and by his surpassing imitation of nature.

Peryllus there might go put vp his pypes, and blush with his deuised Bull, and *Hiram* the Iewe must heere giue place, or what founders els soeuer.

The *Pagma* base or subiect for this metaline machine to stand vpon, was of one solyde peece of marble (of fit and conuenient breadth, heighth, and length, for that purpose accordinglye proportioned) full of streaming vaines, sondry coulered, and diuerslye spotted, maruelous pleasant to the eye, in infinite commixtures, confusedly disposed.

Vpon the brest or formost part, and end of the marble base, that was opposite against the porch, there was a garland of greene marble, like the leaues of bitter *Alisander*, commixt with dead leaues of Maydenweede, of a hayre coulour, within the which there was a smoothe round, pure, white stone, wherein was ingrauen these capitall Romaine letters.

.D. AMBIG .D.D.	EQVVS INFOELI CI TATIS

At the hinder end in like sort was a garland of deadly Woolfwoort, with this inscription, *Equus infœlicitatis.* And vpon the right side there was ingrauen certaine figures, shapes, and representments of men and women dauncing together, byformed or faced, the formost smiling, the hynmost weeping: and dauncing in a ring, with theyr armes spred abrode, and hanfasted, man with man and woman with woman. One arme of the man vnder that of the woman, and the other aboue, and thus closing together, and houlding by the hands, they floung about one after another, that alwayes still in one place, a smyling countenance incountered a foregoing sad. Their number was seauen and seauen, so perfectly and sweetely counterfeited with liuelie motions, their vestures whisking vp and flying abroad, that the workman could not be accused of any imperfection, but that one had not a liuely voyce to expresse their mirth, and the other brinish teares to manifest their sorrow: the said daunce was in fashion of two Semicircles, with a seperating partition put betwixt. f. 12b

None liue in this world in that pleasure, but they haue also their sorowes in time.

Vnder which Hemiall figure, there was inscript this worde TEMPVS. On the contrary side I beheld many of greene adolestencie of like proportion to the former, and in such like compasse or space, the grounds of both beautified and set foorth with an exquisite foliature or woorke of leaues and flowers, this companie was plucking and gathering of the flowers of sundrye hearbes and tender bushing stalkes and braunches: and with them diuers f. 13.

Gift vainely bestowed, in time wantonlie spent, is a great losse, and breedeth repentance.

faire Nimphes pleasantly deuising, and sportinglie snatching away their gathered flowers, and in such sort as

abouesaid vnder the figure were ingrauen certaine capitall letters, to shew this one worde AMISSIO, conteyning the ninth part to the Diameter of the quadrature.

At the first sight hereof I was amased and astonished, but with better regard & great delight curiously reouerlooking the huge founded Machine the shape and forme of a horse made by humane industry and skill most commendable, for that euery member without defect had his perfect harmonie, and euery limme his desired proportion, I straight called to remembrance the vnfortunate horse of *Seian*.

And thus helde still to beholde the same artificiall mysterie another spectacle and obiect no lesse worthy to be looked vpon than the former, offered it selfe to my sight, which was a mighty Elephant, whereunto with a desirous intent I speedely hyed me to approch and come neere.

In which meane while on an other side I heard a mournefull noise and humane groaning, as proceeding from a sicke body euen vnto death: whereat I stoode still at the first, my haires standing right vp, but presently without further stay, I addressed my steppes towards the place from whence I heard this wofull noyse and dolefull lament, forcing my selfe vp vppon a heape of ruinated, broken and downe-fallen marbles. Thus willingly going forward, I came to a vast and wonderfull large Colose, the feete thereof bare, and their soles hollowe, and the legges as if their flesh had beene wasted, consumed and fallen way. From thence with horror I came to looke vpon the head, where *I* did coniecture and imagine that the ayre and winde getting in and comming foorth of his wide open mouth and the hollow pipes of his throat, by a diuine inuention did cause this moderated noise and timed groanes: it lay with the face vpward all of molten mettal, like a man of middle age, and his head lifted vp as with a pillowe, with a resemblance of one that were sicke, breathing out at his mouth, sighes and groanes gaping, his length was three score paces. By the haires of his beard you might mount vp to his breast, and by the rent and torne peeces of the same to his stil lamenting mouth, which groningly remained wide open and empty, by the which, prouoked by the spurre of curious desire, I went downe by diuers degrees into his throat, from thence to his stomacke, and so foorth by secret wayes, and by little and little to all the seuerall partes of his inward bowelles, Oh wonderfull conceit. And euery part of mans

body hauing vpon it written his proper appellation in
14. three ideomes Chaldee, Greeke and Latine, that you might know the intrailes, sinews, bones, veines, muscles and the inclosed flesh, and what disease is bred there : the cause thereof, the cure and remedy, Vnto which inglomerated and winding heape of bowelles, there was a conuenient comming vnto and entrance in : with small loope-holes and wickets in sundry places diuersly disposed, yeelding thorough them a sufficient light to beholde the seuerall partes of the artificiall anothomie, not wanting any member that is found in a naturall body.

When I came to the heart, *I* did see and reade how Loue at his first entrance begetteth sorow, and in continuaunce sendeth out sighes, and where Loue doth most greeuously offend : wherewithall *I* was mooued to renew my passion, sending out from the botome of my heart deepe set and groaning sighs inuocating and calling out vpon *Polia*, in such sort as that the whole Colose and Machine of brasse did resound, striking me into a horrible feare : an exquisite Arte beyond all capacity, for a man to frame his like not being an Anotomy indeede.

Oh the excellency of passed wittes, and perfect golden age, when Vertue did striue with Fortune, leauing onely behind him for an heritage to this our world, blinde, ignorant, and grudging desire of worldly pelfe.

Vpon the other side I perceiued of like bignes to the former Colose, the vpper part of a womans head some deale bare, and the rest buried with the decayed ruines, as I thought, of such like workmanship as the other, and being forbidden by incomposite and disordered heapes of decayed and fallen downe stones, to view the same I returned to another former obiect, which was (and not farre distant from the horse straight forward) a huge Elephant of more black stone than the Obsidium, powdered ouer with small spottes of golde and glimces of siluer, as thicke as dust glistering in the stone. The extreame hardnes whereof the better did shew his cleere shining brightnes, so as euery proper obiect therein did represent it selfe, excepte in that parte where the mettall did beare a contrary colour. Vpon his large backe was set a saddle or furniture of brasse, with two gyrthes going vnder his large belly, betwixt the which two being streight buckled vp with buckles of the same stone, there was inter-set a quadrangle corespondent to the breadth of the Obeliske placed vpon the saddle, and so iustly set, as no perpendicular line would fall on either side the diameter. Vpon three parts or sides of the foure square Obelisk, were ingrauen Egiptian caracters. The beast so exactly and cunningly proportioned, as inuention could deuise, and art performe. The aforesaid saddle and furniture set foorth and beautified with studdes hanging iewels, stories and deuises, and houlding vp as it were a mightie Obeliske of greene couloured stone of Lacedemonia, vpon the euen square, two paces broad, and seauen in height, to the sharpe pointe thereof, waxing smaller and smaller, vpon which pointe there was fixte a Trigon or rounde Ball of a shinyng and glystering substance.

This huge beast stood streight vpon all foure, of an exquisite woorkmanship vpon the plaine leuell, and vpper part of the base, hewen and cunningly fashioned, beeing of *Porphyr* stone. With two large and long teeth, of puer white stone, and cleare appact, and fastned. And to the fore gyrth on eyther side was buckled a riche and gorgeous poiterell beautified with diuers ornaments and varietie of Iewels, the subiect whereof was of the same substance of the saddle : vppon the middest whereof was grauen in Latine *Cerebrum est in capite.* And in like manner brought about the outsides of his neck to the foretop of his large and big head, it was there fastned together with an artificiall knot ; from the which a curious ornament and verie notable, of Gouldsmithes worke, hung downe, ouer spredding his spacious face : the same ornament being twise so long as broade, bordered about, in the table whereof I beheld certaine letters *Ionic* and *Arabic*, in this sorte.

His deuouring trunke rested not vpon the leuel of the base, but some deale hanging downe, turned vppe againe towardes his face. His rigged large ears like a Fox-hounde flappingly pendent, whose vast stature was little lesse, then a verye naturall Olyphant. And in the about compasse, and long sides of the base, were ingrauen certaine *Hierogliphs*, or Egiptian caracters. Being decently and orderlye pullished, with a requisite rebatement. *Lataster gule thore orbicle*, *Astragals* or *Neptrules*, with a turned down *Syme* at the foote of the base, and turned vp aloft with writhin trachils and denticles, agreeable and fit to the due proportion of so large a substance, in length 12. paces, in breadth fiue, and in heigth three, the superficiall and outward part whereof was hewen in forme of a hemicycle.

In the hynder parte of which base and stone, wherevpon this mightie beast did stande, I founde an assending place of seauen steps, to mount vp to the plaine superficies of the base, wherevpon the Olyphant did stand. And in the reserued quadrangle perpendicularly streight vnder the aforesaid brasen saddle, there was cut out and made a little doore and hollowed entrance, a woonderfull woorke in so hard a substance, with certaine steppes of brasse, in manner of stayres, by the which a conuenient going vp into the body of the Olephant was offered me.

At the sight whereof I extreamely desired to see the f. 16.
whole deuise & so going in, I assended vp to the heigth of the base wherevppon the cauernate, hollow, vast, large and predigious monster did stand, except that same part of the Obelisk, which was conteyned within the voyde body of the beast, and so passing to the base. Leauing towards both sides of the Olyphant so much space as might serue for any man to passe, eyther towarde the head or hynder haunches.

And within from the bending downe of the chine or backe of the beast, there hunge by chaynes of copper an euerlasting lampe, and incalcerate light, thorough the which in this hinder parte I sawe an auncient sepulcher of the same stone, with the perfect shape of a man naked, of all naturall parts. Hauing vpon his head a crowne of black stone as iet: his teeth eyes and nayles siluered and standing vpon a sepulcher couered like an arke, of scale woorke, and other exquisite lyneaments, poynting with a goulden scepter, and houlding forward his arme to giue direction to the former part.

On his left side he held a shield in fashion like to the keele of a ship, or the bone of a horse head, wherevppon was inscript in Hebrew, Attic, and Latine letters, this sentence that is placed on the other side with the figure.

16b.

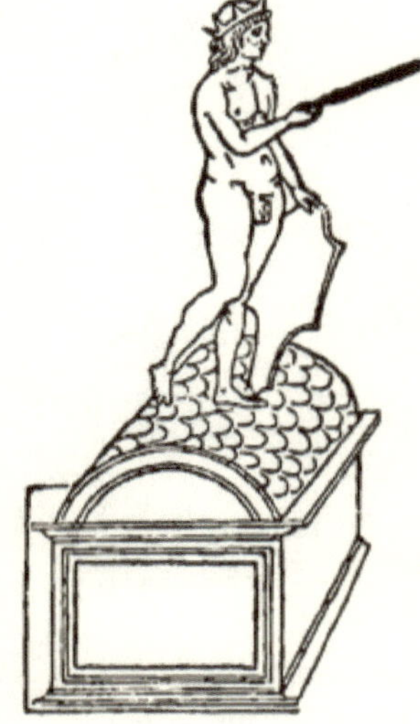

אם לא כי הבהמה כסתה את בשרי
אזי הייתי ערום חפש ותמצא הניחני

ΓΥΜΝΟΣ ΗΝ, ΕΙ ΜΗ ἊΝ ΘΗΡΙ-
ΟΝ ΕΜΕΚΑΛΥΨΕΝ. ΖΗΤΕΙ. ΕΥ-
ΡΗΣΗΔΕ. ΕΑΣΟΝ ΜΕ.

NVDVS ESSEM, BESTIA NIME
TEXISSET, QVAERE, ET INVE
NIES. ME SINITO.

At which vncoth and straunge sight I stood not a little amased and somewhat doubtfull what to imagine, turning my eyes to the contrarie part, I sawe in like sorte an other, as before burning light, and passing thorough betwixt the side of the beast, and the therein inclosed part of the Obelisk; I came towards the forepart of the Olyphant, where in like manner I found such an other fashioned sepulcher as the former, with a stature or image standing therevpon as the other, sauing that it was a Queene, who, lyfting vp hir right arme with hir formost finger, poynted towards that part behinde hir shoulders, and with the other shee helde a little table fast in hir hand, in which was written in three languages this epygram.

היה כי שתהיה קח מן האוצר הזה כאות נפשך
אבל אזהיר אותך הסר הראש ואל תיגע בגופו

ΟΣΤΙΣ ΕΙ. ΛΑΒΕ ΕΚ ΤΟΥΔΕ
ΤΟΥ ΘΗΣΑΥΡΟΥ, ΟΣΟΝ ΑΝ Α
ΡΕΣΚΟΙ. ΠΑΡΑΙΝΩ ΔΕ ΩΣ ΛΑ-
ΒΗΙΣ ΤΗΝ ΚΕΦΑΛΗΝ. ΜΗ Α
ΠΤΟΥ ΣΩΜΑΤΟΣ.

QVISQVIS ES, QVANTVN
CVNQVE LIBVERIT HV-
IVS THESAVRI SVME AT-
MONEO. AVFER CAPVT.
CORPVS NE TANGITO.

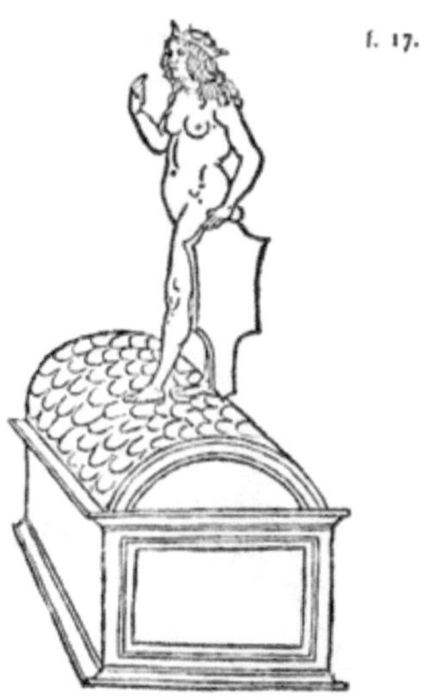

f. 17.

This noueltie worthie to be manifested, and secret riddle often to be read ouer, was not knowen to me, so as I rested doubtfull what the interpretation of this sophisme should signify, not daring to trie the conclusion. But stricken with feare in this dark vnlightsome place, notwithstanding the dimme burning lampe, I was more desirous to beholde and peruse that triumphant porch and gate as more lawfull to remaine there than other-where. Whereupon without more adoe, I determined to leaue this place vntill another time, that I might more quietly at lesure looke vpon the same, and to prepare my selfe to beholde the woonderfull worke of the gate: and thus descending downe I issued foorth of the vnbowelled monster, an inuention past imagination, and an excessiue labour and bolde attempt to euacuate such a hard substance ouer that other stones be, the workemanship f. 17b.
within as curious as that without. Lastly, returned cleane

downe, I beheld in the Porphire laste along the sides notably insculpt and grauen these hierogliphies.

First, the horned scalpe of an oxe, with two tooles of husbandry fastned to the hornes.

An altar standing vpon goates feete, with a burning fire aloft, on the foreside whereof there was also an eie, and a vulture.

After that a bason and an ewre.

A spindle ful of twind, an old vessel fashioned with the mouth stopped and tied fast.

A sole and an eye in the bal[l]e thereof, and two branches trauersed one of Oliue, an other of Palme tree.

An Anchor and a Goose.

An olde lampe, and a hand holding of it.

An ore of ancient forme with a fruitefull Oliue branch fastned to the handle.

Two grapling yrons or hookes.

A Dolphin and an Arke close shut.

These hierogliphies were passing well cut on this manner.

18. Which ancient maner of writing, as I take it, is thus to be vnderstoode.

EX LABORE DEO NATURÆ SACRIFICA LIBERALITER PAULATIM REDUCES ANIMUM DEO SUBIECTUM. FIRMAM CUSTODIAM VITÆ TUÆ, MISERICORDITER GUBERNANDO TENEBIT, INCOLUMEMQUE SERUABIT.

Letting passe this most excellent rare, strange, and secret deuise and worke : Let vs returne againe to the prodigious horse, whose head was leane and little, of a small proportion and yet fitting the body, which seemed continually staring, fieerce and impatient, the flesh in his muscles trembling and quaking, in such sort as that hee seemed rather aliue than a fained imitation, with this Greeke worde in his face ΓΕΝΕΑ. There were also other great peeces and fragments of diuers and sundry lineaments among the broken and decayed ruines, which I looked not on, still running and sliding, time giuing me onely leaue to consider and peruse these foure rare wonders, the porch or gate, the horse, the Colose and the Elephant.

Oh reuerend arthists of times past, what despite hath gotten the vpper hand of your cunning that the same is buried with you, and none left for vs to inherite in this age.

At length being come to this ancient porch, a worke woorthie the looking vpon maruellously composed by exquisite rules, and by art notably beautified, with diuers and sundry sorts of cuttings, which did inflame a desire in me to vnderstand and finde out the lineaments and practise of the architect. I beganne after this maner, making a square from the two collumnes on either side in a perfect sort, in the which I tooke the due proportion of the whole porch.

A tetragon figure A.B.C.D diuided by three lines straight, and three ouerthwart equally distant one from another will make sixeteene quadrats, then adde to the figure halfe as much more in like proportion, diuiding the adiunct you shall finde foure and twenty squares. This figure shall serue of credycels to make the inlepturgie and briefe demonstration that followeth.

Draw then in the first fygure A.B.C.D. two diagons, make also in the same two lines, one straight downe, and the other ouerthwart, which make foure quadrats mutually intersect.

Then in the voide ouer the Isopleures make foure

18b. mediane prickes, drawing lines from one to another, and they wil make the Rhombas.

When I had drawne this figure after this manner I straightway mused with my selfe, what reason should mooue many of our woorkemen in these dayes eyther to thinke well of themselues, or take the art of building in hand, not knowing what it is? Making such grosse faults in churches and great mens houses, defaming arte, and so ignorant, that they seeme as though they could not consider what nature hir selfe dooth teach vs in behoulding of hir woorkes.

And what parte soeuer is not agreeable with his principle, is foule and naught. For take away order and rule, and what thing can any man make, eyther beautifull to the eye, or of commendable proportion and durable: then it must needes follow, that the cause of such inconuenient errors doth proceed from ignorance, and hath his beginning from illiterature. And this notwithstanding, that although the perfection of this arte dooth not varie, & fall from his rectitude, yet the discreet and cunning architect to grace the obiect, to the behoulders: may lawfullye eyther with adiection or deminution, beautifie his worke, keeping whole the sollid part, with his vniuersall composition.

I call that solid which is the bodye of the frame, which is the principall intent, inuention, fore setting downe, and symmetrie, or dew proportion of the building without any additions, rightlye examined, and perfectly composed, which will manifest the skill of the workeman, and the same afterwardes to adorne and beautifie, which adiuncts is an easie matter. Wherein is also to be considered, the dew ordering and placing of euery thing, and not to set a crowne vpon the feete, but vpon the head, and so oualing and denticulating, and other cuttings of sundrye sorts in their seuerall and best fitting places, the chiefe inuention and disposing whereof, resteth in the rare and cunning architect, but the labour and woorking therof to the vulgar and common sort of manualifts and seruants to the architect, who if he will do well, he must in no wise be subiect to auarice.

And besides his skil he must be honest, no pratler full of words, but courteous, gentle, bening, tractable, patient, mery & pleasant, full of new deuises, a curious searcher into all artes, and well aduised in his proceeding, least with rashnes he comit a fault or absurditie in his worke, and heereof f. 19.
thus much shall suffice.

THE FIFTH CHAPTER.

After that *Poliphylus* had at large made a demonstration of the dew proportion of the Gate, hee proceedeth to describe the ornaments thereof, and their excellencie.

HAUING BEENE SOMEWHAT prolix and tedious in my former purpose, it may be that it hath bred some offence, to such as dayly indeuour to occupietheyr sences in the pleasaunt discourses of loue. But it wyll also prooue no whit displeasant, if with a lyttle patience they restraine to glutte themselues with the walowish sweetnes of deceyueable delightes, and trye the taste of a contrarye vyand.

And for as much as the affections of men are naturally variable and different one from an other: vpon this occasion I may bee excused. For although that bread sometime denyed and kept backe from the hungrie body, may cause a hard conceit, yet when it is eftsoones offered vnto him, the mallice is forgotten, and the gift very gratefully receyued.

Nowe hauing in some sorte spoken of the right vse of architecturie, and the direct waye and meanes by order and rule, to finde out, the set downe deuise, and solyde bodye or grounde of the woorke, with facilitie that beeing found out, the architector may vse sundrye deuisions in diuerse perfections, not vnlike vnto a cunning Musition, who hauing deuised his plaine grounde in right measure, with full strokes, afterwarde wyll proportion the same into deuisions, by cromatycall and delyghtfull minims crotchets, and quauers, curiously reporting vpon his plaine song. Euen so after inuention, the principall and speciall rule, for an Architector is a quadrature, the same deuided into smales the harmonie and sweete consent of the building, setteth foorth it selfe, and the conuenient adiunctes, agreeable to theyr principall.

In all which this porche was most excellent, both for the rare inuention and woonderfull composition thereof, and the strange additions to beautifie the same, in such sorte so exquysite, so fitly placed, and so curiouslie cut and f. 19b. ingrauen, as the smallest part thereof could not bee accused of anye fault, but the woorkman commended for the perfection of his skill.

First vpon my right hande belowe, I beheld a stilypode or square stone, like an aulter vnder the bases of the columnes, which hauing vpon the vpper parte a conuenient and meet coronice, and accordingly imbowed, the bottome and lowest part in like manner was fashioned, so as the quadrate and aforesayd stilypode, was no broder then long, but a right quadrangule. Which aulter (as I may tearme it) sidelong about, wrought with leaues, hollowed vnder with a gulaterie, and wrapt ouer with the same foliature and leafeworke, hemming in the smooth face or table of the Stilypode of shining white alliblaster, polished and plaine, the outward part of the quadrangule, equilaterally compassing about the same, wherevpon with a woonderfull curiousnes was ingrauen a man neere his myddle-age, of a churlish and swarffie countenance, with an vnshaply beard, thick, and turning into his chyn, by the towghnesse of the hard skinne, and vneasie growing out of the hayre.

He sat vpon a stone with an aporne of a Goates skinne, the hinder parts compassing his waste, and tyed behynde with a knotte, and the neck part, with the hayrie side next him, hung downe betwixt his legges. Before him in the interstice of these grose and tumorus calfes, there was an anuill fastned vpon a knottie peece of a tree, wherevpon he was fashoning of a bryganine or habergion of burning mettall, houlding vp his Hammer, and as it were striking vpon his worke.

And there before him was a most noble woman, hauing two fethered wings set vpon hir delicate and tender shoulders, houlding hir sonne an infante naked, which sate with his little hyppes vpon the large and goodly proportioned thighes of the faire goddesse his mother, and playing with hir, as she held him vp, and putting his feete vpon a stone, as it had beene a little hill, with a fornace in a hollow hole, wherin was an extreame whote burning fire.

This Ladye had hir fayre tresses curiouslie dressed vpon hyr broad and highe forhead, and in like sorte compassing about with abundance, hir head in so rare and delicate a sort, that I marueyled why the Black smithes that were there busie at theyr worke, left not all to looke still vpon so beautifull an obiect.

f. 20. There was also fast by, of like excellent woorkemanship, a knight of fierce countenance,[1] hauing vpon hym an armour of brasse, with the head of *Medusa* vpon the curate or brest plate, and all the rest exquisitely wrought and beautified, with a bandilier ouerthwart his broad and strong brest, houlding with hys brawny arme a halfe Pike, and raysing vp the poynte thereof, and bearing vpon his head a high crested helmet, the other arme shadowed and not seene by reason of the former figure: There was also

[1] Mars.

a young man in silke clothing, behynde the Smith, whome I could not perceiue but from the brest vpwarde, ouer the declyning head of the forenamed Smith. Thys rehearsed hystorie, for the better and sweeter pleasing to the eye, the workeman had graced in this sort. The playne grounde that was hollowe and smoothe in euery cutting out of a limme or body, vpon the table of the stylipode, was like vnto red coroll and shyning, which made such a reflection vpon the naked bodyes, and theyr members betwixt them, and compassing them about, that they seemed lyke a Carnation Rose couler.

Mercurie.

Vpon the left side of the doore in the like aulter or stylipode vpon the table thereof, there was ingrauen a yoong man of seemly countenance, wherein appeared great celerity: he sate vpon a square seate adorned with an ancient manner of caruing, hauing vpon his legge a paire of half buskens, open from the calfe of the legge to the ancle, from whence grew out on either ancle a wing, and to whome the aforesaide goddes with a heauenlye shape, her brests touching together and growne out round and firme without shaking, with her large flankes conformable to the rest of hir proportion before mentioned with a sweet countenance offered [her] yoong and tender sonne ready to be taught: the yong man bowing himselfe curteously downe to the childe, who stoode before him vppon his pretty little feete, receiuing from his tutor three arrowes, which in such sort were deliuered as one might easelye coniecture and gather after what manner they were to be vsed: the goddesse his mother holding the empty quiuer and bowe vnbent, and at the feete of this instructor lay his vypered caduce.

Amor mi troua di tutto disarmato.

There also I saw a squier or armour-bearer and a woman with a helmet vpon her head carying a trophæ or

signe of victorie vpon a speare after this manner. An ancient coate-armor hung vp, and vpon the top thereof or
20b. creast, a spheare vpon two wings, and betwixt both wings this note or saying, *Nihil firmum*, Nothing permanent: she was apparelled in a thin garment carried abroad with the wind, and her breasts bare.

The two straight pillars of Porphyre of seuen diameters vpon either of the aforenamed stilipodes and square aultars did stretch vpward of a pumish or tawnie colour, the out sides shining cleere and smoothly pollished, chamfered, and chanelled with foure and twenty rebatements or channels in euery collumne betwixt the nextruls or cordels.

Of these the third part was round, and the reason of their cutting in such sort (that is two parts chamfered, & the third round) as I thought was this: the frame or temple was dedicated to both sexes, that is, to a god and a goddesse, or to the mother and the son, or to the husband and the wife, or the father and the daughter, and such like. And therefore the expert and cunning workemen in elder time for the feminine sex, did vse more chamfering and channelling and double varietie then for the masculine, because of their slippery and vnconstant nature.

The cause of so much rebating was to shew that this was the temple of a goddesse, for chamfering dooth set foorth the plytes of feminine apparell, vpon the which they placed a chapter with prependent folding, like vnto plyted and curled haire, and feminine dressing, and sometimes instead of a chapter a womans head with crisped haire.

These notable and faire collumnes aforesaide did rise vp in length vpon their vnderset bases of brasse with

Thores and Cymbies be the outward parts of a chapter or head of a pillar sticking out further than the pillar wrything and turning in, wrought with leaues, the worke is called of caruers & painters draperie and celerie.

their *Thores* and *Cymbies* wrought with a foliature of oke leaues and acornes winding about their chapters standing vpon their subiect *Plynths*.

The Chapters of the same substance of their bases, with requisite meete and conuenient proportion aunswerable to the harmonie of the wholeworke Such as *Callimachus* the chiefe caruer to *Calathus* the sonne of *Iupiter* did neuer performe or come neere in the erected sepulcher of the *Corinthian* Virgin, beautified with draperie of double *Achanthis*.

The Plynthes whereon the chapters did stand wrought with winding and turning workes, and in the middest decorated with a Lillie, the bowle garnished with two rowes of viii leaues of Achanthus, after the Romaine and Corinthian maner, out of which leaues came little small stalkes,
closing together in the middest of the boule, shewing foorth f. 21
a fayre and sweet composed Lyllie in the hollowing of the Abac or Plynth, from the which the tender stalkes did turne round together, vnder the compasse of the square Abac, much after the woorke that *Agrippa* caused to bee made, in the porche of his woonderfull Pantheon.

Let vs come now to the lymet and lowest parte of the doore, for entrance, which was of a great large and harde stone, powdered with sundry sorted spottes, white, black, and of a clay couler, and diuers other mixtures: vppon this stood the streight cheekes and sides of the doore, with an interstitious aspect, inwardly carued with as great cunning as the rest. Without any signe of eyther hookes or hinges, below or aboue.

The arche of which doore compassing like a halfe cyrcle, was wrought curiouslye and imbowed, and as it were bounde about with laces like beads of brasse, some round, and some like Eglantine berries of a reddish couler, hanging downe after an auncient manner, and foulded and turned in among the tender stalkes.

The closing together and bracing of which hemicycle or arch, worthie of admiration, of a rare and subtile deuise, and exquisite polyture, did thus obiect and present it selfe to my sight.

Then I beheld in a hard and most black stone, an eagle displayed, and bearing out of the bignesse of a naturall eagle, which had louingly seazed and taken in hir foote a sweete babe in the swadling cloutes, nicely, carefully, and gently houlding the same, least that hir strong, sharpe, and hooking pounces, should by anye meanes pierce thorough the tender skynne of the young infant.

The Eagle of Jupiter that carryed Ganimed.

Hir feete were fixed about the rising vp chist of the childe, whome she had made bare from the nauell vpwarde and downeward so as the naked hippes might be seene betwixt the fethered thighes of the Eagle. This little infant and most beautifull babe (worthie and meete for him that he was seazed for) by his countenance shewed as if he had beene afraide of his fortune.

And thus lying in the foote of the Eagle, he stretched both his armes abroade, and with his little fat hands tooke fast hould vpon the remigiall bones of the Eagles pinions displayed, as aforesaid. And clasping his swelling prittie legges and feete, about hir subvaging spreding traine, which laye behinde the rising vppe of the arche.

The bones next the back, in the wing, whiche in a hawke excelleth all proportions of other birdes.

This little childe was cut of the white vayne of Achates or Onix, and the Eagle of the other vaine of the same stone called Sardins which is of black couler of some called Cordeoll ioyning both in one selfe same stone. Whereat I stood musing and commending to myselfe the ingenious and apt inuention of the Arthist, in the vse of such a stone, which of his owne nature to contrarie pro-

Achates is a pretious stone wherein are represented the figures of the nine Muses; of Venus and such like beautiful personages.

portions affoorded contrarie coulers, and in such sort as by the raysing vp of hir small plummage aboue hir seare, hir beack halfe open, and hir toung appearing in the middest thereof, as if she had beene resolutely intended, and eagerly bent to haue gorged hir selfe vpon it.

The hemicicle or arche rising rownd from the vpper part of the streight cheeke of the entrance, according to the thicknes thereof, was disposed into losenges or squares, wherin were carued Roses, theyr leaues and branches hanging in a curious and delightfull order to behoulde, ouer the entry of the Gate.

In the two Triangles occasioned by the bow of the arche there were two fayre Nymphes of excellent proportions and shapes, theyr clothes which couered theyr Virgins bodyes, giuing place for theyr legges, brests, and armes to be bare, theyr hayre loose and flying abroad, and towardes the brace, and knitting together of the arche aboue, they held a victorious trophæ.

The ground of which tryangle was of black stone, the better to shew the perfection and truthe of the mettals in the trophæs, and the beautifull bodyes of the delycate virgins.

Zophor is a border wherin diuers things are grauen.

Aboue these mentioned partes, was the Zophor, in the myddest whereof, I beheld a table of goulde, wherein was this Epigram in Cappitall Greeke Letters of Syluer. In thys sorte reporting.

ΘΕΟΙΣ ΑΦΡΟΔΙΤΗΙ ΚΑΙ ΤΩΙ ΥΙΩΙ ΕΡΩΤΙ ΔΙΟΝΥΣΟΣ ΚΑΙ ΔΗΜΗΤΡΑ ΕΚ ΤΩΝ ΙΔΙΩΝ ΜΗΤΡΙ ΣΥΜΠΑΘΕΣΤΑΤΗΙ.

Diis veneri et filio amori, Bacchus, & Ceres de propriis, (S. substantiis) Matri pientissimæ.

Eyther sides of which table was reteind and held vp with two babes or wynged spyrits of perfect and liuelye f. 22.

shapes, as if they had beene celestiall bodyes, vppon a ground of Iasul or blew Saphyrs to grace the mettals and imagerie.

Vpon the face of the Zophor extending and stretching along ouer the columnes of porphir stone were ingrauen certain spoiles or curates, gorgets of mayle, Vaumbraces, gauntlets, shields, Targets, head-peeces, maces, battell Axes, spurres, quiuers, arrowes, dartes, broken launces, curtilaxes, and other auncient instruments of warre. As well ayerie and marine, as for the field singularly well cut, and manifesting to the behoulder both victories, force, and triumphes, after a mortall effusion of bloud.

Vpon this in order stood the Coronice, wrought with such lyneaments as decently concurred, and were aunswerable to the excellencie of the rest of the worke: for otherwise, as in a mans body one qualitie being contrarie to another, sicknesse dooth follow, the humors oppressing one an other in abundance: so in building if the adiuncts be vnaptly disposed, and vndecently distributed there will fall out a fowle deformitie.

For a frame and building growes weake and vnseemely wherin cannot be found a sweete harmonie and commodulate order and concent.

Which thing many moderne ideots doe confound, being ignorant in Locall distribution. For a cunning crafts master will in his worke shewe an allusion or resemblance to a humaine shape and proportion beautifully adorned in apparrell.

Aboue ouer the coronice, by an inuers gradation there were fowre Quadratures or square Tables, two right ouer the chamfered columnes, and channelled pyllars, and two within them. In an other deuision, betwixt the said two contrast and inwarde tables, there stood a Nimph in

Anagliph is smothly chased out with the hammer and not carued.

hir Anagliph most rare and excellent of Orichalke or yealow Latin, houlding in eyther hand a Torche, one of them reuersed and turned downeward, beeing extinct and put out, and the other burning towardes the Sunne. The burning Torche in hyr righte hande, and the extincte in hyr left.

Clymene the mother of Phaeton.

In the quadriture vppon the right side, I behelde the f. 22[b]. iealous *Climene*, with her heare transformed into an hearbe called *Venus* maid, or Lady hearbe, & *Phœbus* in a cruell indignation & wrathfull displeasure, she following of him weeping, from whom he fled hastening on forward hys swift horses, as one that flyeth from hys mortall and deadly enemie.

Vppon the Table ouer the Columnes on the left side in a curious and rare vnusuall caruing, there was the resemblance historyed of the vncomfortable and still mourning *Cyparissus*, holding vp hys handes and armes toward the Sunne, and making his mone to *Apollo* for the wounded *Ceruа*.

In the third Table nexte the last mencioned, in a worke answerable to the presedent and former, I behelde *Leucothoe*, wickedly slayne of hyr own Father, chaunging and transforming her fayre yong and tender flesh into smooth barke, shaking leaues and bending wandes.

In the fourth Table, was represented the discontented & displeasant *Daphne*, at the burning desires of the curled headed *Delius*, rendring vp by little and little her virgins body vndefiled, towards the hote heauens, beeing metamorphised most pyttifully into a greene Laurell.

Nowe successiuely in order ouer the afore-mencioned Tables and quadratures in the *Zophor*, wherein these Histories were represented in shapes, there was extended and laide ouer a Coronice denticuled & oualled with inter-set stralets, betwixt the iates of the Oualls, and leafe worke and the Imbrices with the rest that appertayneth to the setting forth of the same (past my skill to report) without any fault or defect: and lastly the syme was adorned heere and there with the leaues of *Achanthis.*

And to return to the view of the whole frame, in the disposing thereof as aforesaide, the Coronices by a perpendycular lyne were corrospondent and agreeing with the faling out of the whol worke, the Stilliced or Perimeter, or vtter part of the vppermost Coronice onely except. A periment in corrupt English.

It followeth to shew and speake of the Table or inward part of the Trigonall: within the which, according as the extreames of the same triangle would permit, there was presented to my view, a Crowne or Garland of diuers leaues,
f. 23. fruites, and stalkes, foulded vppe and wrapte together of a greene stone knitte in foure partes, the byndings of the selfe same stalkes, holden by two Mermaydes, the vpper partes of them of a humayne shape, and that vnder the nauell like a Fyshe, their one hande vp, and the other belowe on the Garlande, their scalye tayles extending to the nethermost corners of the Triangle, vppon the top of the Coronice hauing at theyr extreeme partes theyr fishy winges or finnes. Theyr faces like vyrgines, theyr tresses of haire, partly curling vppe vppon their forheades, some turned about their heads and rowled vp, some depending downe vppon theyr temples, and crisping and inanulating by their eares. From betwixt their shoulders grewe their winges like Harpies, stretching downe and extending to the foulding and turnings of theyr tayles, vpon their monstrous flankes grew out their fynnes to swimme withall, their beginning, their fishie and scalye

substance, and from thence so continuing theyr nether parts downewarde.

Within the saide Garland I beheld a rough Milche Gote, which a little child did suck, sitting vnder hir side vpon his fleshie young legges one streight foorth, and the other retract and bowed vnder him. VVith his little armes houlding himselfe by the hearie and rough locks, his countenance and eyes vpon the byg and full vdder thus sucking. And a certaine Nimphe, as it were speaking woords, and giuing voyces of contentment, to the Goat and bowing downe hir selfe with the left hand, held vp one of the feete, and with the right hand putting the pappe to the smacking kissings of the sucking infant, and vnder hir were these letters *Amalthea*.

Iupiter.

Iupiter's nursse.

Another Nimphe stood against the head of the Goate, with one arme carefully compassing the neck, and with the other shee held hir by the horne.

In the middest stood the third Nimphe with greene bowgh leaues in one hand, and in the other an oulde fashioned drinking bowle, more long then broad, like a boate by a little handle. Vnder hir feete was written *Melissa*.

The daughter of Melissus and Iupiter's nursse.

Betwixt one and other of the three fore specified Nymphes there were two other hauing Cymbals in theyr handes, as it were playing and dauncing, euery one apparrelled according to the perfection of theyr beauties, f. 23b
with an artificiall performance of workmanship in the vndertaken proportions, that they rather seemed the substances themselues then a Lythoglyph an Imagerie, either by *Policletus*, *Phidias*, or *Lysippus*, neyther did ẏ *Anaglipts* to *Artemisia* the Queene of *Caria*, *Scaphes*, *Briaxes*, *Timotheus*, *Leocaris* and *Theon*, come any thing neare for the workemanship heereof seemed to excell the

Anaglipts be cunning caruers and Grauers.

cunning of any humaine Lapicidarie, caruer, grauer, or cutter whatsoeuer.

Aboue this foresayde Triangle, and vnder the vpper coronice in a smooth plaine were these two Attic wordes in capitall Letters, ΔΙΟΣ ΑΙΓΙΟΧΙΟΝ.

This conspitious porche and gate, most woorthye to be behelde, thus stoode of a maruelous composition, excellently disposed. If I had not explaned the commodulation, and harmonie heereof particularly, I might haue beene blamed for my prolixitie and tediousnesse, and for wanting of fit words in the discription. And thus for this time heereof so much.

f. 24b. It must needes follow, that all the rest of the aforesaide court on euery side was beautifull to behold, and of stately workemanship by that which still remained standing: as in the inward parte the naues and columnes carrieng and bearing vp an immesurable and monstrous weight, and Corinthies of a lesser sort, a diuine and vnknowen work abounding in variety of perfections as proportion required and needfullnes did desire to beare vp the burthen that was laide vppon them. Their ornature and decking with woorkes, and deuises imitating the apparreling of princely bodies indewed as it were with an artificiall reason. For as to a large big and corpulent body strong legges, and broad feete, are necessarie to beare and carry the same: so in a modulate and well composed building, to sustaine great weights, Naues are appointed, and for beautie, columnes, Corinthies, and slender Ionices, are set vpon them. And this whole woorke euen after such sorte as was requisite for the harmonie thereof, euen so it stood in an approoued excellencie.

With diuersite of coulers, sweetlye set, and aptlye disposed, the reflexion of one beautifing an other, and all together making a gratious obiect. Of *Porphyrit*, *Ophit*, *Numidian*, *Alabastrit*, *Pyropœcil*, *Lacedemonian* greene, and white marble, diuerslie watered, and of *Andracine* with white spottes, and many others of strange sorts and diuers commixtures.

I found one rare forme of a base, in fashion like a cushion vpon the plynthe whereof stood two trochils or torrules, with an interposition of Hypotracles or shaftes, and Astragals, with a supreame Thore.

Diuers places were hidden and couered ouer with winding felted and spreding Iuie, full of black berries, and greene soft leaues heare and there growing vp, and hindering the inwarde obiect of the auncient worke, with other Murall and wall weeds comming out of the chinkes and clifts, as the bell-flowre, Venus Nauill, & Erogennet, of some called Loue, to whom he is gratefull, bushing downe againe toward the ground, in other ryfts grew Mowse-eare, Polypodie, Adientus or Lady hayre, the iagged and curled Cithracus the knotted Lunarie minor, Prickmaddam, Polytricon, or goulden lockes and such like, which vse to grow in decayed buildings, and ould stone wales, so that many woorthie peeces were inuested and hydden from me, with such like f. 25.
weedes and greene Olyues the garnishers of ruines.

There was in diuers places inestimable huge downe falles of many columnes or rather confused piles of broken stones, and vnshapely Culpins mounting vp from the earth.

Among which downefallen peeces I might see the remaynders of diuers shapes of men of sundrie sortes, many naked, other some hauing their members couered with folded and plited induments, fast sticking to their naked proportions. Some standing vpon the left foote, others vpon the right in a streight sort, with their heads perpendicularly, euer the center betwixt their heeles, and some looking sidewaies in height, foure Cubites of sixe foote.

Others standing vpon both feete, some deale distant one from an other, and each one in a maiestie sitting in their thrones, and the rest with a rare and modest grace in their best pleasing and appointed seates.

There also I beheld innumerable *trophaes*, spoyles of armor, and infinite ornaments, with the heades of Oxen and Horses of conuenient bignes, and about their hornes part of their garlands of leaues, fruites, twigges, braunches and floures, and some about part of their bodies, with little children riding vpon them and playing, in so perfect a sort and wished order, as the most skilfull workemaister full of varietie, labour, studie, and industrie could deuise and performe. With what care and paine his abounding skill did plainly manifest, and with what pleasure the effect of his purpose did no whit obscure.

And with such an *Eurithmie* or apt proportioning of members, hee did shewe the subtiltie of the art of *Lapicidarie*, as if the substances had not beene of the hardest marble howsoeuer, but of soft chaulke or Potters claie, and with what conclansture the stones were couched, and by what Artillerie, rule and measure they were composed and set, it was woonderfull to imagine.

This was the true Art enucleating and discouering the ignorance that wee worke in, our detestable presumption, and publike condemned errors.

This is that cleare and perfect light, which sweetly and with our vnconstrained willes draweth our dimme sighted eies to contemplate and behold the same. For none (vnles it be he which of set purpose refuseth to behold it) but his eyes would dasell with continuall desire to see it.

This is that which accuseth horrible couetousnes, the deuourer and consumer of all vertue, a stil byting and euerlasting greedie worme in his heart that is captiuated and subiect to the same, the accursed let and hinderance to well disposed wittes, the mortal enemy to good Architecturie, and the execrable Idol of this present world, so vnworthily worshipped, and damnably adored. Thou deadly poison to him that is infected with thee, what sumptuous workes are ouerthrowne, and by thee interdicted.

Herewithall I beeing rauished and taken vp with vnspeakeable delight and pleasure in the regarding of this rare and auncient venerable monument of such a grace and admiration, that I knew not to which part to turne me first, here and there willingly looking about, and thereat amazed, considerately perusing ouer what the ingrauen histories presented vnto me, as I remoued my selfe from place to place, with an vnknowne delight, and vnreportable pleasure to beholde the same, gaping at them with open mouth, forgetting my selfe like a young childe, neuer satisfying my greedie eyes and vnsaciable desire to looke and ouerlooke the exquisite perfection of the auncient worke, I was spoiled and robbed of all thoughts whatsoeuer, the remembrance of my desired *Polia*, often accuring, onely excepted. But with an extreeme and deepe fet sigh, let vs leaue her a litle, and returne again to our continued purpose.

THE SIXTH CHAPTER.

f. 26. **Poliphilus entring a little waye in at the described porch, with great delight he there also beheld how it was garnished and adorned, and after as he was comming out he met with a monstruous dragon whereat he was extreemlie afraide, and compelled to runne backe into the building, and at last getting foorth with much adoe hee came into a fertile place.**

GREAT AND COMMENDABLE thing without dout it shold be, trulie to discribe, & from point to point, to set down the incredible work, and vnimagined composition, of so vast a frame, and huge bignes, of so great a buildinge with the excellencie of the entrance, in a conspicuous and sightly place, conueniently situated, where of my delight to behold them, did exced the greatnes of my admiration breeding in me such a conceit so as I perswaded my self that *Iupiter* durst not vndertake the like to the rest of the gods, & certainly beleeuing that no workman, or human witt could compase so huge a frame, expresse so notable conceits, or imagine and inuent so rare deuises and so gorgiouslie to garnishe them, in so singuler an order and simmetry, to dispose them, and without supplement or correction perfictlye to finishe them. A rare and insolent pride in a building. Vppon which occasion I was in some doubt and that not a little that if the naturall historiographer had seene or heard of this, hee woulde haue scorned that of Egipt, and the cunning and industrie of the woorking thereof, for that heerein the sundrie and diuers woorkes effected by many seuerall woorkmen seemed in the perfections, of their dewe proportion sas if they had been performed by one himselfe.

He would also as lightlie haue regarded the skillfull cunning of *Satirus* the architect and other of fame, especiallye *Simandrus*, for the woorke of *Memnon*, who cut the three statures of *Iupiter* in one stone, the feet being aboue seauen cubits long.

To this the representation of the magnanimous *Semiramis* carued out of the mountaine *Bagistanus* must geue place.

And letting passe to speake of the insolent greatnes of the Piramides of Memphis, those writers at large would haue bente themselues to this description. And leauing vnreported, the famous Theaters, Amphitheaters, Bathes, and building sacred and prophane, carriages, of waters, and colosses, and that of Appolline translated by *Lioculus*. Or the temple dedicated to *Iupiter* by *Claudius Cæser*. Or that of *Lisippus* at *Tarentum*, or the wonder of *Carelindius* at the Rhodes, and of *Xenorodus* in France, and in Roome. And the colosse of *Scrapus* nine cubits longe of Smarage or *Emerauldes*, or the famous Labyrinth of *Egypt*. Or the representacion of *Hercules* at *Tyre*. f. 26[b].

They woulde haue accommodated their sweete styles, to the commendation heard of as aboue all other most excellent, although the Obelist of Iupiter, compact of fower frustes, fortie Cubits high, fower Cubits broade, and two Cubits thick, in his deluber within the temple dooth manifest it selfe to be a wonderfull miracle.

Vnsaciable thus casting mine eyes, and turning vp my countenance now this way & now that way, towards this huge & mighty frame, I thus thought with my selfe. If the fragments and remaynder of so sacred an antiquitie, and if the greet and dust of such a decayed monument, can breed a stupifaction in the admiration thereof, and cause so great delyght to behould the same, what would it haue done in chiefest pride.

After this my discourseing, reason perswaded mee to suppose, that with in might bee the Aultar of *Venus* for hir misticall Sacrificees and sacred flames, or the representation of hir Godhead, or the *Aphrodise* of hir selfe and hir little Archer, and therefore with a deuoute reuerence, my right foote beeing set vppon the halowed lymit of the doore, there came towards me flying a white *Horix*.[1]

But I sodainlye with out any further regard or curious forcaste which with my searching eies went in as the spatious and lightsome entrie gaue me leaue, representing vnto me such sights as merit, and are Condigne of euerlastinge remembrannce, in ether sydes stilled with smoth poollishede Marble, in the middle parte where of there was impacte a rounde table, inclanstrede and compassede about with a greene Stonne verye pretious and accordinglie asosciated with curious workemanship. And the opposite of verie blacke stone, scorning and contemning the hardnes of iron, and cleare and shining as a mirror. By meanes whereof as I passed by (vnawares) I grew afrayd at my owne shadow, neuertheles I was by an by comforted with vnexspected delight, for the place that occasioned my disquiet nowe offered vnto me the grounde of all sciences, historied in a visible manifest and experte painting.

And on either sides vnder the same beautifull and most noble tables, there were placed all a long seates of stone. The pauement neat and cleane from dust, being made of *Ostracus*.[2]

[1] A bird of slow flight & long liuing, in old monuments by Augurs dedicated to Saturne.

[2] Ostracus be pounded shels mixed with lime, whereof a plaister is made to floor withall.

And so in like manner the coloured vpper seeling was pure and voyd of Spiders and Cobwebs, by reason of the continuall fresh ayre both entring in and going out.

The seeling of the walles as aforesayde, mounted vp to the bendyng of the Arche from the Chapters which stood vpon their strict and vpright Antes euen to the vttermost ende of the entrie, which was by my perspectiue iudgement twelue paces.

From which perpolyte ligature and fastned ioyntes, the roofe of the entrie all the length thereof, did march with a hemicircubate flexure, answerable to the Antes and streight sides of the afore described porche full of varieties and exquisite representments, rarely ingrauen and of little water monsters, as in the water it selfe in their right and well disposed plemmyrules, halfe men and women, with their fishie tailes: some imbracing one an other with a mutuall consent, some playing vppon Flutes, and others vpon other fantasticall instruments.

Some sitting in straunge fashioned Charriots, and drawne in them by swift Dolphines, crowned and adorned with water Lillies sutable to the furniture of the garnished seates: some with diuers dishes and vessels replenished with many sortes of fruites, Others with plentiful copies, some coupled togither with bands, and others wrastling as they did, riding vppon *Hipposatamics*, and other sundrie and vncoth beastes, with a Chiloneall defence.

Some wantonly disposed, others to varietie of sportes and feastes, with liuely indeuours and quicke motions, most singularlye well set foorth, and filling all ouer the afore- f. 27b.
sayde arched suffite.

Along vnder the bending ryse of the entrie, I beheld a singular woorkemanship of sundrie representments and counterfeits, in an excellent Thessellature, bright shining lyke goulde, and of diuers other coulers, with a border two foote broade, compassing about the turning couer of the roofe, both vnder and aboue, and deuiding them from the woorke, vpon the plaine sides, of so perfect and fresh coulers, as if they had beene new set, with a naturall leafewoorke of an emerawld greene, vppon a punice or tawnie grounde, with Flowers of *Cianees* and *Phœnicees* adulterated with curious knottes and windings, and in the conteyned space of the aforesayde sides, I sawe this auncient Hystorye paynted.

Europa, a young Ladye, swimming into *Creete* vppon a prestigious Bull. And the edict of King *Agenor* to his Sonnes *Cadmus*, *Fœnice*, and *Cilicia*, to finde out theyr defloured sister, which thing they could not do, but after that they had valiauntly kylled the skalie fierce Dragon that kepte the fayre Fountayne: and consulted with *Appollo*, they determined with theyr followers, and agreed to builde a Cittie, where the bellowing Heyffer should appoynte, wherevppon that countrey, euen to this daye carryeth the name of the bellowing of a Cowe *Europe*. *Cadmus* builte *Athens*. The other brother *Fœnicia*. The third *Cilicia*.

Thys woorke and musaicall painting, was rightlye placed in order, as the beginning and end of the historie required with fictions in theyr naturall coulers, theyr actions and degrees rightlye expressed.

On the contrarie side, I beheld in the same manner the wanton and lasciuious *Pasiphæ* burning in infamous lust, lying in a Machine or frame of wood, and the Bull leaping vpon that hee knew not.

f. 28. After that the monstrous mynotaure with hys vglye shape shut and inclosed in the intricate Labyrinth. And after that the imprysoned *Dedalus*, artificially making of winges for hymselfe, and his young sonne Icarus, who vnhappylye not obseruing hys Fathers rule, fell downe headlong into the deepe see, leauing vnto the same seas his name, after his drowning. And his discreete father, being safe according to his vowe, hanging vp his wings in the temple of *Appollo*.

Vppon the which I stoode with open mouth attentiuely gazing with my eyes, and rauished in minde with the beautie of the hystorie, so well disposed, so perfectly ordered, so artificiallye paynted and curiouslie expressed, whole and sounde, without any signe of decaye, the strength of the glutinous substance, which ioyned and held the Thessalature or checkers, together was such and so perfect. For therein the workeman had taken great paine and shewed a rare cunning.

And thus foote by foote I went forward bowldly, examining and behoulding what direction and arte of painting hee had obserued with a pensiled distribution to make whole proportions in a smoothe and flat playne. Some lynes drawing neere to my obiect, and some seeming as they had beene a farre of hardely to bee deserned, and yet both of a like neerenesse. And the same againe which was hardlie to bee seene, to offer it selfe more and more, to the iudgement of the eye, with exquisite parergie and shadowing.

Waters, Fountaines, Mountaines, Hilles, woodes, and beasts, in theyr naturall coulours, and distante one from an other, with opposite light. And in apparrell the plyghts and fouldes so cunninglye perfected and shaddowed that as well in that as in all the rest, the arte did seeme to enuye nature it selfe, and that not a little whereat I greatly woondered.

After this manner I came to the further ende, where

the beautifull hystories finished, and beyond the same more inward the darknes was such as I durst not enter, & comming back againe I heard among the ruines a continuing noise like the cracking of bones or their ratling
f. 28b. together, whereat I stood still forgetting my fore conceiued delight being interrupted therewith from the sweetnes of the obiects. At length I might heare a rustling as if a dead Oxe had been dragged vpon the ground, the noyse still approaching and comming neerer and neerer the poarch that I was to passe out at, where I heard a great hissing of a huge Serpent: the sodaine feare I was in, made mee past crying out for helpe, neither did I see how to escape, but by running into the darke and obscure vastnes whiche before I was afraide to enter into.

Oh vnhappie wretch oppressed with aduers and sad fortune, I saw in the entrie of the doore comming towardes mee, no hurtfull Lyon crowching to *Androclus*, but a fearefull and horrible Dragon shaking her trifulked and three parted tongue against mee, grating her teeth, and making a skritching or critching noyse, her squamy and scaly hide trailing vpon the flowerd pauement, clapping her winges vpon her wrimpled backe, with a long taile folding and crinckling like an Eele and neuer resting. *O hi me*, the sight was sufficient to haue affrighted *Mars* himselfe in the assurednes of warlike Armour, or to haue made tremble the strong and mightie Hercules, for all his molorchied and clubbed but. And to call *Theseus* backe from his begunne inprese and bold attempt, and to terrifie the Gyant *Typhon*, and to make the proudest and stoutest heart whatsoeuer to quaile and stoope. I wished my selfe the swiftnes of *Atalanta*, beeing but young and vnarmed, no way able to encounter with such a poisonable force, and perceiuing his blacke infectious breath smoaking

The Dragon is that Abaddon and Apolion, the enemy to mankinde.

out at his mouth. Beeing past all hope to slip by him, I deuoutly cried for diuine helpe. And sodeinly turning my backe, as fast as I could runne, I conueighed my fearefull bodie by the helpe of my swift pacing feete, into the inward part of the darke places, penetrating through diuers crooked torments, ambagious passages and vnknowne waies.

The darke places is ignorance, and the wisedome of this world which is no thing els but meere folly.

So that I thought to bee in the inextricable frame of the prudent *Dedalus*, or of *Porsena*, so full of wayes and winding turnings, one entring into another, to deceiue the intent of the goer out, or in the romthie denne of the horrible *Cyclops*, or the hollow Caue of the theeuish *Carus*. In such sort, that although my eyes were somewhat wel acquainted with the darkenes, yet I could see iust nothing. f. 29. But was glad to stretche out my armes from before my face, groping about mee (lyke one that played blynde Sym) least I should runne my face against some pyllers, and feeling with my feete softlye before I did rest vpon them for feare I should tumble downe into some vaulte vnder thys mighty Pyramides.

And looking backe, whether this fearefull Dragon did still followe mee or no, the light was cleane gone. And I remayning in a darke place, full of sundrie turnings and crossing passages, in a greater terror and more deadly heauinesse of minde then *Mercurie*. Making himselfe *Ibis* and *Apollo*, *Threicia*, *Diana*, into the lyttle byrd *Cholomene*. And *Pan* into two shapes. I am more afraide then euer was *Oedipus*, *Cyrus*, *Crœsus*, and *Perseus*. And more trembling then the theefe *Thracilius* in his beares skinne. In sorrowe more abounding then poore *Pscyphes*. And in more laboursome daungers then *Lucius Apuleus*, when hee heard the theeues consulting to knocke him on the head and kyll him.

Cosby for killing the L. Browgh.

Oppressed and laden with all these aforenamed frightes and terrors. I began to imagine that the Dragon was flying about my head, and with the noyse of hir scritching teeth and tearing clawes to take hould vpon me with hir deuouring iawes: my heart giuing mee to vnderstand, that the carniuorus Woolfe which I drempt of, was a presage of this my last doubted end. And thus running vppe and downe like a little poore Pismeere or Aunte, when the Partrich is scratching vpon their hillocks and picking of them vp. With my watchfull and attentiue eares, listning if the horrible monster with her slimie and filthie poyson and stinking sauour were drawing towards mee. And fearing whatsoeuer came first into my thought.

Finding my selfe vnarmed, voyde of all helpe, in this mortall daunger, and miserable perplexitie, although that death is naturally bytter and hated, yet notwithstanding at that time, I did gratiouslie esteeme of it, which mee thought I could suffer willinglye, but that will was insufficient: hope still looking, and perswading mee of an vncertaine, fearefull, and vnquyet lyfe.

Alas howe my soule and bodye were lothe to leaue one
an another, the sorrowe whereof made me vnwilling to
f. 29b. intertaine so cruel an enemy as death: whereupon I plucking vp a good heart, thought thus.

Shall the greatnes of my loue so sweetly set on fire, now decaie, frustrated of anie effect, for if at this present I had been but presented with a sight thereof, I could haue beene yet the better satisfied.

But yet forthwith returning to the inward impression of my sweetest obiect, stil dwelling in the secret of my heart, I fell into blobering teares, for the losse of two so worthie iewels. That was *Polia* and my precious life. Continually calling vpon her with deepe sighes and singultiue sobbings, sounding in the thicke ayre, incloystered vnder the huge arches and secret darke couering, saying thus to my selfe.

If I die heere thus miserably, sorrowfully, and vncomfortably, all alone, who shal bee a woorthie successour of so precious a gemme? And who shal be the possessor of such a treasure of so inestimable valure? And what faire heauen shal shew so cleare a light? Oh most wretched *Poliphilus*, whether dost thou go vnfortunate? whether dost thou hasten thy steppes? hopest thou euer to behold againe any desired good? Behould all thy gratious conceits and pleasant highe delyghtes builded in thy apprehensiue thoughtes, through the sweetenes of loue, are deadly shaken, and abruptlie precipitated and cast downe? Looke how thy loftie *Amorous* cogitations are shaken in peeces and anihilated. Ah me what iniurious lot & maleuolent constellations, haue so perniciously driuen, and deceitfully allured thee into this miserable obscure darknes? and now haue despitefully ledde thee in a heape of mortal feares, and drowning in a deepe sea of vnspeakeable sorrowes. To the vnmercifull deuouring and sodaine gobbling vp of so filthie a monster, and to bee rotted and digested in the stinking intrailes of so fowle a beast, and to bee cast out in so vile a place. Oh lamentable and vnaccustomed death. O miserable end of my desired life. Where are my eyes? what be they barreine? Is their humor gone? Are there no more teares left to fall trickeling downe my blubbered cheekes? Well then I perceiue that death is at my backe, who did euer see such a change of fortune? Behold vnhappie and wayward death, and the last houre, and accursed minute thereof at hande, in this darkesome shade, where my bodie and flesh is appointed to bee a f. 30.

ſoode for so ſowle a beast. What furie? what crueltie? what miserie more monstrous can a mortall creature suffer. That sweete and pleasant light should bee reſt from them that bee aliue, and the earth denied to them that are dead. What hoggish calamitie, and deformed mishap, so greeuously and vntimely shall abandon from mee my most desired and ſlorishing *Polia*. Farewell the merror of all vertue, and true perfection of beautie, ſarewell.

And thus beyond all measure tost and tumbled in such and so great afflictions, my verie soule was vexed within me, striuing to be set at libertie from my vnfortunate and feeble bodie, passing vp and downe I knew not where. My legges weake, feeble and fowltering vnder mee, my spirites languishing, and my sences in a maner gone from mee. Sauing that I called deuoutly vppon the omnipotent God to haue pittie vppon mee, and that some good Angell might bee appointed to conduct mee out. And with that beholde I discouered a little light. To the which, how gladly I hasted, let euerie one iudge what hee would doo in such a perplexitie.

I saw an euerlasting Lampe, burning before an Aultar that was fiue foote high, and tenne foote broad, with the images of golde standing thereupon, which I could not verie perfectly behold, notwithstanding the burning Lampe, the grossenes of the ayre was such and so great an enemy to the light.

And alwayes with attentiue eares I diligently harkened, as not yet ridde of feare, and somewhat I saw, the dimme images and the large foundations, and feareful vaultes, and subterraneal buttresses or vpholders and strengthes, heare and there in infinite places distributed, and many huge and mightie pillers, some foure square, some sixe square, some eight square, aptly set vnder and approportioned to sustaine the vast bignes of the waightie *Pyramides.*

There I hauing small delight to make anie long staie, I intended to take an vnknowne way further in, which my vndertaken course, I espied a light whiche so long I had wished for, comming in at a litle wicket as small as I could see.

Oh with what ioy, and with what a glad heart, I f. 30b.
beheld it, and with what cheare did I hasten my steppes towards it. Perchance faster then *Canistius* or *Philonides* my vnbrideled gladnesse and extreame desire to come neere therevnto was such, that I reuoked and haled backe againe the diuorse of my discontented and irkesome life, successiuely comforting my perturbed minde and quailed hart. Somewhat refreshing and reassuring my selfe : filling vp againe my euacuated and emptie heart, and replenishing the same with his ould cogitations.

Two blockish lasie lubbers, one of Melite an other of Athens, that thought it a great labour to eate their owne meate.

Nowe I settled my selfe more towardes my louely *Polia,* and bound my affections more surely to hir. Being perswaded and firmely opinionated, that this sight was a traunce in loue, for shewing that I should dye and lose my loue. Oh how extreamely did it vexe mee. Neyther did it refuse or make resistance to anye sharpe and newe assaulte of loue, which in my stroken and sore wounded heart woulde lye festering and feeding of himselfe.

And by this time, all lets and hynderances past ouer, a spatious and large going out was offered vnto me. Then by meanes of the cleere light I was somwhat comforted, and reassuming and gathering together againe my wandering thoughts, and restoring my prostrate force, my suspected and vnknowne voyage, made me to set out in running : so as the nearer I came to the doore, the bigger mee thought it grewe. To the which at last by Gods wyll, *Polia* in my amorous brest bearing a predominante vigor, I came, not ceasing to continue forward my fast course: my hands which before I groping helde foorth, to keepe me from running against pyllers, I nowe vsed like a payre of Ores to hasten mee awaye.

Thus traueling on safely, I came into a verie pleasaunt sighte and countrie, in the which I was not yet without feare, and not daring to rest me downe, the impression of the horrible monster was so fresh in my minde, that mee thought I still heard him behinde me, and therefore I could not so easily forget him. But was raythar perswaded to goe on further: first because the countrie was so fertile, pleasaunt and beautifull: Secondly, that I might get farre enough off from the place wherein I was so lately affrighted. That then I sitting downe, might rest my selfe,
f. 31. and set my minde together againe, and forget this conceiued dread, at my entrance in of the gate, the apparation of the white Sorix gratiously comming againe into my reteyning memorie, an exhortatorie prouacation, and good occasion to animate and comforte me, because that to *Augures* it was a gratefull and propitious signe of good luck.

At last I was resolutely perswaded to commit my selfe to the benignitie of my good fortune, which some time might bee vnto me an officious and bountifull handmaide, of prosperous euents. And therewithall pricked forward and prouoked to continue on my walke, whether my wearie and feeble legges would conduct and bring mee. Capillata ministra.
And yet I was (as in good sorte became mee) somewhat doubtfull to enter into such a place, (beeing vnknowne vnto me) where perchaunce it was not lawfull for me to come. Albeit that I was heerin more audacious and bould a great

deale, then in the enteraunce of the gorgeous Porche. And thus my brest fast beating, and my minde perplexed, I saide to my selfe.

There is no cause that should lead mee to turne back againe, all things considered : is not this a safer place, and more fit to flie from daunger ? Is it not better to hassard a man's lyfe in the light and cleere Sunne, then to dye and sterue in a blinde darkenesse ? and so resolued not to turne backe anye more : with a deepe fet sighe, I called into memorie, the pleasure and delight that my sences had well neere lost : for the woorke which I had seene was full of maruelous woonders, and thinking by what meane I was depriued of them, I called to remembrance the brasen Lyons, in Salomons Temple, which were of such fierce countenances, as that they would bring men to forgetfulnes.

And into such an estate I was afrayde that the Dragon had brought me, that so excellent and maruellous woorkes, and rare inuentions, in a manner vnpossible for any humaine creature to performe, worthie to be manifested, and by my selfe diligentlye perused, should now be fled out of my sucking remembrance, so as I should not bee able to make a true reporte of them : but therein I contraried my selfe : neither did I finde that I was in a Lithargie passion : But that I verrie well remembred and helde without any defaulte in order and proportion f. 31b.
whatsoeuer I had seene and beheld. And that the monstrous and cruell beast was a verrie liuelye substance, and no fiction, the like of any mortall man sildome seene, no not of *Regulus*. The verie remembrance whereof, made my hayre stand right vp, and foorthwith mooued me to mend my pace.

Afterward returning to my selfe, I thought thus.

Heere without all doubte (for so I imagined by reason of the glorious bountie of the beautifull soile) is no habitation but for ciuill people, or rather for Angles and noble personages, and a place for Nimphes to frequent vnto, or for the Goddes and Auncients, Monarches and princes, in so much as my perswasiue desire did prouoke forwarde my restrained pace, causing a perceuerance in my late begun iourney. And thus as one captiuated and subiect to the sharpe spurre of vnsatiable desire, I purposed to houlde on whether the fayrenesse of my fortune should conduct mee, as yet but indifferent and rather languishing.

Nowe come to behoulde a fayre and plentifull countrie, fruitefull fieldes, and fertill groundes, I did exceedinglye commend the desire that mooued mee first to enter into them. But especially to giue thankes to him that had brought mee out from the fearefull place, which now I little regarded being far enough off from it.

THE SEVENTH CHAPTER.

Poliphilus sheweth the commodiousnesse of the countrie where-into hee was come, in his trauailing within the same, he came vnto a goodlie Fountaine, and howe hee sawe fiue faire Damsels comming towardes him, and their woondering at his comming hither, assuring him from hurte, and inuiting him to bee a partaker of their solaces. f. 32.

HUS GOTTEN FOORTH OF this fearefull hell, darke hollownesse, and dreadfull place (although it were a sacred Aphrodise and reuerend Temple :) and beeing come into a desired light, louelye ayre, and pleasaunt countrie, full of contentment : I turned my selfe about to looke backe at the place from whence I came out, and where my life, my life that latelye I esteemed so lightlie, was so greatlye perplexed and daungered, where I beheld a mountaine vnnaturall, with a moderate assention and steepe rising, ouer-growne and shaddowed with greene and tender leaues of mastic Okes, Beeches, Wainescot Okes, Holmes, *Cerries Aesculies*, Corke trees, Yew trees, Holly or Huluer, or Acilon.

And towardes the plaine, it was couered with Hamberries, Hasels, Fylbirds, prune, print, or priuet, and whitened with the flowers thereof : bycoulered Xeapie, beeing red towardes the north, and white against the Southe, Plane trees, Ashe trees, and such like, spredding and stretching out their braunches : fowlded and imbraced with the running of Hunnisuckles or woodbines, and Hoppes, which made a pleasaunt and coole shade. Vnder the which grewe Ladyes Seale or Rape Violet, hurtfull for the sight, iagged Polypodie, and the Trientall and foure inched Scolopendria, or Hartes toongue, Heleborous Niger, or Melampodi, Trayfles, and such other Vmbriphilous hearbes and Woodde Flowers, some adorned with them, and some without.

So that the mouth of the darke place, out of the which I had escaped, was in a manner within the highe Moun-
32b. taine all ouergrone with trees.

And as I could coniecture it was iust against the afore spoken of frame, and in my iudgement it had been some rare peice of woork, more auncient then the other, and by time wasted and consumed, now bearing Iuie and other wall trees, and so was become an ouer growne wood, that I could scarce perceiue any comming out, or mouth for easie passage but euen for a necessitie, for it was rownd about compassed and enuironed with bushie and spreeding trees, so as I was neuer determined to enter in there againe.

In the streight passage of the valie betwixt the extensed and highe mounting rockes, the ayre was dim by reason of the retained vapores, and yet I was as well pleased therewith as *Apollo* at his deuine birth.

But letting passe this hole, from the which I gat out by stooping, let vs come forward to the sweet liberties which I next beheld and that was a thicke wood of Chestnuts at the foote of the hill, which I supposed to be a soile for *Pan* or some Siluane God with their feeding heards and flockes, with a pleasant shade, vnder the which as I passed on, I came to an auncient bridge of marble with a very great and highe arche, vppon the which along winning to eyther sides of the walls, there were conuenient seats to rest vppon, which although they were welcome to my wearye bodie, yet I had more desire to go on forwarde, vppon which sides of the bridge, iust ouer the top of the arche, there was placed a porphirit table with a gorgeous border of curious workmanship, one table on the one side and an other on the other side, but that one the left side was of *Ophite*.

Vppon the table on my right hand as I went I beheld *Egiptie hierogliphies* on this sorte, An auncient Helmet crested with a Dogges head.

The bony scalpe of an oxe with two green braunches of trees bound fast to the hornes. And an ould lampe. Which hierogliphis the braunches excepted because I know not whether they were of Firre tree, Pineapple, Larix or Iuniper, or such like: I thus interpret.

PATIENTIA EST ORNAMENTVM, CVSTODIA ET PROTECTIO f. 33.
VITAE.

On the other side there was ingrauen a cyrcle, then an Anchor with a Dolphin winding about the strangule thereof, which I coniectured should signifie this, ΑΕΙ ΣΠΕΥΔΕ ΒΡΑΔΕΟΣ. *Semper festina tarde.*

Vnder which auncient, sure, and faire bridge, did runne a most cleare swift water, deuiding it selfe into two seuerall currents, the one one way and the other an other, which ranne most colde, making a soft continuall still noyse, in their freesed, broken and nibbled Channels, by their eaten in and furrowed bancke, full of stones, couered ouer and shadowed with trees, their spredding rootes appearing in the same bare, and about them hanging *Tricomanes*, *Adiantus* and *Cimbalaria*, and bearded also with diuers small hayres as vse to growe about the banckes of Ryuers.

The wood that I haue spoken of, was to looke vppon verye pleasant, neyther ouer thick or more large in compasse than a man would wish, but building a delightfull shadowe, the trees full of small birdes and foules.

Right forwarde, the Bridge did extende it selfe, and leade towardes a large plaine, resounding all ouer with the sweete chirpings, melodious recordings, and loude singing of them. Wherein were leaping and running little Sqirrels, and the drowsie Dormouse, and other harmeles beastes.

And after this manner as aforesayd, this wooddie Countrie shewed it selfe, enuironed about with high mountaines as much as a man might looke vnto, and the plaine couered all ouer with a fine varietie of sundrie sweete hearbes, and the cleare channels of Christaline streames, sliding downe a long the hilles with a murmuring noyse into the leauell vally.

Adorned and beautified with the flowring bitter Oliue, Lawrell, white Poplar, and Lisimachia, blacke Pople, Alders, and wilde Ashe.

Vpon the hils grew high Firre trees vnarmed, and the weeping Larix, whereon Turpentine is made, and such like.

When I had well considered of this so fruitfull and so commodious a place for cattel and beasts to be fedde in and kept, (for it looked as though it would desire a shepheardes company and a pastorall song) I mused what should be the occasion, that so commodious a place should lye vninhabited. And casting my eyes further on forward into the plaine before mee, and leauing this fore discribed place, I might perceiue a building of Marble, shewing the roofe thereof ouer the tender toppes of the compassing trees. At the sight whereof, I grew wonderfully glad and in good hope, that there yet I should finde some habitation and refuge. To the which without delaie I hastined my selfe. And being come thereunto, I found a building eight square, with a rare and wonderfull fountaine: which was not altogither amisse. For as yet I had not quenched and slaked my thirst.

This building was eight cornered, small towardes the top and leaded. Vpon one side there was placed a faire stone of pure white Marble foure cornered, half as long again as it was broad, which latitude as I supposed was some sixe foote.

Of this goodly stone were exact two litle halfe pillers,
chamfered with their bases, holding vp a streight Sime,
with a gule and adiected denticulature & cordicules, or
worke of harts, with their chapters vnder a Trabet,
Zophor and Coronice, ouer the which was a trigonall con- f. 34.
teined, in the fourth part of the stone smooth and plaine
without any workemanship in the table thereof sauing a
litle garland, within the which were two Doues drinking
in a small vessel.

Al the space vnspoken of inclusiue was cut in and euacuated, betwixt the Pillers the Gulature and ouerthwart Trabet, did containe an elegant Cigrued Nimph. And vnder the Syme was another quarter wrought with Thors, Torques, Ballons and a Plinth.

Which faire Nymph laye sleeping vppon a folded cloth, lap, and wounde vp vnder her head. An other part conueniently brought ouer her, to hide that bare which was womanly & meete to be kept secret. Lying vpon her right side with that subiected arme retract, and her open palme vnder her faire cheeke, wherevpon she rested her head.

The other arme at libertie, lying all along ouer her

left loyne, stretching to the middle of her goodly thigh. By her smal teates (like a yong maids) in her round brests did sprowt out smal streamings of pure and cleare fresh water from the right brest as it had been a threed, but from the left brest most vehemently. The fall of both of them, receiued in a vessel of *Porphyrit* stone, with two Receptories ioyning togither in the same vessel, seperated and distinct from the Nimph sixe foote, standing vppon a conuenient frame of flint stone. Betwixt either of the receptories, there was another vessel placed, in the which the waters did striue togither and meete, running out at the cut and appointed places, in the middle lymbus of their Receptories, which waters comixt out of that vessel, vnladed themselues into a little channel sliding away, and what with one and what with the other, al the hearbes and flowres adioyning, and about were bountifullye benifited.

That of the left brest did spin vp so high, that it did not weat or hinder any that would sucke or drinke of the water that streamed and sprung out of the right brest.

And this excellent Image was so difinitelye expressed, that I feare mee *Praxiteles* neuer perfourmed the lyke for *Venus*, to *Nichomides* the King of *Caria* which Idoll he appointed to be adored of his subiects, although the beauty therof were such that it moued that filthie people to fleshly concupiscence.

But I was perswaded that the perfection of the image of *Venus* was nothing to this, for it looked as if a most bewtifull Ladye in hir sleep had beene chaunged into a stone, hir hart still panting, and hir sweete lipps readie to open, as if she would not be so vsed.

From hir head hir loose tresses laye wauing vppon the suppressed couering, fowlded and plited and as it were scorning the haires of the inglomatede cloth, hir thighes of a conueniente bignes and hir fleshie knees somwhat bending vpp, and retract towards hir.

Showing hir streight toes as it were intreating hir fingers to handle and streine them, the rest of hir bodie aunswerable to the perfections of these seuerall proportions.

And behind hir the shadowing of the leaffye *Memerill* or *Arbut* full of soft small Apples and fruite, and prettye byrdes as yf they had beene chirping and singing of hir a sleep.

At hir feet stood a satire in prurient lust vppon his gotishe feet, his mouth and his nose ioyning together like a gote with a beard growinge on either sides of his chin, with two peakes and shorte in the middeste like Goates hayre, and in like manner about his flankes and his eares, grewe hayre, with a visage adulterated betwixt a mans and a Goates, in so rare a sort as if the excellent woorkman in his caruinge had had presented vnto him by nature the Idea and shape of a *Satire.*

The same *Satire,* had forciblie with his lefte hand bent an arme of the *Arbut* tree ouer the sleepie nimphe, as if he would make hir a fauorable shadowe therewith, and with the other hand howldinge vpp a curtaine by one of the sides that was fastened to the body of the tree.

Betwixt the comare *Meimerill* or *Arbut,* and the *Satire,* were two little *Satires,* the one howlding a bottell in his hands and the other with two snakes fowlding about his armes.

The excellencie, dilicatnes and perfection of this figment and woorkmanshippe cannot be suffi[ci]entlie expressed.

f. 35. This also helping to adorne the sweetnes thereof that is the whitnes of the stone, as if it had been pure iuorie.

I wondered also at the woorking of the clothe coueringe as yf it had been wouen: and at the bowes, braunches, and leaues, and at the little birdes, as if they had been singing and hopping vpp and downe vpon their pretie feet in euerie ioynt single and pounce made perfect, and so the *Satire* like wise. Vnder this rare and woonderfull carued woork betwixt the gulatures and vnduls in the plaine smothe was grauen in *Atthic* characters this poesye ΠΑΝΤΑ ΤΟ ΚΑΔΙ.

f. 36. The thirst which I had gotten the daie before was so increased, that I was prouoked now to slacken the same, or rather inticed with the faire beautie of the instrument, the coolenes whereof was such, as betwixt my lippes me thought it stirred and trembled.

And rounde about this pleasant place, and by the pipplyng channels, grew *Vaticinium*, *Lilly-conuallie*, and the flowring *Lysimachia* or willow hearbe, the sorrowfull Reedes, Myntes, water Parsley, Baume, *Hydrolapathos*, or water Sorrell, and other approued hearbes, and fine floures, a little Channel comming by a sluce from the Bridge, entering in and vnlading it selfe, was the cause of a goodly faire Poole, broad and large, in a verie good order, trimmed about and beautified with a fence of sweete Roses and Gessamine. And from thence running ouer it, dispersed itselfe, nourishyng and visiting the nexte adioyning fieldes and grounde, abounding in all sortes of hearbes, floures, fruites, and trees.

There grewe also great store of *Cynarie*, gratefull to *Venus*, wylde *Tansie*, *Colocassia*, with leaues like a shielde, and garden hearbes.

And from thence beholding the plaine fieldes, it

was woonderfull to see the greennes thereof, powdered with such varietie of sundrie sorted colours, and diuers fashioned floures, as yealow Crowfoote, or golden Knop, Oxeye, *Satrion* Dogges stone, the lesser Centorie, Mellilot, Saxifrage, Cowslops, Ladies fingers, wilde Cheruile, or shepheardes Needle, *Naucus* Gentil, Sinquifolie, Eyebright, Strawberies, with floures and fruites, wild Columbindes, Agnus Castus, Millfoyle, Yarrow, wherewith *Achilles* did heale *Telephus*, and the rust of the same speares head that hurt him. With the white Muscarioli, bee floures and Panenentes in so beautifull and pleasant manner, that they did greatly comfort mee (hauing lost my selfe) but euen with the looking vppon them. And heere and there in a measurable and wel disposed distaunce and space betweene. In a conuenient order and sweete disposed sort by a iust line, grew the greene and sweete smelling Orenges, Lymons, Citrons, Pomegranettes, their water boughes bendyng downe within one pace of the ground, couered with leaues of a glassie greene colour, of a great height and turning downe againe their f. 36b. toppes, laden with the aboundance of their floure and fruites, breathing forth a most sweet and delectable odoriferous smell. Wherwithall my appaled heart did not verie lightly reuiue himselfe (it might bee in a pestilent ayre and contagious and deadly sauour.)

For which cause I stood amazed and in great doubt what to thinke or doo, and the rather because in that place I had seene such a marueilous fountaine, the varietie of hearbes, the colours of floures, the placing orderly of the trees, the faire and commodious disposition of the seat, the sweet chirpings and quiet singing of Birds, and the temperate and healthful ayre. And which I could verie well haue been contented withall, and the worst of them might wel haue contented me, if I had found any inhabitant there. And somewhat I was grieued that I could no longer abide in such a place where so many delightful sightes did present themselues vnto mee. Neither was I aduised to my better safetie and content which way to turne me.

Standing thus in such a suspence of minde, calling to remembraunce the daunger that I had lastlye escaped and the present place that I was newlye entered into, and thinking vppon hieragliphes that I did see in the left side of the bridge, I was in doubt, to hasten my selfe towards any vnaduised aduers accident. And that such a monument and warning woorthie of golden letters, should not be set in vaine to them that passed by, which was *Semper festina tarde*. Behold of a sodaine behinde me I heard a rusling noyse, like the winde or beating of a Dragons winges. Alas I knew not what it should bee. And sodeinly ispasurated and turning my selfe about, I might perceiue vpon one side of me many silique trees of *Aegypt*, with their ripe long coddes hanging and beating one against an other with the winde, had felled downe themselues, which when I perceiued, I was soone quieted, and beganne to make sport at my owne folly.

I had not continued long thus, but I hard a singing company of gallant damoselles comming towardes mee (by their voyces of young and tender yeares) and faire (as I thought) solacing and sporting themselues among the flowering hearbes and fresh coole shadow, free from the suspect of any mans sight, and making in their Gate a great applause among the pleasant flowers. The in-
37. credible sweetnesse of hir musicall and consonant voyce, conueighed in the roriferous ayre, and spredding it

selfe abroade with the aunswerable sounde and delectable report of a warbeling harpe (for the tryall of which noueltie, I couched downe vnder the lowe bowghes of the next adioining bushes, and saw them come towardes mee with gratious gestures) hir Maydenlie head attyred and bound vp in fillets of glystering gould, and instrophiated redimited, garnished ouer and beset with floured mirtle, and vpon hir snowye foreheade, branched out hir trembling curled lockes, and about hir fayrest showlders, flew her long tresses after a nymphish fashion artyfitiallye handeled.

They were apparrelled in carpanticall habites of fine sylke of sondrye coulers, and weauinges of three sorts, one shorter, and distinct from the other. The nethermost of purple, the next of greene silke, & goulde or tissew, and the vppermost of curled white sendall, gyrded about their smale wastes with girdles of goulde, vnder the lower partes of their round breasts. Their sleeues of the same curled Sendall, often doubled, which bettered and graced the subiect couler. And tyed about their wrists with ribands of silke, tagged with Gouldsmithes woorke. And some of them with Pantophles vpon their shooes, the vpper part of the Pantophle of gould and purple silke, leafeworke, shewing thorough betwixt the voyde spaces of the leaues, the fine proportion of their prittie illaquiated and contayned feete. Their shooes comming straightly vnder their anckles, with two lappes meeting vpon their insteps, and closed fast eyther with Buttons or claspes of gowld after a fine manner. Aboue the hemmes of theyr nether garments, there compassed about insteed of gardes and imbrodered woorke of hearts, which now and then blowne vp with the gentle ayre, made a discouerie of their fine legges.

And assoone as they were aware of mee, they left of their song and stayed theyr nimpish gates, being amazed with the insighte, and of my comming into this place, maruelling together, and whisperinglye inquiring of me, one of another, for I seemed vnto them a rare and vnusuall thing, because I was an aliant and stranger, and by chaunce come into so famous and renowned a countrie, Thus they staide still, sometimes looking downe vpon me, & again muttering one to an other, I stood still like an image. Oh wo was me, for I felt all my ioynts quake like the leaues of an Aspe, in a bitter winde, And I was affraide of the presaging poesie that I had read, otherwise aduising me, whereof I now thought to late to experience the effect thereof, and looking for no other euent, I remained as doubtfull of the deuine vision, therewith as much deceyued as *Semele* with the fayned shape of the *Epidaurean Beroe*. Alas I trembled and shooke like the fearefull hinde calues at the sight of the tawnie Lyons roring out for hunger.

Contending and striuing with my selfe, whether it were better for me submissiuely to kneele downe, or els to turne me about and flye from them (for they seemed to mee by their behauiour, to be courteous young women, and besides their humanitie of a deuine beningnitie) or to remaine still vnmoueable. At length I determined to make tryall, and put my selfe forwarde to whatsoeuer would follow, being very well assured, that by no means I should finde any inhumanitie or cruell dealing by any of them, and espetially, because that innocencie carryeth alwayes his protection with him. And thus somewhat comforting my fearefull minde, and yet restrained with shamefastnesse, knowing that I was vnwoorthily come into this shadowie place, and solicious company of deuine and delicate nimphes, my guiltie and troubled minde, telling mee that it was rashly and ouer-bouldly doone, and that they were it might be, prohibited places, and a forbidden countrie for a strainger to frequent. And thinking thus and thus with my selfe : one amongst the rest of a more boulde and audatious spirite, very hardly spake vnto me, saying. Ho who art thou ? at hir speeche I was halfe afraide, and of my selfe ashamed, both ignorant what to say, or howe to aunswer : my voyce and spirit being interdicted, I stoode stone still like a dead image. But the fayre Damsels and beautifull Nimphes well aduised, that in me was a reall and humaine personage and shape, but distempered and afrayde, they drew all of them more neerer vnto me, saying,

Thou young man, whatsoeuer thou art, and from whencesoeuer thou art come : Let not our present aspects any whit dismay thee, or occasion thy discourage-

ment nor be no whit afrayde, for here thou shalt not finde any cruell customes, or cause of discontent, but free
f. 38. from displeasures, and therefore be not afrayde to discouer thy selfe, and tell vs what thou art.

By this motion hauing called backe againe my forgotten and lost sences, comforted with theyr faire, pleasant, and fauourable aspects, and recouering my selfe with their sweet speeches, with a very good will I made this aunswer vnto them.

I am the most disgraced and vnhappiest louer that the whole world can aforde. I loue, and she whom so greatly I esteeme, and so earnestly I desire, I neyther know where eyther she or my selfe is.

And by the greatest and most daungerous hap that can be imagined I am come hither. And now with prouoked teares downe falling from my waterie eyes along my pale cheekes, and bowed downe to the earth prostrating my selfe to your virginall feete I humblie craue and sue for your fauourable graces: whereat theyr soft and tender heartes mooued with pittie towardes mee, and halfe weeping with mee for companie, and as it were dutifullye striuing with theyr armes to lift mee vp from the grounde, with sweete and comfortable speeches, they courteouslye spake vnto me.

Wee are certainly perswaded and know full well (poore wretch) that few or none can escape by that way which thou art come, and therefore bee not vnthankfull to that diuine power, which hath thus preserued thee. And now be not doubtfull or afrayde of any aduers accident or greefe to assaile thee. Therefore quyet, comfort, and settle thy heart to rest. For nowe thou art come as thou mayest euidently perceiue, and plainely see, into a place of pleasure and delight, abandoning strife and discontent. For our vniformed ages: the seate vnchaungeable, the time not stealing away, the good oportunitie, the gratious and sotiable familiaritie, inticingly dooth allure vs therevnto, and graunteth vnto vs a continuall leysure. And this also thou must vnderstand, that if one of vs be merrie and delightsome, the other sheweth her selfe the more glad and pleasaunt, and our delectable and perticipated friendship, is with an attentiue consideration perpetually vnyted and knitte together. One of vs increasing an others content, to the highest degree of delight, and moste conuenyent solace.

Thou seest also that the ayre is healthfull, the lymittes, and bounds of this place verie large: of hearbes full of f. 38b.
varietie. Of plants diuerslie abounding, and with fruites plentifully laden, inuironed and defended with huge mountaines and rockes, well stored with harmelesse beasts, and fitte for all pastimes and pleasures, replenished with all kinde of fruites and graynes, vniuersally growing, and full of goodly fountaines.

An other said: vnderstand, vnknowne, (and yet assured guest,) good friend, that this territorie is more fruitfull then the fertill mountaine *Taurus* in the aquilonall aspect, whose frame dooth swell so much, that their clusters of grapes bee two cubits long, and that one Fig tree will bear seauentie bushels.

The third: this famous and spatious countrey, exceedeth the fertilite of the Hyperborean Island in the West India, or the portugalles of *Lucitania*, nowe vsurped and tyrannized by the insolent Spanyard.

Nor *Talga* in the *Caspian* mountaine. The fourth affirmed in hir commendation of that countrie, that the plentifulnesse of Egypt was but to be accounted scarsitie, in respect of that although that it were thought to be the garden of the world.

And the last, of a choyse countenance and sweete pronuntiacion aboue the rest, added thus much, saying,

In this fayre countrie you shall not finde any large fennie groundes, or offensiue or sicklye ayres, or craggie and fertlesse mosses, but faire and pleasaunt hilles, inuironed and walled about with steip and vnpassageable rockes, and by meanes thereof, secure and free from all daungers and feare, we want not any thing which may breede delight, and cause a sweete content. Besides all this wee are attendant vppon a renowned and most excellent Queene of large bountie and exceeding liberalitie: called *Euterilyda* of great pittie and meruelous clemencie, ruling with great wisdome, and with kingly gouernement, with great pompe, in an accumolated heape of all felicitie, and shee wyll bee greatly delighted, when we shall present thee vnto hir sacred presence, and maiesticall sight. And therefore cast away, shake of, and forget all afflicting sorrowe, and frame thy selfe and thy affrighted spyrits to intertaine of our comforts, solace and pleasure.

THE EIGHTH CHAPTER.

Poliphilus setling himselfe vnder the assurance of the fiue Nymphes, went with them to the bathes where they had great laughter in the deuise of the fountaine, and also by his vnction. Afterward being brought to the Queene Eutherillida, he did see many thinges worthie of regard, but chiefly the worke of a fountaine. f. 39.

BEING THUS CURTEOUSLY intreated of these gracious and pitiful Nymphes, and hauing my safetie by them sufficiently warranted with sweet comforts, reuiuing my decaied spirites. To whatsoeuer might seeme grateful and pleasing vnto them, so much as was conuenient for mee, I framed my selfe to offer my seruice. And because that they had boxes of sweete perfumes, and casting bottels of golde and precious stone, looking Glasses in their delicate and faire handes, and pure white Vailes of silke plited and folded vp, and other necessaries to bee vsed in bathing, which I offering to helpe them to beare, they refusing say thus vnto mee : that their comming into this place was to bathe, and therewith shewed mee that it was their pleasure that I should goe with them, for (saide they) the fountaine is here hard by, haue you not seene it. And I reuerently made them this answere.

Most faire Nimphes, if I had a thousande tongues and knew how to vse them al, yet could I not render sufficient thankes for your gracious desertes, and make requital of your great fauours, because you haue restored vnto mee my life. And therefore if I should not consent and yeeld vnto you my seruice and company, I might wel bee accounted of a churlish disposition. For which cause, amongst you I had rather be a seruant, then in an other place a Lord and commander, for that (so farre as I can coniecture) you are the tenantes and chamberfellowes of al delight and true felicitie.

You shal vnderstand that I did see a maruellous fountaine of a rare and wonderful workemanship, as neuer before my eyes did beholde, and so much my minde was occupied in the regard of the straungenes thereof, and to quench my great thirst, that I did looke for no further benefit.

One pleasant Nymphe spake thus merrily vnto mee saying, giue mee thy hand, thou art verie welcome. Thou seest at this present here, that we are fiue companions, and I am called *Aphea*, and she that carrieth the boxes and white cloathes *Offressia*. This other with the shining Glasse (our delightes) her name is *Orassia*. Shee that carrieth the sounding Harpe is called *Achol*, and shee that beareth the casting bottle of pretious Lyquor, is called *Geushra*. And we are al now going togither to these temperate bathes to refresh and delight our selues, Therefore you also (seeing that it is your good hap to bee amongst vs) shal bee willing to doo the like, and afterwardes with a verie good wil wee wil make our repaire to the great Pallais of our soueraigne.

These nimphs were his fiue sences.

Who is most merciful, bountiful, and liberal, and willing to helpe and further you, in your intended loues, burning desires, and high conceites. Plucke vp a good heart, man, come let vs goe on.

With pleasurable actions, maydenly iestures, swasiuious

behauiours, girlish sportes, wanton regardes, and with sweet words they ledde mee on thither, beeing wel content with euerie present action, but that *Poliä* was not there to the suppliment of my felicitie, and to haue been the sixt person in the making vp of a perfect number.

Further, I found my selfe agrieued, that my apparel was not conformable to this delicious consort, but growing into some houshold familiaritie, I disposed my self to be affable with them, and they with mee, til at last wee came to the place.

There I behelde a marueilous buildyng of a bathe eight square, and at eueryе Exterior corner, they were doubled together twoo Pyles, in fashion of a Pyke, from the leuell of the foundation, the subject Areobates Circumcinct and ribbed about. And after them followed the vtmost of like bignes, from the ground of the other, with their chapters set vnder the streight beame, with a border aboue, vnder a Coronice going round about. Which border was beautified with excellent carued worke, of litle naked children passing wel set forth, and equally distant one from an other, with their handes intricately tyed and f. 40.
wrapped about, and in them holding little bundels of smal greene boughs, instrophiated togither. And aboue the said Coronice, did mount vp (by an elegant arching) an eight square Spyer, imitating the subiect. Which from corner to corner was cut through with a marueilous workemanship of a thousand sundrie fashions, and closed againe with quarrels of Christal, which a farre of I did take to bee Leade. Vpon the top of which arched Spyer was placed a Trygon, and from the vpper center thereof, did ascend vp a strong steale, wherinto was ioyned an other steale whiche was turned about, and to the same was fastened a wyng, which with euerie blast of winde carried

about, the piping steale which had vpon the top thereof a ball, whereupon stood a naked Boy, streight vpon his right foote, and the left holden out. His head was hollow to his mouth like a Tunnel, with the Orifice euacuated to his mouth, to the which was sowdered a Trompet, with his left hand holding the Lanquet to his mouth, & his right hand extending towardes the middle ioynt, iust ouer the pinyon of it the wing or fane. Al which was of thinne brasse, excellently wel cast and guilt. Which wing, ball, and boye, with his cheekes and countenance as if hee were sounding, with the hinder part of his head euacunated towardes the blustring winde, as that blew, so he sounded, and as the winde caused a strange noyse among the rods of *Siliques* of *Egypt*, euen so did it heare in the Trumpet. Vppon which cause I merily thought to my selfe, that a man being alone in an vnknowne place and out of quiet, may easilie bee afrighted with such like strange noyses.

f. 40b. In that part of the building that was on the other side of the Nimph was the enteraunce into the bathe performed as mee thought by the same Lithoglyphe, that couered the sleepyng Nimphe, vppon the phrise whereof, were certaine Greeke Caracters, signifying ΑΣΑΜΙΝΘΟΣ.

Within there were foure seates whiche went rounde about, and one vnder an other, and close knitte togither, wroght with Iasper and Calcedony stone, in all kinde of colours. Two of the compassing about seates were couered ouer with water, and to the vpper margine of the third. In the corners, & in euerry corner stoode a Chorinthian Collumne of diuers colours, waued with so pure & beautiful Iacintes as nature could affoord, with conuenient bases and their chapters curiously made vnder the beame, ouer the which was a *Zophor*, wherein were

carued little naked Boyes playing in the water, with water monsters, with wrastling and childish strifes, with cunning slights and agilities fit for their yeares, in liuely motions f. 41.
and sportes. Al which was beautiful ouer compassed about with a Coronice. Ouer the which, according to the order of the little Collumies, from the perpendicular poynt in the toppe of the Cupul or Suffite and couer of the Bathe, there went a Tore moderator, increasing bigger and bigger of Oke leaues, one folding and lying ouer an other of greene Diasper, hanging vppon their braunshing stalkes gilt, which ascending vp met togither, and ioyned rounde in the aforesaide Cupul: where was placed a Lyons head, with his haire standing vp round about his face, and holding a Ring in his iawes, vnto the whiche were fastened certaine chaines Orichalke or Copper, that held a large goodly vessel, with a great braine or lyp, and furrowed of the aforesaide shyning substance, and hangyng two Cubites aboue the water, the bowle of the vessel whiche was of Christal onely except, the rest as the ribbes thereof and lippings, was of Azure blew, with bubbles of gold and shining sprinkled here and there.

Not farre of, there was a cleft in the earth, the which continually did cast foorth burning matter, and taking of this, and filling the bottome of the vessel, they did put certaine gumes and sweet woods which made an inestimable suffumigation as of the sweetest past, afterwardes closing the same, and putting downe the couer, both partes being holow, and the lipping and ribbing perforated and pearced through the transparent, Christal cleare and bright, they rendered a pleasant and diuers coulered light, by the which through the smal holes the bathes were lightened, and the heate stil incarcerated and interdicted.

The wal equally interposite betwixt Columne and Columne was of most blacke stone, of an extreame hardnes and shining incloystered about and bordered with a conuenient border of Diasper redde as Coral, adorned with a Lyneament and worke of double Gurgules or Verticules. In the middle part of which table, betwixt the Collumnes, there sate an elegant Nymph naked, as if she had been staying and attending of the stone Gallatitis, of colour like Iuorie, the lower partes of euerie of the said borders, circulating iustly with the bases of the Collumnes.

Oh how exquisitely were the same Images cut, that often times my eyes would wander from the real and liuely shapes, to looke vpon those feyned representations.

f. 41b. The paued ground vnder the water being of a diuers emblemature of hard stone, checkered where you might see marueilous graphics through the diuersitie of the colours. For the cleare water and not sulphurous, but sweete and temperatelye hotte, not like a Hotte-house or Stew, but naturally cleansing it selfe beyond all credet, there was no meanes to hinder the obiect from the sight of the eye. For diuers fishes in the sides of the seates, and in the bottom by a museacall cutting expressed, which did so imitate nature as if they had beene swimming aliue. As barbles, lampreys, and many others, the curiousnes of whose woorke I more regarded, then their names and natures.

The black stone of the walles was ingrauen with a leafe worke, as if it had beene an illaqueated composition of leaues and flowers, and the little shelles of cytheriaces, so beautifull to the eye, as was possible to be deuised.

Vpon the doore, the interstice whereof was of stone called Gallactites, I beheld a Dolphin swimming in the calme waues, and carrying vpon his back a young man, playing vpon an harpe. And on the contrarie side vpon the colde Fountaine, there was another dolphin swimming, and *Posidonius* riding vpon him with a sharpe eele speare in his hand.

These histories were perfected within the compasse of one selfe same stone, and set out in a most blacke ground. Then deseruedly I did commend both the archytect and the statuarie. On the other side, the pleasant dignitie of the fayre and beautiful sporting nimphes did highlye content mee, so as I could not compare to thinke whether the excesse of my passed sorrow, or present solace should be greatest. And there was so sweete a smell as Arabia neuer yeelded the like.

Vppon the seates of stone, in steed of an Apodyterie, they did impouerish theyr apparell, richely inuoluped, in the casting of it off, from their celestiall bodyes. Theyr fayre tresses bound vp in nettings of gould, wouen after a most curious sort. And without any respect at all, they gaue mee leaue to looke vpon theyr fayre and delicate personages, theyr honestie and honour reserued. Flesh vndoubtedly like the pure Roses and white Snowe. Ah woe is me, I found my heart to rise
and open it selfe and altogether to be adicted to a volup- f. 42.
tuous delight. Wherevpon I at that present thought my selfe most happie, onely in the behoulding of such delights, because I was not able to resist the burning flames which did set vpon mee in the fornace of my heart. And therefore sometime for a refuge and succour I durst not looke so narrowly vppon theyr inticing beauties, heaped vp in their heauenly bodyes. And they perceiuing the same did smile at my bashful behauiour, making great sport at me. And thereat I was glad, and contented

that I might in any way occasion their pastime. But I was greatly ashamed, in that I was an vnfit companion for such a company, but that they intreated mee to enter in with them where I stood like a Crowe among white Doues, which made me partly ashamed to behould, and ouerlooke such choyse obiects.

Then *Offressia* a very pleasant disposed piece, said vnto mee. Tel me young man what is your name? And I reuerently aunswered them, *Poliphilus:* it will please me well saith she, if the effect of your conditions be aunswerable to your name. And without deceit, said the rest. And how is your dearest loue called? Whereat I making some pause, aunswered, *Polia:* then she replyed. A ha I thought that your name should signifie that you were a great louer, but now I perceiue that you are a louer of *Polia:* and presently shee added more, saying: if shee were heere present, what would you doo? I aunswered, That which were agreeable with hir honour, and fit for your companies. Tel me *Poliphilus* doest thou loue hir wel indeed? Then I fetting a deepe sigh, aunswered: beyond all the delights and cheefest substance of the greatest and most pretious treasure in the whole world, and this opinion hath made an euerlasting impression in my still tormented heart. And she: where haue you lost or abandoned so loued a iewel? I know not, neyther where I am my selfe I know. Then she smyling aunswered. If any should finde hir out for you, what rewarde would you giue. But content thy selfe, be of good comfort, and frame thy selfe to delights, for thou shalt finde thy *Polia* againe. And with these and such like pleasaunt and gratious questions, these fayre young Virgins, sporting and solacing themselues, we washt and bathed together.

f. 42b At the opposite interstice of the beautifull fountaine without, of the faire sleeping Nymph before mentioned, within the Bathe there was an other of seatnes of fine mettal, and of a curious workemanship, glistering of a golden colour, that one might see himselfe therein. Which were fastened in a Marble, cut into a squadrature and euacuated for the Images to stand in there proportions, with two halfe Collumnes that is Hemiciles, one of either side, with a Trabet, a smal Zophor, and a Coronice, all cut in one sollid Marble, and this peece of worke was nothing inferior to any of the rest, which before I had seene, but with a rare art, and marueilous inuention, both deuised and performed. In the voyd and plaine euacuated quadret, there stood two Nimphes, little lesse then if they had been liuely creatures, apparelled, so as you might see somewhat aboue their knees, vppon one of theyr legges, as if the winde had blowne it vp, as they were doing theyr office, and their armes bare, from the elbow to the shoulder except. And vpon that arme, wherewith they sustained the Boye, the habite that was lifted vp was reiect. The feete of the Infant stood one in one of the handes of the Nymphes, and the other, in the others hand. All their three countenances smiling : and with their other handes, they held vp the Boyes shirt, above his nauil.

The Infant holding his little Instrument in both his hands, and continued pissing into the hotte water, fresh coole water. In this delicious place of pleasure, I was verie iocund and full of content, but the same was much apalled, in that I thought my selfe a contemptible bodie, among such beauties, and dewe conicaled into Snowe, and as it were a Negro or tawnye Moore amongst them.

One of them called *Achoe*, verie affably and with a pleasant countenance said vnto mee, *Poliphile* take that Christal vessel and bring mee some of that fresh water.

I without staie intending to do so, and thinking nothing but to do her seruice in any sort that she would commaund me, went to the place. And I had no sooner set my foote vpon the steppe, to receiue the water, as it fell, but the pissing Boye lift vp his pricke, and cast sodeinlye so colde water vppon my face, that I had lyke at that instant to haue fallen backward. Whereat they so laughed, and it made such a sounde in the roundnes and closenes of the bathe, that I also beganne (when I was come to my selfe) to laugh that I was almost dead. Afterward, I founde out the concauitie, and perceiued that my heavy weight, being put upon the moueable stepping, that it would rise vp like the Keye and Iacke of a Virginall, and lift vp the Boyes pricke, and finding out the deuise and curious workemanship thereof, I was greatly contented. Vpon the Zophor was written in *Atthic* letters this title

ΓΕΛΟΙΑΣΤΟΣ

After our great laughter and bathing, and all hauing washed with a thousand sweete, amorous, and pleasant wordes, maydenly sportes, and pastimes, wee went out of the water, and leapt vp vppon the accustomed seates, tripping on their toes, where they did annoynt themselues with sweete Odours, Diasdasmatic, and with a Myristic liquor, or water of Nutmegges. And they offered a boxe vnto mee also, and I annoynted my selfe therewithall, and I founde great pleasure therein, for besides the excellent smel and sweete sauour, it was verie good to comfort my bodie, legges, and armes, that had been so wearied in my daungerous flight.

Afterward when we had made our selues redy, which was somwhat long after the manner of other women, by reason of so many gewgawes and gimmerie whatchets, they did open their vesselles of daintie confections, and refreshed themselues, and I amongst them, and with precious drinke. When they had eaten sufficiently, they returned againe to their looking Glasses, with a scrupulous examination, about their bodies, and the attire of their heades, and dressing of their yealow curling haires depending, and hemicirculately enstrophiated about their diuine faces. And when they had made an ende, they sayd vnto mee.

Poliphilus, wee are now going vnto our gratious and most excellent souereigne the Queene *Eutherillida*, where you shal finde and conceiue greater delight, but the water is still in your face, whereat they beganne to renew their laughter, without all measure at mee, glauncing and turning their eyes one on an other, with a louely regarde. At last they set foorth, and as they went rounde to gither, they beganne to sing verses in a Phrygial tune, of a pleasaunt metamorphosing of one, who with an oyntment thought to haue transformed himselfe into a Byrd, and by mistakyng of the Boxe, was turned into a rude Asse.

Concludyng, that manye tooke Oyntmentes to one purpose, and founde the effects to contrarie their expectations.

Whereat I beganne to be in a doubt, that they had sung that by mee, because that they still smiled as they turned towardes mee. But seeing that I perceiued no alteration in my selfe, but wel I was contented to let them laugh on. Vpon a sodaine I founde my selfe so lasciuously heat, and in such a prurient lust, that which way so euer I turned, I could not forbeare, and they as they sung laughed the more, knowing what had happened vnto mee. And it did so increase in me more and more, that I knew not wherewithal I might bridle and restraine my selfe from catching of one of them, like an eager and hot Falcon comming downe out of the ayre, vpon a couie of Partriges. I was with such a violent desire prickt forwarde, which I felt more and more to increase in a sault burning. And the more I was to that venerious desire by the violent offers of so oportune and sweete obiects. A ſoode for suche a pernitious plague, and vnexperienced burning.

Then one of these flamigerous Nymphes named *Aphea* said vnto mee, How is it *Poliphilus?* Euen now I did see you verye merry, what hath altered your disposition? I answered. Pardon mee that I binde and vexe my selfe more than a willow Garland. Giue mee leaue to destroy my selfe in a lascivious fire. And then as they burst out all in a laughter and said, Ah ha, and if your desired *Polia*, if shee were here, what would you do, how? Alas my desire, euen by the deitie which you serue, I beseech you put not Flaxe and Rosin to the fire, which burneth mee out of all measure. Put no Pitch to the fire in my heart, make me not to forget my selfe I beseech you.

At this my lamentable and sorrowing answere, they were provoked to such a loude laughter, wherein they did exceed so much, that neither they nor my selfe with the wearines thereof could goe any further, but were constrained to rest our selues for want of breath, vpon the odoriferous floures and coole grasse, by means wherof, I became somewhat oportunely to bee eased, my heate aswaging and relenting by little and little.

And as they thus contentedly rested themselues awhile, vnder the coole vmbrage of the leafie Trees, I beganne to bee bolde with them saying. O you women, that are burners and destroyers, doo you use mee thus? See what an offered occasion I haue, which wil holde mee excused, to breake foorth and doo violence vnto you. And therevpon somewhat boldly moouing myselfe and fayning as if I would haue done that which by no meanes I durst, but then with a newe pastyme and laughter they called one for anothers helpe, leauing heere and there their golden Pantoffles and Vailes, to bee carried about with the winde, and their vesselles neglected in the grasse, they ranne all awaye and I after them, that I might well perceiue that they had neither crampes nor stringhawldes or leaden heeles, and thus continuing our pastimes a pretie space, being somewhat pleased that I had made them to runne. I returned backe to gather up their Pantophles and such things as they had scattered behind them. And comming neere to a fresh coole Riuer, they began to cease off from laughter, and to take pittie vppon mee, and *Geussia* behinde all the rest, bowed herselfe downe to the water, beautifully adorned with the bending Bull Rushe, water Spyke, swimmyng Vitrix, and aboundance of water Symples, she dyd pluck vp the *Heraclea* Nympha, of some called water Lillye or *Nenuphar*, and the roote of Aron or wake Robyn, of some, *Pesvituli* or *Serpentaria Minor*.

And *Amella* or Bawme Gentill, all whiche grew very neare togither and not farre distant, whiche shee fauourably offered vnto mee saying, of these whiche I haue made choyse of take and for my freedome taste.

For which cause I reufused the Nenuphar, and reiected the Dracuncle for his heate, and accepted of the *Amella*, whiche she had cleane washed, by meanes whereof, within a verye short space, I founde my venerious Lubric and incessing spurre of desire to leaue of, and my intemperate luste was cleane gone.

And when my vnlawfull desires of the fleshe were brideled, the pleasant Nymphes came again to mee, and as wee walked on, we came into a frequented place, and wonderfully fruitfull.

Vnlawful concupiscence blindeth a man, and drieueth his sences from him.

And there in a fine order and appointed distance was a waye set on either sides with Cyprus Trees, with their corner clefted Apples; and as thick with leaues as their nature will suffer them, the leauele grounde beeyng couered all ouer, with greene Vinca Peruima, or Laureols and Chammee, *Daphne*, and full of his asurine flowers. Which adorned way of a meete and conuenient breadth, did lead directly on into a greene Closure, from the beginning of whiche walke, iust betwixt the Cypress Trees, to the entrance and opening of the aforesaide enclosure, was some foure furlonges. Vnto which enclosure when wee came I founde it equilaterall, with three fences like a streight wall, as high as the Cyprus Trees vpon either side of the waye, that wee had passed along in: which was altogether of Cytrons, Orenges and Lymonds, bushing with their leaues one within an other, and artifitially knitte and twisted togither, and the thicknes mee thought of sixe foote: with a gate in the middest of the same Trees, so wel composed as is either possible to be thought or done. And aboue in conuenient places were made windowes, by means whereof, the boughes in those places were to be seene bare, but for their greene leaues, which yeelded a most sweet and pleasant verdure. Betwixt the curious twistings of the braunches and their greene leaues the white flowers did aboundently shewe themselues a singular Ornament, breathing foorth a most delectable and sweete odour. And to please the eye, the faire fruite was in no place wanting, where it should yeelde content. And afterwardes I might perceiue that in the interstitious thicknes, the bowghes (not without a wonderful woorke) were so artificially twisted and growne togither, that you might assend vp by them, and not be seen in them, not yet the way where you went vp.

At length comming into this greene and delightful grounde to the eye, and in a mans understanding woorthie of estimation, I perceiued that it was a great enclosure in the fore front of a marueilous Pallaice of a noble simmetriated architercturie which of this frondiferous conclausure, was the fourth part in longitude sixtie paces. And this was the *Hypaethri* to walke in, for open ayre.

In the middest of this great base court, I did behold a goodly Fountaine of cleare water, spinnyng from the verie toppe as it were to the foundation, whiche stoode vpon a smoothe pauement through little streight Pypes, falling into a hollowed vessel, which was of most pure Amethist, whose Diameter conteined three paces, the thicknes agree-ing therewithall, leauyng the twelfth part for the thick- f. 46.
nesse of the brimme, rounde about the same were carued water monsters, after the best sort that euer any auncient inuentor or woorkeman for the hardnes of the stone could deuise to woorke, it might bee the woorke of *Daedalus* for the wonderful excellencie thereof. *Pausania*, if he had seene this, would haue taken small pleasure to boast of the standing cup which he made to *Hipparis*.

Which same was founded vpon a steale or smal Pillar of Iasper of diuers colours, beautifully adulterating one with an other, being cut in the middest and closed vp with the cleare Calcidonie of the colour of the troubled Sea water, and brought into a marueilous woorke, beeing lifted vp with guttured hollowe vessels, one aboue an other, with a reserued seperation, by artificiall and woonderful ioyntes. It stood streight vp, fastened in the center of a Plynth, made of greene Ophite which was rounde, and somewhat lifted vp aboue, about compassing Porphyr, some fiue inches, whiche was curiously wrought with diuers lyneaments.

Rounde about the steale whiche helde vp the vessell, foure Harpies of Golde did stand, with their clawes and tallented feete vpon the smoothe Table of the Ophite.

Their hinder partes towardes the steale, one iust opposite against an other, with their winges displaied and spredde abroad, they rested vnder the vessell with their feminine countenances, and hauing haire vpon their heades, from the same, it spredde downe to their showlders, their heades vnder, and not touching the vessell : with their tayles like Eeles, and turning rounde. And vpon their nauels, an Antique leafe worke. These were verie necessarie for the strengthening of the Pype within the steale and smal Pillar.

Within the middest of the wombe and bellye, or nauel of the vessel, vpon the Subiect steale, there was proportionately raised vp of the same vessel of *Amathyst*, a substance like a Challice, inward, or the inwarde moulde for a Bell, so high as the vessel was deepe the middle thereof, leuell with the brimme of the vessell.

Vppon the which was made an artificious foote set vnder the three graces naked of fine Gold, of a common stature, one ioyning to an other.

From the teates of their breastes the ascending water did spin out lyke siluer twist. And euerie one of them in their right hand did holde a copie full of all kinde of fruites, whiche did extend in length vp aboue their heades, and at the opening, all three of them ioyned rounde into one, with diuers leaues and fruites hangyng ouer the brimmes or lippes of the wrythen Copies.

Betwixt the fruite and the leaues, there came vp sixe

small Pypes, out of the whiche the water did spring vp through a small hole.

And the cunning Artificer, because that he would not trouble one Cubit with the tuch of another. With a signe of shamefastnes, the Images with their left handes did hide that part which modestie would not haue seene, but accounteth worthie to bee couered.

Vppon the brimme of the hollow vessell, whose compasse was a foote moreouer about, then the subiacent of it, with their heades lifted vp vpon their Vipers feete, with a conuenient and decent intercalation, there were placed sixe little scaly Dragons, of pure shining Golde, with such a deuise, that the water comming from the teates of the Ladies, did fall directly vppon the euacuated and open crowne of the head of the Dragons, afore spoken of, with their winges spredde abroad, and as if they had been byting, they did cast vp and vomit the same water whiche fell beyonde the roundnes of the Ophict, into a receptorie of Porphyr, and rounde, whiche were both more higher then the flatnesse of the pauement before spoken of: where there was a little Channell going rounde about betwyxt the Ophit and the Porphyrite, in breadth one foote and a halfe, and in depth two foote.

Whiche Porphyrite was three foote from the playne ouermost parte to the Pauement, with an excellent vndiculation. The reste of the partes of the Dragonnes, for the moderate deepenesse of the vessell did grow on, vntill all met together, transforming the extreame partes of their tailes into an antique foliature making a beautifull illygament with the azule or foote set vnder the three images without any deforming hinderance to the hollownesse of f. 47.
the precious vessell. And what with the greene assayling of the compassing Orange trees, and the bright reflections

of the shining matter, and the pure water, there was such a gratious couler, in that singular and most pretious vessell, as if the Rainbowe and the clowdes had made theyr habitation there.

Then in the corpulent bearing out of the belly of the vessell, betwixt one, and the other Dragons, in an equall distance, and of a most excellent melting or casting, there stood out *Lyons* heads of an exquisite exaction, and driuing, casting foorth by a little pype, the water that distilled from the six fistulets, placed in the copie aboue. Which water did so forciblie spring vpward, that in the turning downe it fell among the Dragons in the large vessell, where by reason of the high fall, and fashion of the vessel, it made a pleasant tinckling noyse.

f. 48. All which rare worke, by so sharpe and fine a wit composed, as this insolent and precious vessell was, the foure perfect harpies, the woonderfull and curious azule, wherevpon the three Images of pure gould stood, with what Arte, ordinance, and rule, digested and made perfect: as I am ignorant in them altogither, so much the lesse able am I to describe the whole as it did deserue, being a woorke past any humaine reache and capacitie to frame the like.

And I may bouldly say, that in our age there was neuer seene in stone and mettle such a peece of woorke embost, chased, and engrauen. For it was a woonder to see, that stones of such extreame hardnesse, as that which was the steale to hould vppe the Vessell, should be cut and wrought to that purpose, as if it had beene as soft as wax. A woorke raither to bee woondered at, then vndertaken.

The square base court, (in the middest whereof stood this notable woorke of the sumptuous Fountaine), was paued with fine Marble of diuers coulers and fashions.

Amongst which were appact very beautifully, roundes of Diasper, equally distant, and disagreeing from the couler of the pauement, and the corners closed vp with leaues and Lyllies. Betwixt the square marble pauing stones, there was a space left like a list, which was filled vp with diuers coulered stones of a lesser cut, some proportioned into greene leaues, and tawnie flowers. Cyanei, Phænicei, and Sallendine, so well agreeing in theyr coulers, so glistering and seuerly set of a diligent Xesturgie. As full of coulers as a Christall glasse, repercust and beaten against with the beames of the sunne. Because the circumduct and compassing coulers, meeting together in the selfe same smoothe and cleane stones, did yeeld a reflection, no part being faultie, eyther of the square checkers or scutuls and Trigons. But with a smoothe and streight ordinance well ioyned together.

Whereat I remained woonderfully amased by my selfe, diligently considering vpon the noblenes of the woorke, such as I had not beene vsed to see, and verye willinglye I would haue beene content, to haue made more staye in the contemplating thereof, for so the dignitie of the worke required, but I could not because it was necessarie for me to follow after my leaders.

Then the aspect of this sumptuous magnificent and f. 48b.
statelye pallace, the approoued situation thereof, the dew proportion, and the maruelous composition in my first comming to it, did make me woonderfully contented to view the woorthines thereof, and in continuance I was prouoked to behould more, for which cause I perswaded my selfe, as I might very well, that the expert builder, excelled all other whatsoever. What kinde of rafters? what manner of roofe? after what sort the Parlors chambers, closets, and lodgings, were disposed? with what kind of seeling they

were enclosed and incrusted? wherewithall hanged? with what couler and kinde of painting ouerhead? What order of columination, and what space betwixt. No other building maye goe beyonde this whatsoeuer, but may giue place verye well, of what kinde of Marble, and what manner of engrauing.

There I beheld the laboures of Hercules grauen in stone with halfe the representation standing out or bearing foorth, in a woonderfull sort, the skinnes, flatnes, tytles, and trophes. What an entry, what a stately porche, what that of Titus Cesar with his stone of Phenicea with all the tinkering and pullishing about it, there is none whose wit is so grosse to commend it, in respect of this, but will rather scorne to speake of it. As for the woorthie and excellent manner of glasing the gallerie without the pallace, the conspitious porche, the manner of building, the arched seeling aboue head, beautified and adorned with foliature and other lineaments of pure gould and asuer couler and excellent painting that whatsoeuer I had seene before I made small acount of, as not worthie of remembrance. And beeing now come to the doore within the porche, the going in was closed vp with a hanging, drawne ouer before it of gould and silke, wrought together, and in the same two images. One of them hauing all kinde of instruments about hir, fitte and readie to goe to worke, and the other with a maidenly countenance, looking vp with hyr eyes into heauen.

The beautye of which two were such, and so fresh, as I looked about mee, whether *Apelles* had painted them with his Pensill.

f. 49. And there my sportfull, faire, and pleasant companions, euerie one putting their right handes to mine, willing to haue me in, sayde, *Poliphilus* this is the vsuall waye, by the which you must come into the presence of our Gracious and moste excellent Queene.

But you cannot haue leaue to enter in here through this Curtain, before you bee receiued of a vigilant and innocent Damosel that is the keeper of this doore, and she is called *Cinosia*. Who hearing vs comming, did forthwith present her selfe, and fauourably held vp the cloth, and wee entered in.

There was a roome hung about and diuided by an other Curtaine of excellent Arras full of Imagerie, as signes, shapes, plants, and beastes, singularly well done.

In this place at our comming, an other curious woman came towardes vs, called *Indalomena*, and she putting by the Curtaine, wee entered in. And there was an other suche like roome, from the second for quantitie, with discourses and reason marueilously wouen, with infinite knottes, bucklinges, tyings, and old fashioned harping Irons, or Hookes, as if they had been fastened and knit togither. In which place without any staying, the third woman came and receiued vs very gratiously, her name was *Mnemosina*, and shee calling vs, gaue vs free leaue to go in. Where lastly my companions did present mee before the sacred maiestie of the Queene *Eleutherillida*.

THE NINTH CHAPTER.

Poliphilus sheweth as well as hee may, how exceeding great the Maiestie of the Queene was, the manner of her Residence and seruice. His fauourable entertainment. Howe shee marueiled at him.

HEN I CAME TOWARDES THE first doore-keeper, I was somewhat abashed, but yet I did salute her in good sorte as became mee to doo. And shee verie curteously badde mee come neere. And in like manner the second.

f. 49b. In whose gard I did see a loftie Gallery as long the content of the Pallaice, the roote whereof, was all painted with a greene foliature, with distinct flowers and folded leaues, and little flying Byrdes, excellently imphrygiated of museacall paynting, as without in the first Court, and the stone walles seeled with Chipworkes of diuers colours.

At the last doore, the Matrone *Mnemosina* perswaded me verie effectually, not to doubt of any thing, but that I should stedfastly follow the royall perswasion, and healthfull counsell of the Queene, and perseuere in the execution thereof, for that the ende without doubt would be to my content.

And thus hauing leaue to goe in, beholde such thinges presented themselues to my eyes, as were lyker to be celestiall then humane.

A most stately and sumpteous preparation, in a gorgeous

and spacious Court, beyond the Pallaice neere and opposite to the other, and foure square.

The bewtifull and precious Pauement within a checkered compasse going about the same, there was a space of sixtie foure Squadrates of three foote, the dyameter of euerye one: Of the which one was of Iasper, of the colour of Corall, and the other greene, powdered with drops of blood not to bee woorne away: and set togither in manner of a Chesse-boord. Compassed about with a border, the breadth of one pace of rare inuention of woorke, with small pieces of stones, of diuers colours, and so compacte together, as if it had beene a straunge paynted woorke euenly cut and set by rule, that you could not perceiue the ioyning, but smoothe and shyning, and so well framed by the Lybell and Squadrate, that no circulating or sphæricall Instrument woulde mooue to either sides without forcing.

About this, lastlye was an other marueylous kynde of Pauing of three paces broad, in knottes of Iasper, Praxin, Calcedonie, Agat, and other sortes of stones of price.

And about by the sides of the walles, compassing the sayde Court paued as you haue heard, there were placed Settles, of the wood of Palme Trees, of colour betwixt a yealow and tawny, passing well turned and fashioned, couered ouer with greene Veluet, and bowlstered with some soft stuffe or feathers easie to sit vpon, the Veluet brought downe to the frame of the Settles or Benches, and fastened to the same with tatch Nayles of Golde, with bossed heades vppon a plaine Siluer Nextrule or Cordicell.

The alament of the claustering walles, were couered ouer with Plates of beaten Golde, with a grauing agreeable to the pretiousnes of the metall.

And in the coæquated and smoothe plaine of the same

walles of stone, by certaine Pilastrelles, Quadrangules, or Lossenges, of an equall dimension and distinct correspondencie in the middest of euerie one, there were perspicuously appact rounde Iewels, bearing out and swelling beyond the plaine leuell of the wall, after the manner of the tores of bases, and of thicknes according to the proportion of the Losenge wherein it stood, compassed about with greene iagged leaues, one bending ouer an other, the tops turned toward the Iewell.

And betwyxt the Foliature and the great Iewell, an other border of pretious stones curiouslie sorted and conspicuouslie set.

And in the rest of the wall circumvallate of these bearing out rownde Iewels, the seuen Plannets with their nature and properties, with an Encaustic woorke were sweetly painted, which I beheld with great delight. The rest of the wall exclusive from the rowndnes of the Iewels within the Pilastrels, were filled vp and bewtified with infinite varietie of workes in siluer, and powdered with diuers inestimable stones, singularly well cut, and of diuers fashions.

The wall on the left side was in like sort, and opposite in rundels. Against the seuen Plannettes were there seuen Tryumphes ouer the subiectes of the same predominent Plannettes, and in such lyke Art of Painting as the other side.

And on the right part I behelde their seuen harmonies and friendly aspectes, and the passage of the blood, with the qualitatiue receiuing and retiring & circulating entrance, with an incredible Historie of the celestiall operation accedent.

The fourth alament made the Pallaice of suche like distribution as the other, the doore except, whiche did occupie an emptie voyde interstice. The other sixe with a regulate correspondence, and harmonye of the rest, in the Iewelles to the opposite and symentriall congresse of the Plannettes, with their vertuous inclinations, were expressed in the shapes of elegant Nimphes, with the titles and signes of their natures.

The seuenth Mediane quarter, was the forefront directlye placed against the seuenth Iewell, representing the Planet *Soll*, which was set vp more higher then the rest, by reason of the Queenes Throne.

Euerie part of matter, number, forme, and lyneament, in distribution equally correspondent to his Lybell, the right with the left, and here and there, with an exquisite loue, and congresse agreeing.

Of whiche moste excellent Court, euerie side was eight and twentie paces. In this sort stood this synarie open Court, all compassed about with fine golde, a worke rather to bee wondered at, then spoken off.

The Pilastrelles were discrepant fowre paces one from another, with a iust partition of seuen (a number gratefull to nature) of fine and orient Azure, Lazull stone, passing well coloured according to his kinde, with a bewtifull bestowing of small glymces of gold. In the fore part of which, betwixt the seuen pilastrels, there were appointed little slender Pillers wrought about with leaues, copies, heades with haire like leaues, boyes their hippes and legges proportioned into brawnches, Birdes and copies, and vesselles full of flowers, with other woonderfull inuentions and deuises, from the top to the bottome of the Anaglyph, as if they had grown out of the foundation, making and diuiding in sunder the spaces, their chapters were wrought of a fashion answerable to the rest.

Ouer the whiche did extend a streight beame with

grauen lineamentes fitting the same. And ouer that a Zophor, conteining this woorke still throughout, that is, the bonye scalpes of Oxen, with myroll bowghes full of berries, tyed abowt theyr hornes by a towell of linnen.

Vpon either sides of them were Dolphines with their gilles lyke leaues, and their Finnes and their extreeme
f. 51. partes of a foliature, and vpon theyr heades and backes certaine naked boyes, getting holde of theyr lifted vp braunching tayles, with leaues and flowers, and bending them downe.

The head of the Dolphine hauyng a Syme, whereof the one part turned towardes the Boye, and the other bent against the vessell with an open gaping, and endyng in the head of a Storke, with her beake against the open mouth of a Monster, lying with his face vpwarde, and certaine Whorelles or Beades rysing vp betwixt his mouth and her beake.

Whiche heades in stead of haire, were couered with leaues one ouer an other, filling the Orifice of the vessell, and from one lyp to an other, and vnder the bowle thereof towarde the foote, there compassed a fine towell of linnen, the endes hanging downe from the knottes, in suche an excellent sorte as was conuenient both for the place and matter. And in the middle ouer the heades, was the face of a childe vppon a payre of winges.

And with suche lyke lineamentes was the Zophor adorned and couered, with a Coronice full of excellent workemanship. Vppon the plaine toppe whereof, by a perpendicular lyne ouer the Pillars, in the ordeining of the squadrangalles, there were placed and framed certaine olde fashioned vesselles, by an appointed distribution, three foote high of Calcedonie, some of Amethist, some of Agat, some of Iasper, with their bellies furrowed and

Channelled, and cut of a rare and maruellous cunning, and with excellent eares.

In a perfect order ouer euerie Iewell aboue the Coronice, were aptlye ioyned traunsomes, squared seuen foote high, and the middle space betweene them of glistering Golde, with a superadiect extention, closing ouer the streight extended transomes. And by a turnyng downe the transomes, did ioyne decently one with the other, with a Topiarie woorke. Intending that out of the vesselles standing vpon the Coronice as aforesaide, in the cornes the transome and the vyne should ryse vp togither, but out of the other vesselles, either a vyne or some Woodbine of Golde, by courses meeting ouer the transwerst traunsomes, with a thicke stretching out of theyr spreadyng braunches, one ioyning f. 51b.
with an other, and twisting togither with a fine and pleasant congresse, couering ouer all the whole court with a riche and inestimable suffite with diuers fashioned leaues of greene emeralde, gratefull to the sight, more perfect then that wherein *Amenon* was impressed, and the flowers dispersed and distributed of Saphires & byrrals. And with an excellent disposition and artificiall, betwixt the greene leaues and the grosse vaynes, so precious hunge downe the clusters of grapes made of stones, agreeable and fitting to the naturall coulers of Grapes.

Topiaria, the feate of making Images or Arbours in Trees.

All which most rare deuises, of pryse incomparable, incredible, and past imagination, did shine all ouer most pretiouslie: not so much to be marueyled at for the costlinesse of the matter, but for the large greatnesse of the worke.

For not without great cause, from place to place, with a diligent and iealous examination I did carefully consider the large extention of the inmost intricate braunches, and their proportionate strength and thicknesse, so cunninglie doone, by such an arte, boulde attempt, and continued intent, they were so aptly led out, whether by sowdering, or by the Hammer, or by casting, or by all three, me thought it an vnpossible worke to make a couering of such a breadth and so twysted and twyned together.

In the midde prospect, opposite against our going in vpon a degreed regall throne, set full of glystering stones in a maruelous order, farre more excellent then the seat in the temple of *Hercules* at *Tyre*, of the stone *Eusebes*. The Queene with an imperiall Maiestie sitting vppon it, goddesse like, and of a woonderfull magnanimitie in countenance: gorgiously apparrelled in clothe of goulde, with a sumptuous and curious attyre, vpon hir head of a purple couler, with an edging of Orient Pearle, shadowing ouer hir large forhead, aunciently and princelike, euer pressing hir plemmirrulate trammels of hayre, as blacke as iet descending downe hir snowie temples, and the rest of the aboundance of hir long hayre, fastned rounde in the hinder parte of her head, and deuided into two partes or tresses, lapt about this waye and that waye, behind hir small eares, ouer hir streight proportioned head, and
f. 52. finished in the crowne, with a flower of great Orient, and rownd Pearles, such as be found in the Indian promontorie *Perimula*.

The rest of hir long spreding hayre was not seene, but couered ouer with a thinne vayle, edged with gould, hanging downe from the said flower and knot of pearle, to hir delicate shoulders, and flingering abroade with the ayre.

In the middle of the edging of hir dressing, vpon the highest parte ouer the middest of hir forhead hoong a rare iewell. And about hir round and snowie neck, went an inestimable Carkenet with a pendent ouer the diuision of hir rownde brests, of a table Dyamond, in fashion of an Egge, sparkling, and of a monstrous largenes, set in gould with wyer woorke.

At hir eares moste richelye were hanged in the typpes two earinges, two great shynyng Carbunckles of an inestimable price.

Hir shoees were of greene silke & hir pantofles of gould embrodered in a leafe woorke. Vppon a foote stoole aboue the which, and vnder hir feete, was layde a cushion of white Veluet, with a purfeling of silke and Orient Pearles of *Arabia*, within the persick golph, with foure Buttons wrought with pretious Stones, and tasseld with goulde twist, and crimosen silke, depending.

Vppon eyther sides along vpon the aforesaid benches couered ouer with greene veluet, sate hir Ladyes of honour, attendant in a goodly and commendable order, according to their estates, apparrelled in clothe of goulde in an incredible brauerie, as in the world may bee seene. And in the middest of them this renowned and famous Queene in great pompe and vnspeakeable statelynes, and the hemmes of hir vestures so edged and set with pearle and stone, as if nature had rayned and powred them down vpon hir.

At hir high and imperiall aspect, with great reuerence bowing their knees to the ground vnto hir, hir women did rise vppe from their seates, occasioned by the noueltie of the spectacle, & greatly marueiling that I should come into such a place.

But I founde my selfe more amazed, my hearte quayling, and dilating both of the troubles that I passed, and the present estate that I was brought into, which did f. 52b.

enuiron and fill me with an extreame amasement, reuerend feare, and honest shamefastnesse.

And they asking the fiue Nimphes that brought me in, whysperinglie what I was, and the strangenesse of my hap, directing, bending and intentiuely fixing all their eyes vpon me. Where finding my selfe so base a worme in such an excellent conspect, I was woonderfully astonished, and lyke one that had no spyrite.

But the successe and manner of my comming being demaunded of them, the Nymphes plainly, open and manifest the same at large, whereat the gratious Queene beeing mooued to compassion, caused me to stand vp, and vnderstanding what my name was, began to say,

Poliphilus, be of good comfort, and pluck vp a good heart, and tell me how thou commest hither, and by what meanes, and how thou diddest escape that mortall and horrible Dragon ? and how thou diddest finde a way out of that odious and blinde darkenes, I haue beene tould of it: But I maruell me not a little, because few or none dare aduenture that waye. But seeing that grace hath safelye brought thee hither vnto vs, I will not denye thee (any cause notwithstanding) a gratious and fauourable intertaynement.

To whose liberall inuiting, royall woordes and intertaynement, better then I could haue imagined to desire, with diuote and honourable thankes, giuen aboundantly from pointe to pointe, I tould how I escaped and fled from the Dragon, a fearefull monster. And consequently with what trauell and payne I came to the desired place. And how the fiue Nimphes did finde me wandering and afrayde. Which when I had at large declared and ended my speeche, I began with great desire to frame my selfe to bee a pertaker of their ſolacious and magnicifient pleasures.

After that she said unto me with a smiling and pleasant countenance. It is a woorthie matter to consider, that an euill and descontented beginning, often time ſalleth out

to a happie and good successe in the end: and before that anye thing bee committed vnto you to perſourme, f. 53.
as touching your amorous and firme conceit, it is our pleasure, ſor the asswagement and mitigation of thy commendable griefes, that in this company thou especially shouldest associate thy selfe with *Philotesia*, seeing that the faire heauens haue shewed thee of thy entertainment,

and brought thee into our triumphant mansion place. And therefore my *Poliphilus*, without any more ceremonies take thy place there and sit downe, for thou shalt see (with a verie good will) part of our sumptuous and stately manner of seruice, the plentifull diuersitie and number of my more then princely dainties, the honourable attendance of my houshold, & excellent order thereof, the inestimable pretiousnes of my great aboundance, and the large effects of my bounty.

At which imperious command, her eloquent and fauourable speech ended, humbly, and with a little more audacitie than before, vppon one of the benches of my right hande I did sit downe (lapping my torne gowne together before me with certaine brymble leaues still sticking in it) betwixt the fiue Nymphes that brought mee in, and amongst them next vnto *Offresia* and *Achoe*, placed behinde the Queene, and six other of the chamber vppon the other hande, and in the middest on high vppon a throne did the Queene sitte in an imperiall Maiestie.

The Couer ouer the Throne was of an inamelled coulorNing contayning in it a beautifull image without any beard, the head bushing with yellow haire, part of his brest couered with a thinne cloath ouer the displayed winges of an Eagle, her head turning vp, and beholding of him. The head of which image was redymited with an azure Diademe, adorned with seauen beames, and at the foot of the Eagle two braunches of greene Lawrell, one one way, the other contrary towards either side. And in euerie garland I behelde the figment proper to his planet, and behind at my backe was the iewell, containing the historie of the winged Mercury, and howe the
f. 53b. benignitie of his good disposition is deprayed, when he is in the malignant taile of the venemous Scorpion. And

looking vpon my selfe, I was ashamed to see my vile habite among suche sumpteous induments, that me thought my selfe no otherwaies but euen lyke that vile and mortiferous beast among the most noble signes of the Zodiac. The bewtifull and honorable damosels sate in order vpon the Benches, compast about all along by the sides of the walles vppon the right side, and the best of the Court, with a rare and strange kinde of womanly dressing vppon their heads, as is in the world, with the tresses of their haire lapt and bowed vp in Caules of gold.

Some with their haires of Amber colour, curled and dressed vp with flowers of the same vppon a wyer, with the endes turning downe and wauing vppon their snowy foreheades and smooth temples, bewtified with Rubies and Diamonds prickt in the haire.

Others of the colour of the Obsidium of *India*, blacke and shining, adorned with floures of Orient Pearle, & Carkenets of the same. They stood all waiting with such a venerate attention, that when the seruice was brought to the table, they all at one instant time alike, made their reuerent curtesies in bowing of their knees, and in like manner when they did rise from of their seates, euerie one apparrelled in cloth of Golde, but they did not sit and eate at the same table.

Streight before the triumphant Queene was the opening of the third Curtaine, couering a great and goodly doore, not of Marble, but of rare and hard Diasper of the East, of an artificiall and ancient worke, wonderfully bewtifull to behold. Vpon either sides of this doore, their yoong damosels Musitians, seuen vpon a side in a Nimpish apparrel, notable for the fashion and verie rich: which at euery change of seruice, did alter their Musicke and Instruments, and during the banquetting, others with an

Angelike and Syreneall consent, did tune the same to their handes. Then in a sodaine was placed frames of Hebony, with three feete, and other temporary tables, without any noyse or brustling. Euerie one readie to his appoynted Office, with a carefull, diligent, and affecting indeuour, wholy to that seruice which was enioyned him.

f. 54. And first before the Queene, there was placed a frame of three feete of this fourme, vpon a rounde of fine Dyasper, with curious Lineaments. To the which were three stypits, the lower partes whereof, did finish in the forme of the tearing claw of a Lyon, with an exquisite foliature, compassing about the steales of the stypets, hauing in the middest of euerie one, fastened the head of a childe betwixt two wings, from the which betwixt one and other of the stypets, there hung in maner of a Garland a bundle of leaues and fruites bounde togither, and biggest towardes the midst, and vppon the top of the stypets or steales, was put a proiection to beare vp the rounde table before the Queene.

This frame was vnmoueable, but the round table was to be quickly taken of and on, according to the substance of the vessels at euery changing of the table.

And streight way as it were in the twinckling of an eye and turne of a hand, there was put vppon this three footed frame a rounde table of Golde, three foote by the Diameter, and of an indifferent thicknesse, and of this forme and bignes were all the rest.

Vpon this table was laide a Carpet perfumed, of cloth of Hormisine of a greene colour, euenly distended large and long downe to the pauement : fringed vpon the sides with twisted threede of the selfe same, and mixed with Siluer and Golde, depending downe vnder a border of imbroyderie of Pearle and pretious stone, with a hand-breadth of the pauement on euerie side hanging downe. And of this sort were all the Carpets bordered and fringed.

Afterwards followed a faire yoong Damosell and quicke, with a great Bason of Gold filled with the flowers of Violets, tawny, blew & white, and sweet smelling, as in the prime spring time, and strewing of them vpon the tables, except that before the Queene.

Her sacred maiestie, hauing put off her robe so gorgeous as *Lolia*, wife to *Paulus Aemilius* neuer saw in her husbandes tryumphes, and shee remayned in a gowne of purple Veluet, hauing wouen in it birdes, little beastes, f. 54b.
leaues and flowers in knottes, the worke somewhat raysed vp with pearle and stone, with a thynne vayle couering it all ouer of silke syprusse, shewing through it the couered workes and cloath by reason of the cleare subtiltie and thinnesse thereof, and imperiall and gratious apparell.

After came in two beautifull Damosels bringing in an artificious fountaine continually running with water, and reassuming the same agayne, which was of fine golde, and in a vessell of a curious workmanshippe, which was brought before the Queene, and after the presenting of it vpon the table of golde they bowed their knees downe to the pauement, and like reuerence at the same instaunt made all the rest of the attendant Ladyes, both at the presenting of euery thing, and at the taking away. Three other faire Damosels followed neare after them, one carrying an Ewer of golde, the second a bason, and the other a towell of white silke.

The Queen whilest shee did wash hir handes, one that caried the golden bason, receyued therin the water, that it might not fall agayne into the reassuming fountaine : and the other with the Ewrie, powred in as much sweete water as was borne away, because that the fountaine shoulde not be emptie, and hyndered in hys course. The third did wipe and drie her hands.

The broad and large Receptorie of this fountaine was carryed vpon foure little wheeles, which they drew vppon
f. 55. euerie table to wash the handes of all that were sette.

The brim of the vessell wherein the rising vp fountaine did stande, was adorned with bubbles of pearle standing vp, and vnder the same was sette an other of an other sorte, and both ioyned together with two claspes of an exquisite dipoliture, fine worke, and pretiously garnished. For among other iewelles of inestimable price, vppon the verie toppe in a flower, there was sette a Diamond in fashion of a peare, glistering and sparkling of a huge and vnseene bignes.

And as neare as my smell could tell mee, I did iudge the water to bee of Roses, mixt with the iuice of Lymon pilles, and a little Amber artificially composed, which yeelded a sweet and pleasant smell.

In the middest of this admirable and stupendious Court, there was set out a maruellous perfuming vessel, not so much for the excellent and perfecte substaunce thereof, which was pure and fine golde: but for the conspicuous, rare, and auncient fashion of the base, standing vpon three Harpyes feete, the which in a foliature made a trianguled illygament to the base, full of deuises, as the mettall required, ouer euerie Angle or corner whereof stoode three naked shapes of flying spirites orderly sette, of two cubites high, with their shoulders turned one towards an other, and somewhat neare together.

They stood vpon the base with the right foot towards
f. 55b. the corner and the lefte stretching towardes the fixed foot of the other boye. Their cubits bending vp, and holding the handle of the perfuming panne, verie slender in the

steale, and vpward in fashion of a bowle, somewhat furrowed and broad lipped.

There were six in a round circuit, one towardes an other: And betwixt theyr shoulders in the Center point of the triangulted base, there rose vp a steale like an olde fashioned Candlesticke, holding on the toppe thereof suche a bowle or vessell as aforesaide, and so broade as did fill vp the voyde place in the middest betwixt the other six.

Which bowles were filled with burning coles couered ouer with embers, and in euery vessell vppon the ashes did boyle a little pot of gold, which contrary liquors infused with sweet odours.

And as I suspected, euery potte had seuerall waters, as it were, one with Rose-water, another with water of Orange flowers, another of myrtle, tender greene Lawrell leaues, elder flowers, and diuers such lyke sociable symples. And these boyling together, they did yeelde a most pleasant and fragrant smell.

In the presence of the magnificent Queene there did alwayes wayte and attend three honourable Nymphes, their apparell beeing of golde and silke, maruelously wouen and adorned, and sette with pearle and stone. The lyninges of theyr gownes going about their snowie shoulders, and comming downe vppon theyr little round brestes to the lower parte of their wastes, of suche colour as the napkins, leauing to be seene the pleasaunt valleys betwixt their faire brestes, an extreame delight and desired nourishment vnto a narrowe looke and greedie eye, with a thousand small chaynes, pretie iewelles and flowers of golde in a fæminine sort, a sweet bayte to carrie a man headlong into forgetfulnes of hymselfe, beeing inchaunted with choyse and amorous regards, farre passing the desire

of any other delycate vyands. Their shooes of golde cutte with halfe Moones, and closed vp at the ioyning of the hornes or corners with buttons and flowers of gold-
f.56. smithes woorke in a curious sorte, and the trammels of their faire and plentifull haire aboue their forheads and temples instrophiated with large and round oryent pearle.

They stoode thus on eyther hande and before the Queene with a singular and reuerent regarde, attending and readilie perfourming that charge whereunto they were appoynted. And these serued but on one Table: which beeing chaunged, they withdrewe themselues by, and stoode still vppon theyr feete arme in arme, other three hauing supplyed their places: And the three that wayted, shee in the middest was caruer.

The other vppon the right side helde vnder a plate if anie thing should fall by: and the thirde vppon the lefte hand held a most whyte and cleane towell of silke to drie her lippes, and in euery action a reuerence.

The towell was not vsed but once, and then cast by vpon the pauement, and carryed away by one that stoode neare. And so many morsels as shee did eate, so many sweete perfumed cleane towelles of silke plyted and finely wrought were vsed.

And the like was doone to euerie guest, for not one at that banquet did touch anie thinge sauing onelye the cuppe.

After that the Queene had washed, and had her first seruice, then all the rest did wash at the same fountaine, casting out water of it selfe, and reassuming the same in a wonderfull manner by two small pypes on eyther sides, and running vp straight in the middest from the bottome of the vessell, the deuyse whereof when I did vnderstand, I was much contented therewithall.

After the washing of the Queene first, and successiuely of all the rest, there was deliuered to euery one of the wayters a rounde ball of golde wyer-woorke full of small holes, and within stuft with Amber past of a most perfect composition, set with pretious stones, to the ende their hands, eyes, and sences should not be idle.

Then there at euerie chaunge of course, two *Edeabrices* that had the ordayning of the Queenes meate, did bring into the middest of the royall Court vppon foure turning f. 56b.
wheeles a stately repositorie or cupbord, in fashion like vnto a shippe, and the rest like to a triumphant Chariot, of most fine golde, with many fishes and water monsters, and infinit other exquisite shapes maruelously wrought, and sette full of riche stones, the sparklings and glisterings whereof did shine rounde about the sides of the Court, and reincounter vpon the roundelles of the other before spoken iewelles, on euery side fitly placed, as if Phœbus had beene sette by a Nymph to grace hir eyes and countenance with his shining brightnes.

To all which continuall glistering of ineffable workemanshippe, there could no more bee deuised of equall comparison, although it were the Temple at Babylon with the three golden statues.

Within the which was put all such necessaries perfumed, as were meete and conuenient for the chaunging of the tables, as clothes, flowers, cuppes, towelles, and vesselles, to powre out of, to drinke in, and plates to eate vpon.

Which did draw in the cupbord.

And these two Nymphes plaustraries, did take them downe, and deliuer them (as neede required) to the wayters.

And the first Table beeing chaunged, euerie thing was brought backe agayne to the plaustraries, at whose going away the Trumpettes sounded in such a sorte, as *Piscus*

Therrenus neuer came neare vnto, nor *Maletus* Trumpetor to the King of Hetruria.

And then they did wind their Cornettes, thus dooing euerie time that the repositorie was drawne out, vntil that it came in againe, at what time they ceased.

And when the Table was chaunged, they altered their musicall instruments, which beeing ceased, the singers began so heauenly, that it would haue caused the Syrens to sleepe, hauing mixed with their voyces still winde instruments of wood, such as the *Troezein Dardanus* neuer inuented.

And by this appoynted order, there was continually heard melodious soundes, and pleasaunt harmonies, sweete consortes, with delightfull Musicke presented, odoriferous perfumes smelt, and stately viandes plentifully
f. 57. fedde of. And euerie thing whatsoeuer, without any defect of grace or delight answerable, according to the dignitie of the place.

To this first princely table, all the vessels and instruments togither with the table it selfe, were of pure fine Gold. Wherupon there was appresented a Cordiall confection, and as I could coniecture, it was made of the scraping of Vnicornes horne, Date stones and Pearle, often hette, and quenched and pownded small, Manna, Pineapple kernels, Rose water, Musk and Lyquid, Golde, in a precious composition by weight, and made Losenges with fine Sugar and Amylum.

This was eaten without any drinking vpon it, and it was a Confection to prohibite all Feuers, and to driue away Melancholy wearines.

This being done in a moment, all things were taken vp and remoued, the Violets cast vpon the ground, and the table bare. And assoone as this was done, the table was laide againe couered with cloth of Talasike, and also the wayters, and as at the first, there was cast vpon them the sweete flowers of Cedars, Orenges, and *L*ymons, and vpon that, they did appresent in vessels of Beryl, and of that precious stone was the Queenes table (except the skinking pottes which were all of pure fine Gold) fiue Fritters of paste of a Saffron colour, and crusted ouer with extreeme hotte Rose water, and fine pownded Sugar, and then againe cast ouer with musked water, and with fine Sugar like frost vpon Ise. These Seruices of a most pleasant taste, and of sundry fashions were laid in thus. The first, in oyle of the flowers of Orenges. The second, in oyle of Gilliflowers. The third, in oyle of the ffloures of Gessamin. The fourth, in pure oyle of Beniamin. And the last, in the oyle of Muske and Amber. And when we had wel tasted and eaten of the same delectable meat, there was deliuered to vs a goodly cup of the aforenamed Beryl, with his couer, and couered ouer that also with a thinne Veyle of silke and Gold, curiously folded into the fourme of a Canapie, the ends cast ouer the shoulders of the bearers and hanging down their backe.

And in this sort they did present all drinking vessels and others, with meates and sawces couered. Within the drinkyng that cup they had infused a precious Wine, so f. 57b
as mee thought that the Gods of the *Elysian* fieldes, had transformed their power into the sweetnes of the lyquor: surpassing the wine of *Thassus.*

Without delaie (after our drinking this table being taken away, and the sweete flowers cast vpon the pauement, there was forthwith spred a cloth of murry silke and carnation: with Roses white, redde, Damaske, Muske, and yealow cast vppon the same. And presently new wayters brought in (apparrelled in the same colours) sixe pieces of bread cut for euery one, tossed and dressed with refined marrow, sprinckled ouer with Rose water, Saffron, and the iuice of Orenges, tempering the taste and gilded ouer, and with them sixe pieces of pure manchut were set downe. And next vnto them a confection, of the iuice of Lymons tempered with fine Sugar, the seedes of Pines, Rose water, Muske, Saffron, and choyce Synamon, and thus were all the sawces made with conuenient gradation and deliuery. The vessels were of Topas and the round table.

This third magnificent table being taken vp as before said, there was presently an other innouated, with a cloth of silke smooth and of a yealow colour, (the wayters sutable) and strewed with Lilly Conually, and Daffadil, immediately this course was presented, seuen morsels of the flesh of a Partridge in a sharpe broth, and so many pieces of pure white Manchut. The sauce Acceres, minced and dissolued in Sugar thrice sodden, Amylum, Saunders, Muske and Rose water. The vessels and the rounde table of *Chrysolite*. Lastly, they offered a precious drinking cup, and so obserued in the rest.

The fourth table beeing taken away, the fift was reuested with a cloth of silke, of a crimosen colour, and in like sort the Nimphish apparrel. The flowers of purple, yealow, white, and tawny. The Seruis, eight morsels of the flesh of a Pheasant rosted lying in the grauie, and withall so many pieces of fine white manchet. The sauce was this, water of Orenge flowers, the iuice of Pomegranets, Sugar, Cloues, and Cynamon. The vesselles of Smaragde, and the table of the Souerigne Queene.

This beeing taken away verie solemnely, there was

spred an other cloth of silke of a purple colour, and so the apparrel of the wayters. f. 58.

The flowers were of three sortes, of Iessamine, tawny, yealow, and white. The Seruice was nine morsels of the flesh of a restoratiue Peacocke, moystened in his grauie. The sauce was most greene and tart, with Pistacke, Nuttes pownded, Sugar, Cypricum, Amylum, and Muske, Time, white Marioram, and Pepper. The vesselles of Saphyre, and the Princely Table.

At the seuenth chaunge, they brought in a sumpteous table of white Iuory, bordered, trayled, and finely wrought with many small pieces vpon the precious wood of Aloes, and ioyned & glued togither, and from one side to the other, wrought with knottes and foliature, flowers, vesselles, monsters, little Birdes, and the strikes and caruings filled vp with a black paste and mixture of Amber and Muske. This mee thought was a most excellent thing and sumpteous breathing out, a most delightful sweet smel. The cloth white and subtily wrought with drawne worke and Satten silke, the ground powdered and filled, and the worke white and plaine, with the representation of shapes, byrdes, beastes, and flowers, and in like sort the apparel of the wayters. The flowers Lady steale, Rape, Violet, and all sortes of sweete Gilliflowers. And thus there varied euerie where such diuersitie of smelles, seuerally brought in, and so delightfull to the sences, as I cannot sufficiently expresse.

Then there was giuen to euerie one a confection in three morsels of the shell, fish, Dactilus, with Pistacke, Nut kernels pownded and put into Rose water and Sugar, of the Ilandes, and Muske and leafe Golde, beaten and adulterated therwith, that euerie piece taken vp, seemed as if it had beene all Gold.

The vessels were of Iacynth, and the table circulare. An apt and conuenient stone to so excellent disposition and royall board and straunge banquets, suche as before were neuer heard of.

After the taking away of these wonderfull Confections, f. 58b. and the flowers cast downe vpon the pauement in a princely magnificence, there was presently brought in, a great vessell of Gold full of kindled coales, into the which the table cloathes, napkins and towelles of silke were throwne, whiche presently burned light, and after that beeing taken out and cooled, they were whole, vnhurt and cleane, as at the first. And this yet was the wonderfull straungest of all the rest. And then the tables and frames were taken downe and carried away.

Which most excellent order and sightes, the more that I carefully indeuoured to consider of them, the more ignorant and amazed I founde my selfe.

But in all thinges assuredly I did take great pleasure with my intended admiration, in seeing of such, so great, plentifull, and tryumphant sumpteousnes, of so incredible costly a banket, that it is better to holde my peace then not to speake sufficiently in the report thereof. For that the bankets of *Sicilia* be in respect but beggerly, and so were the stately Ornaments of *Attalus*. The Corinthian vessels, the dainties of *Ciprus*, and *Saliarie* suppers.

Yet notwithstanding so supreame and excessiue alacritie, and cordiall delectation, and that onely and extreeme pleasure (occasioned by such and so vnexpected delightes) by one of those three which in the last chaunge attended, were quayled, ouerthrowne, interrupted, lamed, intercepted and made vaine. For shee did represent in her behauiour, the sweet iesture and resemblance of *Polia*, stirring vp by them in me stealing regardes.

This was no small hinderance vnto mee, in the takyng of those pleasant dainties and princely refection. Yet notwithstanding my eyes would now and then with much adoo, bee withdrawne to beholde the bewtie of the Iewels and precious stones, sparkeling and glistering in euerie place, in such diuersities of straunge and vnseene glorious-nes and conspicuous decoraments, as if they had all ought a duetie to her, which made mee with an immoderate desire, to behold the correspondency of her excellent bewtie.

Lastly, in suche order and sorte, as aforesaide, the tables f. 59.
being taken away, I hung downe my heade, because that I might not followe after the last iunckates which I had lost by minding of her that ministred.

Then first before the sacred Maiestie and royall person of the Queene, and afterwards to vs, fiue fayre Nymphes apparelled in blewe silke and golde curiously wouen togeather in workes, did all together appresent them-selues.

The middlemost of them did beare a braunch of coorrall, lyke a tree, such as is not founde amongst the Ilandes Orchades, of one cubite high, which stoode as vppon a little mountayne, which was the couer of an old fashioned vessell of pure gold, in forme of a Challyce, as high agayne as the couer and the tree of coorrall, full of curious work-manshippe and leafe worke, neuer made in our age, nor the like seene.

Betwixt the gracylament of the foote and the cuppe, it was knitte together with a handle of inestimable worke-manship, and in lyke manner the foote and the bowle were of an excellent anaglyphie of foliature, monsters and byformed Scyllules, so exquisitely expressed, as could be imbossed, chased, or ingrauen by proportionate circulation.

And the mordycant couer of the same was thicke set with incomparable iewelles; and in lyke sorte all the base and handle whereas conueniencie requyred, and glystering about.

Vppon the braunches of the coorrall, there were artificially sette certayne open flowers with fiue leaves, some of Saphyre, some of Iacynth and Berill, and in the middest of them a little round seede of golde, fastening the leaues to the stalke of corrall.

Which yoong woman reuerently bowing to the earth with her right knee, reseruing the other still vp, whereuppon shee helde this couer of coorrall, which also besides the flowers, had vppon the pointes and toppes of other twigges or sprouts curiously infixed monstrous great pearle. And other of them had a cuppe full of pretious lyquor, better then that which the prowde *Cleopatra* gaue vnto the Romane Captaine: The reste did execute their
f. 59b. offices as aforesaid, and plucking off one after another, with a little instrument with two teeth of golde they offering the same fruits vnto vs, to me vnknowne, for that I had neuer seene the lyke, we did tast them.

But the vnexpected pleasure of them, and sweetnes of their tast, was no otherwise to me than like a gratious substance wanting his desired forme.

And there were restored agayne the balles of golde before mentioned.

Vppon this appeared an other maruellous woorke, that was a perpetuall running fountaine artificially deuysed of the aforesaid matter, but of an other notable fashion and workemanshippe, founded vppon an immoueable axeltree, vppon the which two wheeles turned about.

Aboue the which stood an vnequal quadrature three foot long, two foot broad, and six foote high.

In euery angular part did sit a Harpie with both her winges extended and stretched vp to the breadth of a higher vessell, standing vp vppon the middest of the measured quadrangule, coronized at the extreme and vpper parts, and beautified with chanelling and foliature, circumuesting the lower part.

And vppon euerie side the same diuided into three, the middle parte betwixt the fall of the waters intercepted, did contayne in halfe bodyes carued, a tryumph of Satyres and Nymphes, with Trophees, and exquysite actions, excepte the fore-part and hinder parte moderately sinuated and bent in. The which in steade of squadred lyneament, did contayne, a roundnesse waued betweene, in the which was maruellously ingrauen a little sacrifice with an olde Aultar on eyther sides, with manie figures and actions, the rest that was voyde, the tayles of the foresayde Harpyes ioyning togeather, and turning heere and there into leaues, did excellently couer the same.

Out of the medyan center of the equature and quadrangule afore specified and described out of an antyke folyature, did ryse vp an olde fashioned vessell, and verie beautifull, the cyrcuite whereof did not exceede the content of the quadrangulate playne, and this with all the rest of the woorke, and euerie proportionate disquisition, tryall, and examination, both in the highest breadth and f. 60.
thicknesse, with moste conuenient vesseling lineamentes, diligently delymated and fyled, and then finished with an absolute and depolyte deformation.

The which out of the suppressed orifice thereof did ascend vp an other hollowe vessell, the compasse whereof did exceede the aforesaide subiect vessell furrowed and channelled round about, of a great breadth and large brymmes so wel fashioned, as is possible for any goldsmith to beate out with his hammer.

In the center poynt whereof did rise and mount an other vessell of incredible workemanship.

In the bottome of which thirde there were small ridges swelling outwardes, the toppes of them compassed about with a row of diuerse inestimable stones, bearing out and differing in colours, as best might content the eye of a curious Lapidarie and skilfull vnderstanding.

Vppon the same on eyther sides was made a heade of a monster, from the which on both handes did proceede the garnishing thereof in an exquisite and most rare woorke of leaues, inuesting the same about with the congresse of the opposyte head, and finely gracing that parte of the vessell.

And in the bearing out of the lippe of the vessell ouer the perpendicular poynt of the heade there was fastened a rynge, from the which vppon eyther sides there hung downe a garland of braunches, leaues, flowers, and fruites growing bigger towardes the middest, with a perpolyte bynding to eyther ringes.

Ouer the middle bending of the garland, and vnder the proiecture of the lyppe of the vessell, there was fixed and placed the head of an olde man, with his beard and haire of his head transformed into nettle leaues, out of whose mouth gushed out the water of the fountayne by art continually into the hollownes of the broad vessell vnder this.

Vppon the mouth of this last described vessell did mount vppe a pretyous hyll maruellously congest, and
f. 60b. framed of innumerable rounde pretious rocke stones closing one with another vnequally, as if nature had ioyned them growing, making a rounde composed hill,

beautifully glistering of dyuerse sortes and colours in a proportionate bignes.

And aloft vpon the toppe of this little hill, there grewe a fine pomgranate tree, the body, boughes and fruite made all of golde, the leaues of greene Smaragde. The fruit of theyr naturall bignesse heere and there aptly placed, their sides cut open, and in place of kernelles they were full of most perfecte Rubyes, as bigge as the kernels.

After that, the ingenious Artificer wanting no inuention, hee seperated the graynes in steade of the ſylme with siluer foyle.

And moreouer, in other apples, opened, but not rype, hee redoubled the thicknesse of the foyle, making the kernelles of an oryentall colour, so also hee made the flowers of perfect corrall, in the cuppes full of bees of golde.

Besides this, out of the toppe of the hollowe steale, lyke a pype, there came out a turning steale, the lowest part whereof rested in a heade, framed from the middle trunke or pype iust ouer the axeltree.

Which steale or stypet beeing strongly fastened, it bare vp a vessell of Topas of an auncient forme, the bowle whereof in the bottome was broad, and swelling out with rigges in the opening, rarely bewtified with a coronice, and put vnder with another.

In which closing and binding together in foure equall diuisions, there were foure winged heades of a little childe, with four pipes in their mouthes.

The rest mounted vp so much as the lower bignesse of the vessell was, beeing closed vp at the orifice with an inuerse foliature Vppon the which there was placed an other vessell as it were a circular couer of a most curious leafe worke, with a smal coronice, and an artificiall orifice.

From the bottome of which there beganne a flourished tayle of a Dolphin fastened and sowldered to the gracylament of the vessell, descending downe with his heade finned with leaues, to the circulating brymme of the
f. 61. vessell where the boyes heades were fixed. And with a moderate swelling out about the head, and streightning in towardes the tayle, they fitted for the eares in a beautiful manner. And all that inclining part with an exquisite polishing did make an expresse shewe of most curious lineaments.

The vpper vessell was so perfectly wrought, that when the wheele was mooued, the steale with the vessell vppon the toppe thereof, turned about and powred out water through the tree, and when the wheele stoode still, then that lefte turning.

The wheeles were halfe couered with two winges, the typpes turning one way and the other an other way, adorned with a chasing of Mermaydes or Scillaes.

f. 62. This excellent peece of woorke thus running before euerie one, and weeting our handes and feete of an incredible sweetnesse, such as I neuer had felt before, we dryed our hands, and it was carryed away.

And beeing thus sprinckled with this rare and maiesticall water, the wayters with great reuerence presented vnto the Queene first a great cuppe of golde, and her highnesse affably saluting vs, drunke Nectar, and afterwardes euerie one of vs after other, with reuerent, mutual, and solemne honours done, did drinke a most pleasaunt farewell and shutting vp of all the pretious dainties that we had tasted and fed vpon.

Lastly, the redolent flowers beeing diligently taken

away, and all thinges that had beene vsed borne from thence, the pauement remayned pure and shining as a most cleare steele glasse, and as it were emulating the pretious iewelles rownde about.

And euerie one beeing sette in his appoynted place, the high and mightie Princesse did commaund a company to come in, and stande vppon the diasper checkers, neuer the like before seene or imagined of anie mortall creature.

THE TENTH CHAPTER.

f. 62b. Poliphilus followeth to shew besides this great banket of a most excellent daunce or game, and how the Queene did commit him to two of her Nymphes, the which did leade and conduct him to the sight of many wonderfull things, and as they talked, shewed vnto him the secrecies of such things as hee stood in doubt of. Finally, how they came to the three gates, in the middlemost whereof he remained amongest the amorous Nymphes.

AUING SPOKEN SOMETHING of the exceeding & incomparable glorie, triumph, vnknowne treasure, plentiful delights, solemne banket, and the most honourable and sumptuous drinking of this most happie and rich Queene, if I haue not distinctly and perfectly expressed her chiefest dignitie, let not the curious company maruel thereat, for whatsoeuer rype, sharpe, aud readie wit, with a franke, eloquent and plentiful toong adorned, is not able to performe the least part of his duetie.

And much lesse I, who continually suffer in euerie secret place of my burning heart, an vncessant strife notwithstanding the absence of *Polia* my mistres, the owner of all my skil, and imprisoner of my perfections.

Besides that, in truth the many maruels in excellency, and varietie vnhard of, so vncoth, rare and straunge vnlikes inestimable, and not humane, haue so oppressed, laden & born down my sences, with the greedie and excessiue contemplation and beholding of their variable diuersities, as that from point to point I am no whit able to describe them, and much lesse worthie to publish them.

All and the most that I can do, is to thinke of the rich apparrel, exquisite prouision, curious dressings, perfect ambitious and wounding bewties without imperfections, their deepe iudgements, *Aemilian* eloquence, & bountie more then princely, the notable disposition and order of Architecture, the durable Symmetrie and proportion of f. 63.
the building, perfect and absolute, the noblenes of the Art of Masonrie and Lapycidarie, the directions and placing of Columnes, the perfection of statues and representations, the adornment of the walles, the diuersitie of the stones, the stately entrance & princely porch, large Gallery, and artificious pauements, no man will thinke with what cost and charge bewtified and hanged with precious Arras and Verdure. The spacious and loftie inner Court, goodly bedchambers, inner withdrawing chambers, parlours, bathes, librarie and pinacloth, where coat Armors, escuchions, painted tables, and counterfeates of strangers were kept, & with a maiestical comelines and order placed and solemnely distributed.

In which conceiuing capacitie, maruellous performance, incredible charge and high commendation of the most excellent Artificer, woorthily allowed in euerie partition and elegant conuention of exquisite Lineaments. I also beheld a maruellous twisted conlignation or couering of goldsmiths work, ouer a foure square plaine Court, growing vp alike, without comparison like a heauen, with a disposite distance of many sorted proportions, with sundry lybellated Dimensions, shadowing ouer the Court, with an Arched Eminence, which was vnder, adorned with coronised

Lyneaments and grauings, thereunto conuenient, as Fasheols, Gululles, and Oualling, and the leaues of *Achanthus*, licking vp as it were in the corners of the quadranguled Court. With Roses, and the growing order of their leaues, the top leafe least, their iaggings about the leaues, and space betweene leafe and leafe. All thinges couered with pure fine gold and Azure colour, with diuers other proportions and counterfets of substance, equal with their workemanship. The roofing of *Salauces*, King of *Colchis*, may not compare with this.

Then the delightful fruitfulnes of the set hedges Orchards, watered Gardens, springing Fountaines, current streames in Marble Channelles, conteined, framed, and held in, with an incredible Art, greene Hearbes, still freshe and flowering, a sweete ayre, warme and spring windes, with a confused charme of singing and chirping birdes, a pure, faire and bright aire, and stil continuing temperate and
f. 63b. healthfull, country free from danger and cleane, No craggy nor rockie places, nipt and blasted with sharpe windes, nor burnt with an vntemperate hotte Sunne, but vnder a sweet and pleasant temperature, in a moderate meane reioycing, betwixt two extreemes, the fields fruitful and without tillage and manuring, yeelding all commodities, warme hilles, greene woods, and sweet coole shadowes.

Also the inestimable furniture, the attendant housholde and great number, their excellent seruice, the diuersitie of youthes, and all in the prime of their yeares. The delightfull presence of the Nymphes, both attending abroad in the presence and chambers, her baser sort, their honourable and gracious behauiours, their diuersitie of apparrel, attire and dressings set with Pearle and stone, in an allowed, pleasant & louely sort, as any can imagine or expresse. With these infinite riches, supreame delightes, and immeasurable treasure, neither *Darius*, *Crœsus*, or any other humane state, whatsoeuer might in any way compare.

And thus to conclude, being ouercome with the glorie of them, I know not what more to say, but that I stood amazed, and as it were senceles, and yet in great delight and without wearines, beholding those present obiects, and casting with my selfe what fate and destinate should conduct and leade mee into such a place.

But afterwardes finding my selfe in such an accumulation of glorie, pleasant seate, happie Country, great contentment and tryumphant company, such as *Clodius* the Player in Tragedies neuer had scene. I was but moderately conuerted, notwithstanding the promise of the Queene, to fauour my amorous desire, accouating all, but as eye pleasures that hitherto I had seene and had been presented vnto me, stil desiring a greater happines.

For which cause, and for the greater setting out of the excesse and abounding excellency, beyond all the rest of her royall magnificence, euery one sitting in their place after the miraculous, wonderful, and sumpteous banket, without any delaie, she commanded a game to be playd by parsonages, not onelie woorthie the beholding, but of eternall remembrance, which was a game at Chesse, in this sort as followeth.

By the entraunce of the curtaine there came in thirty f. 64.
two Nymphes. whereof sixteene were apparrelled in cloth of Gold (eyght vniformally without difference of degrees) afterwards one of those sixteene was aparrelled in princely robes lyke a King, and the other lyke a Queene, with two tower-keepers or Rookes, as wee tearme them, two counsell-keepers or Secretaries, we tearme them Bishoppes, and two Knights. In like sort were eight other in cloth of siluer, vnder the like gouernement and magistracie as aforesaid.

Euerie one of these according to their duties, tooke theyr places vppon the checkers of the pauement, that is, sixteene in golde of one side in two rowes, and sixteene in siluer of the contrarie side.

The Musicke beganne vppon a sodayne with a rare inuention to sound a charge with a pleasaunt concord, participating togeather a sweete and thundering melodie, hauing in it a deuine furie.

At the measured sounde and time of the Musicke vppon their checkers, as it pleased the King to commaund, the pawns turning themselues with a decent reuolution, honouring the King and the Queene, leapt vppon an other checker before them.

The King of the white men, his musicke sounding, commaunded her forward that stoode before the Queene, and the same with lyke reuerent behauiour marched forward her continent, and stoode still. And according to the mensuration of the musicall time in this order, so they chaunged their places, or continued vppon the checkers dauncing, vntill that they were eyther taken or commaunded forward by the King.

If the musicke kepte still one time, those eyght vnyforme pawnes did spende the time in marching forwardes into another checker, neuer comming backe vntill that worthily without touch or appalement of courage, they had leapt vppon the line of that square where was the residence of the Queene, proceeding straight on, vnlesse she tooke a prisoner by a Diagonick line.

The Bishop went in a Diagonike line, still holding that coloured checker wherein he stood first.

64[b]. The Knight ouer two checkers before him taketh the next of eyther handes, and of a contrary colour to that hee stoode in immediately before.

The Castle-keepers or Rookes might passe ouer manie checkers streight on as they pleased at commaundement, so that they might goe one, two, three, foure, or fiue checkers, keeping a measure, and not staying in their march.

The King might goe vpon anie checker, if none were in it, or backeward, and cause any other to remooue for him, and make him roome.

The Queene might goe any way, but it is best when shee is neare her husband on euery side.

And whensoeuer the officers of eyther of the Kings shall finde one without guarde of helpe, they take her prisoner, and both kissing one another, she that is ouercome and taken, goeth foorth and standeth by.

Thus they continued playing and dauncing according to the time of the musicke, with great pleasure. solace, and applause, vntill the King of the Siluer Nymphes was victour and conquerour.

This solemne sport, what with resistance flying backe, and seconding of one an other, with such a measured circulation, reuerence, pause, and modest continencie, endured the space of an hower, whereat I tooke such pleasure and delyght, that I imagyne (and not amysse) that I was rapt vpon the sodaine from the liking of the sportes of Olympus to a newe felicitie.

This first game beeing ended, and conquest obtayned, all retourned into theyr accustomed places, and in like manner as at the first, so the second time euerie one intheyr appoynted checkers, the Musicke chaunging theyr measure, so the moouings and gestures of the players were altered.

And obseruing the time of the musicke in a conuenient order, and approoued gesture and arte, that it was no neede to commaund or say any thing.

But the cunning and experte Nymphes, with theyr plentifull tresses effused ouer theyr delicate shoulders hung wauing, and in theyr motion forwardes would
f. 59. streame out at length, somewhat shewing their backes, about their heades wearing Garlandes and Crownes of Violets. And when any one was taken, they lifted vp their armes and clapt handes. Thus playing and coursing vp and downe, the first continued still conquerour.

In the last game and daunsing, they beeing all returned to their distributed places, the Musicke againe sounded a measure phrygiall in as perfect and prouoking furie as euer *Marcias* of *Phrygia* inuented.

The King in robes of Golde, caused the yoong Damosell that stood before the Queene, to marche forwarde to the third Checker, direct in the first remooue, whereupon immediately there was seene a battaile and Torney, with so swift and sodaine forces, bending themselues to the grounde as it were lying close vpon their Garde, and presently vpon it capering vp with a turne twise aboue ground, one iust opposite against an other, and vpon their downe come withall a turne vpon the toe thrise about.

All this Action they did at one time, with such a grace and agilitie, as nothing could be better, with their lowe inclinations, high Capers and Turnings, without affectation of strayning, as it should seeme with facilitie and careles ease at pleasure and sweete iestures, as in such a thing may bee imagined, and not else where to bee seene. Neuer any one troubling an other, but who so was taken prisoner, did presently kisse their Conquerour, and voyded the place. And the lesser number that there was, the more pleasure it was to perceiue the pollicies of either sides to ouercome other.

And such an order and motion was vsed of euerie one, in a commendable sort without fault, as the measure and time of the Musike appointed, stirryng euen them that looked on to haue a motion in their sinowes and mindes to doo the lyke, there was such a concord and agreement betwixt nature and the Musike especially, seeing the performance of the same in the actions of others.

Vpon this occasion I was moued to call to remembrance the force of *Timotheus*, the most cunning musitian, who with his voice and measure vppon his Instrument would
prouoke the great Macedonian *Alexander*, violently to f. 6
take Armes, and presently altering his voyce and tune, to forget the same, and sit downe contentedly. In this third game, they apparrelled in gold did triumph in the victoritie.

Thus honourably with exceeding pleasure and great solace, this sumpteous feast beeing ended, euerie one framed themselues to sit downe. And I rysing vp, made reuerence before the Royall seate of her sacred maiestie, and kneelyng downe vpon my knee, she thus said vnto me.

Poliphilus, forget now, and wipe out of thy remembrance all forepassed griefes, occursiue troubles, pensiue conceites, and ouergone daungers, because that I am assured of thy forthwith full contentment of desire.

And seeing that thy determination is to perseuere resolutely in the amorous flames and loue of *Polia*, I thinke it conuenient, that for the recouerie thereof, thou repaire to the three Portes, which are the resident places of the high and mightie Queene *Telosia*, in which place vppon euerie of those Portes and Gates, thou shalt see her tytle and name inscrypt. Read it diligently, but for thy better direction and safegarde, thou shalt haue to accompany thee, two of my handmaydes, which know verie well the way thither, and therefore go on vndoubtedly with a happie successe.

And thereupon with a princely bountie, she drew of from her finger a Ring of gold, hauing set in it an Anchit, and deliuered it vnto me to remember her bountie by.

At this aduise and precious gift, I became amphasiatike, not knowing what to saie or doo, in requitall or giuing of thankes. Which her Highnes perceiuing, motherly and with a naturall promptnes in a maiestical grauitie, turned her countenance to two noble and goodly Nymphes, attending neere vnto her Royall and imperiall Throne, saying thus to one of them vpon her right side.

Logistica, you shall bee one that shall accompanye our guest *Poliphilus*, and with a sacred and honourable grace, shee turned to the left hande, saying, *Thelemia*, you shall also go with him. And both of you shewe and instruct him at what Gate hee must remayne, and then *Poliphilus*, they shall bring you to an other mightie and maiesticall Queene, who if shee shall bee bountifull vnto thee in entertainment thou art happie, if contrarie, then discontented.

Notwithstandyng, none doth knowe her intent by her countenance, because that sometime shee sheweth her selfe full of favour, loue, and pleasant dispositions. An other time shee is malignant, frowarde, disdainefull, with vnstable incursyue passions. And shee it is that determineth such euents as thou seekest after. And for her obscure condition, shee is rightly called *Thelosia*.

Her residence is not in suche a stately Pallaice, as thou seest me to dwell in.

Therefore I would haue thee to vnderstande, that the chiefe woorkeman in the creation of nature, did make no thyng comparable to mee, neyther can the earth shew thee greater treasure then to come to my presence and taste of my bountie, obtaine my fauour and participate of my qualitie.

And therefore esteeme of it according to the value, for that thou findest in me, is a heauenly Tallent aboue all earthly Iewels, for I haue not had my residence in man since his fall.

They may imagine of mee but they knowe mee not, neyther doo I beare any rule with them to the good of my selfe.

Nowe the Queene *Telosia*, shee dwelleth in a place of cloudie darkenes, her house is kept close and shut, for that shee will not shew her selfe vnto man, nor anothomise, discouer, and laye open her selfe vnto any as shee is, and for this cause the euent of her variable determination is kept secret.

But in a maruellous sort considerately, shee transformeth her selfe against the haire, into diuers fashions, not manifesting her selfe, although desired.

And when the auncient Gates shall be opened vnto thee, in euerie one shall bee written what shall befall thee, but thou shalt not perceiue the same, vnlesse that in some part thy vnderstandyng and wisedome enigmatically and f. 66v.
with a right and sincere iudgement looke vnto it, and quickly consider of it, for because that shee ambyguously chaungeth hir selfe in habite and countenance, and through this doubtfull anymaduersion, a man remaineth deceiued of his expectation without remedie.

And therefore *Poliphilus*, that which these my consigned, trustie and appoynted handmaydes by suggestion shall perswade thee vnto, and at what Gate thou oughtest to enter in and remayne, euen which of those two it shall best please thee to giue eare vnto, doe : for they haue some vnderstanding of her.

And hauyng thus spoken shee made a signe or becke with her head to the two Nymphes *Logistica* and *Thelemia*, who presently without delaie, were obedient to hir commaund. And I beeing readie to speake, neyther knew what to say, or yet durst to so high a maiestie, and for so great bounties giue a word.

The two appoynted companyons of my iourney, verie fauourablye, and with a familiar readines and virginlike iestures, tooke holde of mee, one by the right hande, and the other by the left, and reuerently obteyning licence, first of the Queene, and takyng theyr leaue of the rest, went out the same way that I came in.

And I beeyng desirous and not satisfied, turned mee about towardes the conspicuous Poarch, to beholde diligently the artificious Pallaice, wonderfull and perfinite of the Art of building.

The subtiltie of which, no humane excogitation is able to imitate.

And therefore I thought that nature had made that for a maruell of all her woorkes for commoditie, vse, grace, bewtie, ayre, and continuall durablenes.

For which cause, I was excessiuely desirous to staie and looke vppon it, but my leaders and guides would not suffer mee, and yet by the theft of my eye in the Zopher, ouer the gate I noted this inscription, Ο ΤΗΣ ΦΥΣΕΩΣ ΟΛΒΟΣ.

f. 67. And as muche as with my quicke sences I could carrie, I tooke in my going foorth, with as greate pleasure and delight as is possible to expresse. O happie were hee that myght bee but a drudge or kitchin slaue in suche a Paradice.

Nowe beeing come into the base Court, compassed and sette about with Orenge trees, *Thelemia* in great curtesie saide thus vnto me, besides and aboue all the maruellous and woonderfull thinges which thou hast yet seene and behelde, there bee fower yet remayning behynde whiche thou shalt see.

And vppon the lefte side of the incomparable pallace, they brought mee into a fayre Orchyard of excogitable expence, tyme, and subtletie of woorke-manshippe, the contynent and cyrcuite whereof was as muche as the plot of the Pallace, wherein was the resydence and abiding of the Queene.

Ars toparia is the way of cutting of trees in gardens or other places to proportions or shapes.

Round about fast by the walles of the Orchyard there were set conuenyent garden pots in the which in stead of growing plantes, euerie one was of pure glasse, exceeding a mans imagination or beleefe, intorpiaried boxe the rootes and stalkes of golde, whereout the other proceeded.

Betwixt one and other of the which was placed a Cyprusse tree, not aboue two paces high, and the boxe one pace full of manyfolde maruellous symples, with a moste excellent imitation of nature, and pleasaunt diuersitie in the fashions of flowers in distinct colours verie delyghtfull.

The playne labiall compassing about the quadrant Orchyard comming out from the walles as a seate for these aforesayde garden pottes and trees to stande vppon, was subcoronized with golde by excellent lyneamentes wrought and adorned. The vpper face whereof, and whereuppon those pottes and trees did stande, was couered with a playster of glasse gilte, and a curious historographie to be seene in the same, and compassed about and holden in with wyering and netting of golde.

f. 67ᵇ. The wall that compassed about the Orchyard with a conuenient distance, was bellyed out with columnes of the same matter, and inuested with flowring bindings naturally proportioned, and heere and there were quadrangulate columnes of golde chamfered, arching from one to an other, with a requisite beame Zophor and coronice, with a meete and conuenient proiecture ouer the chapter of glasse vppon the round.

The substance of which subiect proiecture of the bryttle matter, was of counterfayte diasper diuersly coloured and shining. Which bryttle substance had some void space betwixt that and the other.

The mouth of the arches were stopped with rombyes of cleare glasse in forme of a tryangle, and the pypes beautified all ouer with an Encaustick painting, verie gratious to the sight of the beholder.

The ground was here and there couered with great round balles of glasse lyke gunne stones, and other fine proportions much pleasing, with a mutuall consent vnmoouеable lyke pearles shining without any adulteration by folyature. From the flowers did breath a sweet fragrancie by some cleare washing with oyle for that purpose.

There most cunningly did *Logistica* lyke an Orator make a discourse in commendation physically of that excellent confection of the noblenes of the substaunce, secrecie of the art, and straungenes of the inuention. The like is not to bee found.

And after shee sayde, *Poliphilus* lette vs goe and ascende vp this mount nexte the Garden, and *Thelemia* remayning at the stayre foote, wee ascended vp to the playne toppe. Where shee shewed vnto mee, with a heauenly eloquence, a Garden of a large compasse, made in the forme of an intricate Laborynth allyes and wayes, not to bee troden, but sayled about, for in steade of allyes to treade vppon, there were ryuers of water.

The which mysticall place was of a verie lustie mould and fruitfull, replenished with all sorts of fruits, beautified with faire springs, and greene hearbes and flowers, full of all solace and delight. Wereupon she spake thus.

I doe imagine (*Poliphilus*) that you doe not vnderstande f. 68.
the conditionate state of this maruellous seate, and therefore giue attendance to my wordes.

Whosoeuer entereth in cannot come backe, but as you see yonder mountaines heere and there distributed, seuen circuits and the about goings distant from another.

And the extreeme molestation and sorrowe of the enterers in, is this: In the myddle mountayne within the center thereof, and open mouth of the same, there lurketh inuisibly a deadly deuouring olde Dragon, hee is vtter destruction to some, and others are not hurte to death by him. Hee cannot bee seene nor shunned, neyther doth he leaue any vnassaulted, but eyther in the entrie, or in their iourney, hee destroyeth or woundeth. And if hee killeth them not betwixt one mountayne and another, they passe the seuen circuites to the next mount.

And they that enter in by the first tower or mount (wherevppon is this tytle inscript ΔΟΞΑ ΚΟΣΜΙΚΗΩΣ ΓΟΜΦΟΛΥΣ). They sayle in a little shippe with a prosperous winde, and securely at pleasure: The fruites and flowers fall downe vppon theyr hatches, and with great solace and pleasure they cut through by the seauen revolutions with a merry winde, vntill the second mount bee discouered and come vnto. And marke and beholde (*Poliphilus*) howe cleare and bright the ayre is in the entrance, ouer that it is in the center, about the which is thicke darknesse.

In the first mount or tower there is alwayes resident a pittifull matron and bountifull, before whome standeth an auncient appoynted vessell called *Vrna*, in a readinesse, hauing vppon it seauen Greeke letters as thus, ΘΕΣΓΙΟΝ, full of appoynted honie, and to euerie one that entereth in, verie curteously and with a good will shee giueth one of them without respecte of state and condition, but according to theyr enterance.

These beeing receyued, they come foorth, and begin to sayle in the Laborynth, the water being enuyroned vpon either sides, with roses, trees, and fruits.

68b. And hauing sayled the first seuen revolutions of *Aries*, and being come to the second mount, there they meet with innumerable troopes of yong women of diuerse conditions, which demaund of euerie one the sight of theyr honye, which beeing shewed vnto them, they straightwayes knowe the propertie of the hony, and the goodnesse thereof, and embracing him as theyr guest, they inuyte him with them to passe through the next seuen reuolutions, and with diuerse exercises according to her inclyned promptnes, they accompany them to the third mount.

In this place hee that will goe on forwards with his companion, shee will neuer abandon or leaue him: for there bee farre more pleasaunt voluptuous women. And many refuse the first and make choyse of them.

In the putting off from the second mount, to come to the third, they finde the current of the water somewhat agaynst them, and stand in neede of oares, but beeing fallen off from the thirde mount, making theyr course towardes the fourth, they finde the tide and streame more against them, and in these seauen oblique courses their pleasure is variable and vnconstant.

Beeing come to the fourth mount, they finde other yoong women combatting and fighting, and those examining theyr pottes of honie, they intice them to theyr exercise, but those that refuse to leaue theyr first companions, they let passe together, and in this cyrcuite the water is yet more contrary and troublesome, where there is neede of great studie and labour to passe on.

And beeing come to the fift mount, they finde it speculable, lyke a mirrour they see theyr representations, and in that they take great delyght, and with a feruent desire they passe on their laboursome course. In that mount they see this sentence and golden saying manyfested, *Medium tenuere beati:* not lyneall, nor locall, but temporall, where by a sincere and perfect examination hee discerneth that meane wherewith he hath ioyned his felicitie, wisdome and riches: which if not well, in the rest of his course he faynteth the more.

And losing off from thence, the Waters by reason of the f. 69.
broken circles, beginne to be verie slyding towards the Center, so that with small or no rowing they are brought to the sixt Mount. And there they finde elegant Women, with a shew of heauenly modestie and diuine worship, with whose amiable aspects and countenaunces the Trauailers are taken in their loue, condemning their former with despite and hatefull abhorrence. And with these they fall acquainted, and passe the seauen reuolucions.

These beeing come ouer with an obscure and foggy close ayre, with many losses and a grieuous voyage, they beginne to remember what they haue past and lost: for the more that the compasse of the reuolucion draweth neere to the discouerie of the Figure of the Center, the sooner they are passed ouer, styll shorter and shorter, and the more swyfter the course of the streame is into the deuouring swallow of the Center.

And then with extreame affliction and bitter anguish remembring the abuse of their pleasures, and companions that they haue forsaken, and sweete places, which so much the more augmenteth their sorrowes, for that they can not returne or goe backe with theyr Shyppe, such a companie still follow them vppon the stearne with their fore-castles. And most of all dysmayeth them the heauie sentence ouer the median Center, *Theoulykos Dys Algetos*.

And there, considering the displeasant tytle, they curse the time of their entrance into the Labirinth, which hath in it so manie sundry delights, and the end of them subiect to such myserable and ineuitable necessity.

And then she smyling, said: *Poliphilus*, ouer the deuouring throat of thys Center, there sitteth a seuere Iudge, balancing euery ones actions, and helping whom hee will helpe. And because that it will be tedious to tell thee all, let thus much heereof suffise. Let vs goe downe to our companion *Thelemia*, who demanding the cause why they staid so long aboue, *Logistica* made aunswer, it doth not content our *Poliphilus*, onely to behold, but also to vnderstand by me the secrecie of those things, which he could not goe to knowe, wherein I haue satis-fied him. And when she had ended, *Thelemia* said.

Ggb. Let vs goe a little while to an other garden no lesse pleasant ioyning to the glasse garden, vppon the right side of the Pallas: and when wee were come in thither, I was amazed with excessiue wondering, to see the curiousnesse of the worke, as vneasie to report as vncredible to beleeue: æquiuolent with that of glasse, wyth lyke disposition of benches or bankes; theyr lyppes set out with coronising and golden ground worke, and such trees, but that the boxes and Cyprus trees, were all silke, sauing the bodies and greater branches, or the strength of the armes: the rest, as the leaues, flowers, and outermost rynde, was of fine silke, wanting no store of Pearles to beautifie the same: and the perfect fine collour, smelling as the glasse flowers before mentioned, and alike, but that they about compassing walles, of meruailous and incredible sumpteousnesse, were all couered ouer with a crusting of Pearle, close ioyned and set together: and towardes the toppe, there sprouted out greene yuie, the leaues thickning and bushing out from the Pearles, with the stringes and veines of golde, running vppe in diuers places betwixt the Pearles, in a most rare and curious sort, as if it had beene very growing yuie, with berries of precious stones sette in the stalkes in little bunches: and in the bushes were Ringe-doues of silke, as if they had beene feeding of the berries, all along the sides of the square plotted garden walles: ouer the which, in master-like and requisite order, stretched out the beame and Zophor of golde.

The plaine smooth of the settles, where-vpon the boxe trees stoode, couered ouer with Histories of loue and venerie, in a worke of silke and threddes of golde and siluer, in suche a perfect proportioned ymaginarie and counterfaiting as none may goe beyonde. The ground of the leuell garden was of leaues, grasse, and flowers of silke, like a faire sweete meddowe: in the midst whereof, there was a large and goodly round Arbour, made with golde wyer, and ouerspread with roses of the lyke worke, more beautifull to the eye, then if they had been growing roses, vnder which couering and within which Arbour about the sides, were seates of red Diaspre, & all the round

pauement of a yellow Diaspre, according to the largenes
70. of the place, with dyuers colloured spottings, confusedly agreeing together in pleasant adulterated vniting, and so cleere and shining, that to euery obiect was it selfe gaine represented. Vnder the which Arbour, the fayre and pleasant *Thelemia*, solaciously sitting downe, tooke her Lute which she carryed with her, and with a heauenly melodie and vn-hearde sweetenesse, she began to sing in the commendation and delightes of her Queene. And seeing what a grace vnto her the company of her fellowe *Logistica* was, I maruailed why *Apollo* came not to harken the Harmonie made by them : it was so melodious, that for the present tyme a man woulde haue thought that there had beene no greater fælicitie. And after that shee ended her diuine Poems, *Logistica* tooke me by the hande and led me foorth of the Arbour, saying unto me,

Poliphilus, thou shalt vnderstande that the deuise of these obiects, are more pleasant to bee vnderstoode then beholde, and therefore lette vs enter in heere, to bee satisfied in both.

And from thence, shee and her companion brought mee from thys garden to an other, where I beheld an arching *Areostile*, from the ground bent to the toppe, fyue paces in height and three ouer, and thus continued rounde about the compasse of the garden, in an orderly and requisite proportioning, all inuested and couered ouer with greene yuie, so that no part of the wall was to be seene. And there were a hundred Arches to the compassing of this garden.

By euery of the Arches was an Aulter of red Porphirite, curiously proportioned with exquisite lyneaments ; and vppon euery one of them was placed, an image of golde, like a Nymph, of rare and beautifull semblances, diuersly apparelled, and varying in theyr attyre and heade dressing, euery one bending their eyes towardes the Center of the garden.

In which midde Centricke place, there was founded a Base, of a cleere Christal-like Calcedonic stone, in a Cubic forme: that is, euery way a like square. And vppon that was set a round stone, but flatte vppon both sides, two foote high, and by the Diameter, one pace and a halfe ouer, of most pure red Diaspre. Vppon the which, stoode a most blacke stone, in forme three square, and in quantitie for breadth, fitting the rounde, and in height one pace and a halfe. The corners of which triangle did iumpe with the sides, and lymbus of the subiacent plynth or round stone.

In the smooth polished fronts of which triangle, there was appact a beautifull Image, of a heauenly aspect, graue and modest, with their feete not touching the stone, but standing out from the same iust ouer the suppressed and vnder-put rounde stone. Theyr statures as tall as the trygonall would beare, vnto the which they did stick fast by their backe parts. Theyr armes were stretched abroade, both the right and left to the corners of the triangle, where they held a Coppy, filled and fastned to the corners of the Trigonall, the length of euery one of which Coppies of fine gold, was seauen foote.

And the Images, the Coppyes and their bandes wherewith they were tyed in the midst and held by, were all shyning, and their hands inuiluped with the sundry stringes, flying about the plaine smothe of the black stone.

Their habits were Nymphish of most rare and most excellent working. The Sepulchre of *Tarnia* the Queene of the *Scythians* in *Asia* was nothing comparable.

In the lowest Cubicall Figure, vpon the smoth plaine

of euery square, were ingrauen Greeke Letters, three, one, two and three on thys sort, ΔΥΣ Α ΑΩ ΤΟΣ.

In the circular there were three Characters Hieragliphicall, perpindicularly vnder the feet of euerie Image. For the first was impressed the forme of the Sonne. Next vnder another, the figure of an olde fashioned Ower.

Thirdly, a dyshe with a burning flame in it.

Vpon the heade of the trygonall blacke stone, towarde euerie corner, I did behold an Egiptian Monster of Gold, fower footed couchant. One of them hauing a face lyke [a] man altogether. The other like half a man, & halfe a beast. And the third like a beast. VVith a linnen vaile ouer euery of their heades, with two Labels hanging ouer theyr eares, & the rest descending downe and couering their necks & backes, with the bodies of Lyons. Theyr lookes directly forward.

Vppon the backs of these three, dyd stande rysing vp a massiue Spyre of Gold, three square, sharpning vp to the toppe, fiue tymes as high as broade below. And vpon euery front or fore side was grauen a circle, and ouer one circle a Greeke Letter, O, ouer another, a Letter Ω, and ouer the third, a Greeke N.

Then *Logistica* beganne to speake vnto me, saying, by these Figures are discribed, so farre as man's reason can shewe, the celestiall harmony. And vnderstand *Poliphilus*, that these Figures, with a perpetuall affynitie and coniunction, are auncient Monuments, and Egiptian Hieragliphs, signifying this, *Diuinæ infinitæque trinitati vnius essentiæ*. Which is now by his holy word, in a most louing sort manifested to the whole world, according to his will : and yet it shall not be a misse to see antiquities, and consider what greater benefite is had by the precious Gospel.

The lower Figure was consecrated to the Deitie, because it is euerie way alike, and all one: and vpon euery side, and turned euery way, of like stablenes; vpon euery base, constant and permanent.

The round Circular standing vppon that, is without beginning or ende. Vppon the circumferent sides whereof, these three lyneaments are contained, directly vnder euerie Image, according to the property attributed.

The Sunne with his comfortable light giueth life to euerie thing, and his nature is attributed to GOD.

The second is the Ower, which is prouident direction and gouernment of all with an infinite wisedome.

The third is a Fyerie Vessell, whereby is vnderstoode a partycipation of Loue.

And although that they be three distinct things, yet they are contained & vnited in one sempeternallie, with great loue communicating their blessings, as you may see by the coppies at euery corner of the trygonall stone.

And continuing her delectable speech, she sayd, vnder the forme of the Sunne, note this Greeke worde, *Adiegetos*. By the Ower looke upon this *Adiachoristos*. And by the Vessel of fier, was engrauen, *Adiercynes*.

And to this ende are the three Monsters placed vnder the golden Obelisque, because that there be three great
opinions like those Monsters: & as that with the f. 72.
humane countenaunce is best, so the other be beastly and monstrous.

In the Spyre there be three plaine sides, lyneated with three circles, signifying one for euery time—The past, the present, and to come; and no other figure can holde these three circles, but in that inuariable. And no mortall man can at one instant perfectlie discerne and see together two sides of the same figure, sauing one integrally, which is the Present: and therefore vppon great knowledge were these three Characters engrauen, O, Ω, N.

For which cause *Poliphilus*, not that I excuse my selfe for beeing ouer prolix and tedious, but briefely to teach thee, and sette thee right vp. In the knowledge heereof, thou shalt vnderstand, that the first basiall Figure is onely knowne to hymselfe, and to one Sonne of man, which hath a humane bodie glorifyed and without sinne: and the brightnes thereof wee see but as in a glasse, and not cleerely as it is, for that it is incomprehensible for a fynite substance.

But he that is indued with wisedome, let him consider of the glorious brightnes thereof. But to the thirde Figure, which is of a darke and blacke collour, wherein be the three golden Images: *The Blacke stone is the Lawe: the Coppies foode: the three Women the preseruation of Man-kind.*

Nowe they which will looke higher, they see a Figure in a tryne aspect, and the higher that they goe towardes the toppe, where the vnion of the three is, be they neuer so wise, their vnderstanding is vnperfect: and although that they see it, yet they knowe not what they see, but that there is such a thing, in comparison whereof, they are fooles, theyr power weake, and themselues nothing.

And there *Logistica* hauing ended her allowed talke, proceeding from an absolute knowledge, deepe iudgement, and sharpnesse of wit in Diuine matters, and vnknowne to weake capacities, I began heereat to take greater delight, then in any other meruailous worke what soeuer, that I had graciously beholden with my greedy eyes. Considering with my selfe of the mysticall Obelisque, the ineffable equality stataric, for durablenesse and perpetuitie vnmoueable, and enduring vncorruptible.

Where there breathed a sweet ayre from heauen, with vnuariable windes, in this Garden round about full of flowers, of a large and circular permanent plot: compassed about with all sorts of fruites, pleasant in taste and full of health: with a perpetuall greenesse, disposed and set by a regular order, both beautifull, pleasant, and conuenient; with the perfect labour and indeuour of Nature to bring it to that passe, and beautified with precious gold. f. 72b.

And *Logistica* holding her peace, they tooke mee both by the hands, and we went out at the mouth of one of the Arches from the precyncts of the Iuied inclosure. And beeing gone from thence, very contentedly passing on betwixt them both, saith *Thelemia*, let vs now hasten on to our three Gates whether we are sent.

Where-vpon, we passing through a plentiful seate and pleasant Countrey, with a reasonable conuenient pace, I beheld the heauens very cleere & bright, & beguiled the tyme with merry, sweet, and delightfull discourses. And I desirous to vnderstand euery particular of the inestimable riches, vnspeakeable delights and incomparable treasure of the sacred Queene, (to the which *Osyris* the builder of the two Temples of Golde, one to *Iupiter*, and the other to the kingdome, must giue place,) I mooued this question.

Tell me I beseech you fayre Nymphes, (if my curiosity bee not to your discontentment) amongst all the precious stones that I could perfectly behold of great estimation and pryce, one I deemed inestimable, and without comparison most precious; The Iasper which had the effigies of *Nero* cut, it was not much bigger. Neither was the Coruscant to passe in the statue of *Arsinoe* the *Arabian* Queene equall with it. Next her, of such value was the Iewell, wherein was the representation of *Nonius* the

Senator, as this sparkling and shyning Dyamond, of a rare and vnseene beautie and bignes, which did hang vpon a rich Carkenet about the snowie necke of the sacred Queene, what cutting was in the same, which I could not perceiue by meanes of the brightnesse and my beeing some-what farre of. And therefore I beeing therein ignoraunt, desyre to knowe the same.

73. *Logistica* considering of my honest demaund, aunswered me incontinently. Know this *Poliphilus*, in the Iewell was ingrauen an imperiall throne, and in the throne the mighty name of *Iehouah* in Hebrew Letters, and before that throne are cast downe and troden vnder foote, the Gyants which proudly haue lift vp themselues against his worde, and resisted hys will: vppon the left side of the throne is a flame of fire, vppon the right hande a horne of saluation, or Copie full of all good blessednes, and this is all that is contained in the Iewell.

Then I presumed further to knowe, what should these two things vpon eyther sides of the throne signifie, that were holden out in two handes. *Thelemia* quickly aunswered me, God of his infinite goodnesse, proposeth to mankind his mercie and his iudgement, chuse which they will.

For thys beeing satis-fied I sayd moreouer. Seeing that most gracious Nymphs, my speeches be not displeasant vnto you, and that I am not yet satis-fied in all that I haue seene, I pray you let me vnderstand this.

Before the horrible feare that I was driuen into by the Dragon, I beheld a mighty huge Elephant of stone, with an entrance into his bellie, where were two Sepulchres, with a wryting, the meaning wherof is too mysticall for me, that was, that I shoulde not touch the bodie, but take away the head.

Logistica forthwith made me aunswer. *Poliphilus*, I

doe vnderstande very well your doubt, and therefore you shall vnderstande, that this monstrous shape and machine was not made without great and wonderfull humane wisedome, much labour, and incredible diligence, with a perplexibility of vnderstanding to knowe the mysticall conceite. Thou remembrest that vpon the face there hung an ornament, with a certaine *Ideonix ionic* and *Arabic*, which in our Mother-tongue is as much to say, as labour, and industrie. Sgnifying thereby, that in thys world, whosoeuer will haue any bessing that shall do him good, he must leaue the body, which is ease and idlenes, and betake himselfe to trauaile and industry, which is the head.

Shee had no sooner ended her words both pleasant & piercing, but I vnderstoode it very well and gaue her great thankes. And yet desirous to be resolued in whatsoeuer I stood in doubt, and seeing that I might speake boldly, I made this third question. Most wise Nymph, in my comming out of the subterraneall vast darksome place, as I passed on I came to a goodlie bridge, and vppon the same, in a Porphyrite stone vppon the one side, and an Ophite vpon the other, I beheld engrauen certaine Hieragliphs, both which I did interprete, but I stoode doubtfull of certaine branches, that were tyed to the hornes of the scalpe of the Oxe, and the rather because they were in the Porphyrite stone, and not in the Ophit vpon the other side.

She aunswered me straight way. The braunches, one is of the Thistle or thorne of Iudea, and the other of the Turbentine. The nature of which Woodes bee, that the one will not easily take fire, and the other will neither bend, rotte, consume, nor be eaten with wormes. And

The crown of the thorne vpon Christes head.

so that patience is commended, which with anger is not kindled, nor by aduersity will bee subdued.

The nature of the Porphyrit stone is of this secrecie, that in the fornace it will neither burne it selfe, but also causeth other stones neere adioyning that they shall not burne. And of that nature is patience, that it will neither be altered it selfe, nor suffer any other wherein it beareth rule to fall into a furie. And the Ophite stone is of such nature also.

Nowe *Poliphilus*, I doe greatly commende you, in that you are desirous to vnderstand such secrets: for to behold, consider, and measure the same, is a commendable vertue, and the way to knowledge: whereuppon I had occasion giuen to render innumerable thanks, for her great and fauourable curtesies.

And thus with allowed and delightfull discoursing speeches, we came to a fayre Riuer, vpon the banck whereof, besides other fayre greene and florishing Trees, and water hearbes, I beheld a fine Groue of Plane Trees, in the which was an excellent fayre bridge ouer the Riuer made of stone, with three Arches, with pyles bearing foorth against the two fronts, to preserue the worke of the bridge, the sides thereof beeing of excellent workmanship.

And in the middle bending of the same, vpon eyther sides, there was a square stone of Porphyrite set, hauing in it a Catagliphic, engrauing of Hieragliphies.

Vpon the right hand as I went ouer, I beheld a woman, casting abroade her armes, sitting onely vppon one buttocke, putting foorth one of her legges as if shee would rise; In her right hand, vpon that side which shee did sitte, shee helde a payre of winges, and in the other hand, vppon that side whereon she was arysing, a Tortice.

Right against her, there was a Circle, the center wherof two little Spyrits did hold, with their backs turned towards the circumference of the Circle.

And then *Logistica* saide vnto me, *Poliphilus*, I am sure that thou doost not vnderstand these Hieragliphs, but they make much for thy purpose : and therfore they are placed for a Monument and thing to be considered, of such as passe by.

The Circle *Medium tenuere beati*.

The other, temper thy hast by staying, and thy slownesse by rysing, consider heereof as thou seest cause.

This bridge was built with a moderate bending, shewing the cunning disquisition, tryall, examination, arte, and discretion of the excellent workman and inuenter, commended in the continuaunce and durablenesse thereof, which manie of our Bayard-like moderne Idiots, without knowledge, measure and arte buzzing on, neither obserue proportion nor lyneaments, but all out of order.

This bridge was all of pure Marble.

When wee had passed ouer the bridge wee walked in the coole shadow, delighted with the variable notes and chirpings of small byrds, to a rocky and stony place, where high & craggie Mountaines lifted vp themselues, afterwarde continuing to abrupt and wilesome hilly places, full of broken and nybled stones, mounting vppe into the ayre, as high as a man might looke to, and without any greene grasse or hearbe, and there were hewen out the three gates, in the verie rocke it selfe, euen as plaine as might be. A worke verie auncient and past record, in a very displeasant seate.

Ouer euery one of the which I beheld in Letters Ionic, Romaine, Hebrew and Arabic, the tytle that the sacred Queene *Eleutherillida* fore-told me that I should find. f. 75.

The Gate vppon my right hand, had vpon it this word, *Theodoxia.* That vppon my left hand, *Cosmodoxia.* And the thirde, *Erototrophos.* Vnto the which as soone as we were come, the Damosels beganne to instruct me in the tytles, and knocking in the resounding leaues of the Gates, vppon the right hande couered ouer with greene mosse, they were presently opened.

And ther dyd an olde woman present herselfe vnto vs, of an honourable countenaunce, out of an olde dawbed and smoakie house, hauing a poore base little doore, ouer the which was painted *Pilurania.* Shee came with a modest and honest shamefastnesse, and her dwelling place was in a solitarie site and shadie Rocke, decayed and crumbly, her clothes were tattered, her face leane, pale & poore. Her eyes looking towards the ground, her name was *Theude.* Shee had attending vppon her sixe Handmaydes basely and slenderly apparrelled. One was named *Parthenia*, the second *Edosia*, an other *Hypocolinia*, the fourth *Pinotidia*, the next *Tapinosa*, the last *Prochina*. Which reuerent Matron with her right arme naked poynted to the heauens.

She dwelt in a place very hard to come vnto, and ful of troubles to passe on the way, beeing hyndered with

thorne and bryers, very rough and displeasant, a mistie clowde cast ouer it, and very hard to clymbe vp into.

Logistica perceiuing by my looke that I had no great lyking in this place, some-what greeued therewith, said, this Rocke is knowne neuer but at the end. And then *Thelemia* sayde, *Poliphilus*, I see you make small regarde of such a painefull woman. Whereat I assenting to her with my countenaunce, wee departed, and the gate being shut we came to the next.

Where knocking, it was presently opened, and wee

entering in, there met vs a browne woman, with fierce eyes rowling, and of a quicke countenaunce, lyfting vp a naked glittering sworde, vpon the middle wherof was a Crowne of golde, and a branche of Palme tree intrauersed.

Her armes brawnie like *Hercules*, in labour and acts magnanimious and nobly minded. Her belly small. A
75b. little mouth, strong and stooping shoulders, by her countenaunce seeming to bee of an vndaunted minde, not fearing to vndertake any enterprise how hard soeuer.

Her name was *Euclelia*, verie honourablie attended vppon with sixe young Women. The first was called *Merimnasia*, the second, *Epitide*, another, *Ergasilea*, the fourth, *Anectea*, the fift was named *Statia*, the last was called *Olistea*.

The situation and place me thought was painefull, and *Logistica* perceiuing my inclynation, presentlie tooke into her hand *Thelemias* Lute, and beganne to strike a doricall tune, and sung to the same verie sweetly, saying, O *Poliphilus* be not wearie to take paynes in thys place, for when labour and trauell is ouer-come there will be a tyme of rest. And her songe was of such force, that I was euen consenting to remaine there, notwithstanding that the habitation seemed laboursome. Wherevppon *Thelemia* inticingly said vnto me, I think that it standeth with verie great reason my *Poliphilus*, that before you set downe your rest heere in this place, you ought in any case to see the third Gate.

Whereunto I consented with a very good will, and therefore going out from hence, we came to the other Gate, where *Thelemia* knocking at a ring of Brasse, it was forth-with sette open, and when wee were come in, there came towardes vs a notable goodly woman, and her name was *Philtronia*.

Her regards were wanton, lasciuious, and vnconstant, her grace wonderfull pleasant, so as at the verie first sight shee violently drew me into her loue.

This place was the Mansion-house of Voluptuousnes. The grounde decked with small hearbes, and adorned with all sorts of sundrie flowers, abounding with solace and quiet ease. Issuing and sending foorth in diuers places small streames of water, pyppling and slyding downe vpon the Amber grauell in theyr crooking Channels heere and there, by some suddaine fall making a still continued noyse, to great pleasure moystning the open fieldes, and making the shadowed place vnder the leaffye Trees, coole and fresh.

Shee had with her also sixe young women of like statures, passing fayre, of pleasant countenaunces, amorously adorned and dressed as may bee desired of an f. 76.
ambitious beautie and gesture.

The first was called *Rastonelia*. The second, *Cortasina*. The thirde, *Idonesa*. The fourth, *Triphelia*. The fift, *Epiania*. And the last was named *Adia*.

These and their companie were very delightfull to my gasing and searching eyes. VVhere-vppon *Logistica* presentlie with a sad and grieued countenaunce, seeing mee disposing my selfe abruptlie to the seruile loue of them, shee said vnto mee, O *Poliphilus*, the alluring and inticing beauties of these are vaine, deceiueable, and counterfeited, vnsauorie and displeasant, and therefore if thou wouldest with aduisement looke vppon theyr backes, thou wouldest then hate, contemne, and abhorre theyr lothsome filthinesse and shame, abounding in stinke and noysome sauoure aboue any dunghill, which no stomacke can abide.

And therefore what is slypperie and transitorie flye and

eschewe, despose that pleasure which bringeth shame and repentance, vaine hopes, a short and small ioy, with perpetuall complaynts, doubtfull sighes, and a sorrowfull life neuer ending.

Oh adulterated and vnkindly pleasure, fraught with miserie, contayning such bitternesse, like honnie, and yet gall dropping from greene leaues.

O lyfe worse than death, and yet deadly, delighted in sweete poyson, with what care, sorrow, pensiue thoughts, mortall and desperate attempts, art thou sought for to bee obtained by blind Louers, who without regarde or aduise cast themselues headlong into a gulfe of sorrowes.

They be present before thine eyes, and yet thou seest them not. Oh what and howe great sorrowes, bitter and sharpe paine and vexation doost thou beare wicked, execrable and accursed appetite.

O detestable madnesse, oh beguiled senses, by your faulte with the selfe same beastlie pleasure, myserable mortall men are ouerthrowne.

Oh filthy lust, absurd furie, disordinate and vaine desire, building nests with errours, and torments for vvounded harts, the vtter destroyer, and idle letting goe by of all good blessings.

Oh blinde Monster, how doost thou blinde, and with what deceipt doost thou couer the eyes, and deceiue the vnderstanding sences of vnhappie and miserable Louers with vailes and mystes.

O monstrous and slauish which compassed with so manie euils, hastenest to so small pleasure poysoned and fayned.

Logistica speaking with vehemencie these and such lyke words, her fore-head frowning, wrympling with furrowes, and veines, rysing vp in a great rage, shee cast her Lute vppon the ground and brake it.

Where-vppon *Thelemia*, with a smyling countenaunce nodded towards mee, as if shee shoulde say, let *Logistica* speake her pleasure, but doe as you see good your selfe.

And *Logistica* seeing my wicked intent and resolute

determination, beeing kindled with disdaine, turned her backe, and with a great sigh hastened away.

And I remained still with my companion *Thelemia*, who with a flattering and smyling grace sayd vnto me, this is the place where thou shalt not continue long, but thou shalt finde the deerest thing which thou louest in the world, & which thou hast in thy hart, without intermission determined to seeke and desire.

And doubtfully then discoursing with my selfe, I waa resolued that nothing coulde breede quiet, or bring content to my poore grieued hart, but my best desired *Polia*. The promise and warrantise of *Thelemia* for my obtayning the same, bred in mee some comfort.

And shee perceiuing that the Mistris of thys place, and the seate it selfe, and her Women dyd bothe please mee well, and entertained mee courteously, shee kissing mee, tooke her leaue and gaue me a fare-well.

The mettalyne gates beeing shut, I remayned incloystered among these fayre and beautifull Nymphes, who began very pleasantly and wantonly to deuise with mee: and beeing hemmed in with their lasciuious company, I found my selfe prouoked by their perswasiue alluring intisements, to vnlawfull concupiscence, feeling in my selfe a burning desire, kyndled with their wanton aspects, an increasing prouocation of a lusting fier. I doubt me that if *Phrine* had beene of that sauour, and force in gesture and speech, colde *Xenocrates* would haue consented to her alluring, and not haue beene accused by her, to be an image of stone. Their countenances were so lasciuious, their breastes naked and intycing, theyr eyes flattering, in their roseall forheads, glystering and rowling, their shapes most excellent, their apparell rich, their motions girlish, theyr regards byting, theyr ornaments, sweete and precious, no part counterfeited, but all perfected by nature in an excellent sort, nothing deformed, but all partes aunswerable one to an other.

Their heades yellowe, their tresses fayre, and the hayre soft and fine, in such a sort dressed vp and rouled into trammels, with laces of silke and golde, passing any ioye that a man may beholde, turned about their heads in an excellent manner, inuiluxed, and bound vppe together, their forheades compassed about and shaddowed with wauering curles, mouably præpending in a wonderfull manner, marueilous delightfull, perfumed & sweet, yeelding an vnknown fragrancie. Their speeches so perswasorie and pleasing, as might robbe the fauour of an indesposed hart, and violently drawe vnto them any mind, though Satyr-like or churlish howsoeuer, to depraue Religion, to binde euery loose conceit, to make any rusty Peasant amorous, and to mollifie any froward disposition. Vppon which occasion, my minde, altogether set on fier with a new desire, and in the extreame heate of concupiscence, prouoked to fall headlong into a lasciuious appetite, & drowned in lustfull loue vnbridled : in the extreame inuasion and infectious contage thereof, the Damoselles forsooke mee and left me all alone in a fruitfull playne.

THE ELEVENTH CHAPTER.

77b. **In this place Poliphilus being left alone, a most fayre Nymphe (when hee was forsaken of the lasciuious company) came vnto him, whose beautie and apparell Poliphilus dooth amourously describe.**

Y TENDER HEART THUS EXcessiuely wounded with amorous prouocation, I think I was mad, I stood so amazed, or blinde at the least, because that I coulde not perceiue in what sort or how this desired and delightfull company gaue mee the slip: and at last not knowing what I did, but casting mine eyes right forward, I behelde before mee, a fine Arbour of sweete Gessamine, somewhat high, lifting vppe and bending ouer, all to bee painted and decked with the pleasant and odoriferous flowers of three sortes commixt, and entring in vnder the same. Wonderfully perplexed for the losse of my company, I knewe not howe or in what sort, and calling to remembraunce the diuers, rare and wonderfull thinges past, and aboue al the great hope and trust which I had conceiued vpon the Queenes promise, that I should finde my loue *Polia*.

Alas said I, with a deepe sigh, my *Polia*, that the greene Arbour resounded againe therewithall, my amourous breathings were such, framed within and sent out from my burning hart. And I was no sooner entered into this agony, and ouerwhelmed in this passion, but as I passed on to the other ende of the Arbor, I might perceiue a farre off, a great number of youthes, solacing and sporting themselues very loude with diuers melodious soundes, with pleasant sports and sundry pastimes, in great ioye, and passing delight assembled together, in a large playne. Vppon this gratefull and desired noueltie, I set me down marueiling at it, before I would step any further on.

And beholde, a most noble and faire Nymph, with a burning torch in her hand, departing from the company, tended her course towardes mee, so as I might well perceiue that shee was a reall mayde indeede and no spirite, whervpon I mooued not one whit, but gladly expected her comming, who with a maidenly hast, modest accesse, star-like countenance, and smiling grace, drewe neere vnto mee with such a Maiestie, and yet friendly, so as I doubt me, the amorous *Idalea* neuer shewed her selfe to *Mars*, nor to her the fayre Pastor *Adonis*. Nor the delicate *Ganimed* to *Iupiter*, or the fayre *Psyches* to her spouse *Cupid*.

For which cause, if shee had beene the fourth among the three contending Goddesses, if *Ioue* had beene Iudge, as in the shady Wooddes of *Mensunlone* was the Phrigian Sheepheard, without all doubt she had beene iudged of farre more excellent beautie, and without equiuolence, more worthy of the golden apple, then all or any one of the rest. At the first sight I was perswaded that shee had beene *Polia*, but the place vnaccustomed & her apparell made mee thinke the contrarie, and therefore my doubtfull iudgement remained in suspence, hauing onely a reuerent suspition therof.

This honourable Nymph, had her virgineall diuine and small body couered with a thinne subtill stuffe of greene silke, powdered with golde, vppon a smocke of pure white coorled Lawne, couering her most delicate and tender body, and snowye skinne, as fine and good as euer *Pamphila* the daughter to *Platis* in the Iland of Coo, did inuent to weaue. Which white smocke seemed as if it had couered damaske Roses.

The coate which she wore ouer that, was not like our fashioned petticoates with French wastes, for that her sweete proporcioned body needed no such pinching in, & vnholsome weare, hyndering procreation and an enemie to health: but rather like a wastcoate, with little plightes and gathers vnder her rounde and pretty bearing out breasts, vpon her slender and small waste, ouer her large proportioned flanckes and little round belly, fast girded about with a girdle of golde: and ouer the same, a gowne or garment side to the ground, and welted belowe.

This garment beeing very side, was taken vp round about the pitch of her hippes, and before vpon her belly, & tyed about with the studded marriage girdle of *Citherea*, the plucking vp of ẏ garment, bearing ouer the girdle about her like a french vardingale, & the nethermost part falling down about her feet in plightes and fouldes, vnstable and blowne about with the sweete ayre & coole winde, causing sometime, by the thinnesse thereof, her shape to be seene in it, which shee seemed with a prompt readinesse to resist and hynder. Her beautie and grace was such, as I stoode in doubt whether shee were be-
78b. gotten by any humaine generation: her armes stretching downe, her handes long and slender, her fingers small and fayre, and her nayles thinne and ruddy, and shining, as if she had beene *Minerua* her selfe. Her armes to be seene through the cleere thinnesse of the Lawne, the winges about the size of her garment where her armes came out, were of golde, in an excellent sort and fashion welted, and

set with Pearle and stone: and in like sort all the hemming about of her vesture, with golde ooes, and Pearle, and spangles of golde in diuers places, distantly disposed in a curious and pleasant sort to beholde.

Vppon either side, vnder the armes to her waste, her vpper garment was vnsowed and open, but fastened with three buttons of great Orient Pearle (such as *Cleopatra* neuer had to dissolue in a Potion) in loopes of blewe silke, so that you might see her smocke betweene the distance of one Pearle from an other, couering her daintie soft snowye thinne skinne: except her small necke and the vpper halfe of her spatious and delitious breast, more desired and contenting mine eyes, then the water brookes and coole Ryuers to the emboste and chased Hart, more pleasing then the fisher boate of *Endimion* to *Cynthia*, and more pleasant then *Cithera* to *Orpheus*.

The sleeues of her smocke of a conuenient largenesse, and about her wristes plighted and tyed with Bracelets of Golde, double and vnited with Orient Pearle. And besides all her ornaments and gracious gestures, she indeuoured nowe and then with stolen and affected regards, in a sweet & pleasant sort, to cast down her eyes vpon her little round swelling breastes, impatient at the suppressing of her soft and fine apparell: so as I iudged vppon good consideration, and thought that in the dignitie and honourable frame of her personage, the Creator had framed and vnited together, all the violence of Loue. The foure Nourses of the royall Kingdome of Babilon, called *The tongue of the Gods*, had not that powre to winne fauour and loue of the King, which this most sweet Nymph had.

About her fayre Necke, more white then the Scithian snowe, shee wore a Carkenet of Oryent Pearle: *Cerna* the

wife of *Cæsar* neuer had the like, and I doubt me that that of *Eriphile*, which she tooke to *Amphiaraus*, was nothing comparable vnto it. And in the bending downe ouer the deuision of her breastes, betwixt two great Pearles, there
f. 79. was laced a corruscant rounde Rubie, and vppon the collaterate sides of the sayde Pearles, two glistering Saphires, and two Pearles, next them two Emeraldes, & two Pearles, and after them two fayre Iacinthes: all these Pearles and Stones were laced in a worke in losenges, in a rare and beautifull manner.

Her fayre heade, sending downe and vnfolding a loose spreading abroade of plentifull hayre, like the smallest threds of golde, wauing with the winde, and vpon her crowne, a garland of tawny vyolets sweetly smelling, and couering the same almost to her forheade: from the middle vpper point whereof, in forme of two Hemycycles to the halfe of her eares, it mounted vppe in curled trammelles, falling downe againe vppon her fayre Temples, moueably wauing and shaddowing the same, and hyding the vpper halfe of her small eares, more fayre then euer was reported of *Mimoria*.

The rest of her yellowe haire, descended downe ouer her fayre necke, well disposed shoulders, and straight backe, to the calues of her slender legges, moderatly wauing and blowne abroad in greater beautie than the proude eyed feathers of *Iunoes* Birde. Such hayre as *Berenice* did neuer vow to in the venereous Temple for her *Tholemæus*, nor *Conus* the Mathematrician did euer beholde the like placed in the Triangule.

In her forehead, vnder two subtile blacke Hemycicles and distinct eye brees, such as *Abacsine* in Æthiopia had not to boast of, or compare with, nor *Iuno* her selfe, did looke out and present themselues two pleasant radious and glistering eyes, which would enforce *Iupiter* to rayne golde, of a cleere sight, quicke and pearcing, with a browne circle betwixt the Apple and the milchie white: neere to the which were her purple and Cherry cheekes, beautified with two round smiling dimples, gracing the pleasure of her countenaunce, of the collour of the fresh Roses gathered at the rysing of the Sunne, and layde in a vessell of the Christall of Cyprus, and shewing through the same, as me thought.

Vnder her nose to her lyppes, passed a little valley to her small mouth of a most sweete forme, her lyppes not blabbered or swelling, but indifferent, & of a rubye collour, couering two vniforme sets of teeth, like yuory, and small, not one longer and sharper than any other, but in order euenly disposed and set: from betwixt the which, Loue had composed an euerlasting sweet breathing, so as I presumed to thinke, that the snow white teeth betwixt f. 79b.
her gracious lyppes, wer no other but Oryent Pearles, & her sweet breath hot Muske, and by her delightfull voyce that she was *Thespis* with her nine daughters.

By all which sight I was greatly mooued and my sences rauished with a kindled appetite, causing among them great strife and bitter contention, such as I neuer felt before, by any other presence or excellent sightes whatsoeuer. My searching eyes commended one part aboue another, to bee more beautifull: but my appetite rapt into another part of her heauenly body, esteeming that aboue the other. And thus my insatiable and wanton eyes, were the euill beginning of all thys perturbing and contentious commotion, whome I founde the seminaries and moouers of all so great strife and trouble, in my wounded and festering heart. Through theyr contumacy, I was now brought from my selfe, and neuerthelesse, I could not be satisfied by them. My greedy appetyte extolled her delicate breast aboue any comparison, my eyes delightfully consenting thervnto, sayd, at least by that we may discouer what yͤ rest is: And they, glauncing from that to the regarde of her grace and gesture, set all their delight therein: and my appetite strengthened and not easilie remooued from thence, I perswaded my selfe, that the plentie and fayrenesse of her head and hayre, and the dressing thereof, and the beautie of her forheade, coulde neuer bee compared with any one or other, like the scrapings of golde alwaies turning into little roundels.

With two eyes lyke morning starres in a cleere heauen, more beautifully adorning her heade, than any that euer the warlike *Neco* beheld among the *Acitanians*, wounding my heart like one of the arrowes of the angrie *Cupid*. And thus to conclude, I dare be bolde to say, that no mortall man hath seene, so gracious, so shyning, so cleere and pleasant lightes as these were, placed in the forhead of this heauenly creature; so that by them my hart was taken prisoner; & was filled with such continuall controuersies of desire, as if a leafe of the Laurell of the Tombe of the king of *Bibria* had bin placed betwixt, & that strife should neuer cease while it was there: so I thought that this strife would neuer cease, vntill the pleasure were taken away, by reason wherof, I could not perceiue howe I shoulde obtaine the fulnes of my desire or howe it coulde agree with either one or other. Like one extreamely
f. 80. hungry among a number of prepared meates being
desirous of all, feedes of none, his burning
appetite remayning satisfied with
none, but still hungry.

THE TWELFTH CHAPTER.

The most fayre Nymph beeing come to Poliphilus, bearing a Torch in her left hand, with the other tooke him and inuited him to walke with her, and there Poliphilus by her loue was more inflamed.

HUS SEING BEFORE ME, A reall and visible obiect of a most excellent representation, louely presence and heauenly aspect, of a plentifull store, and vniuersall gathering of vnseene beautie, and inhumaine comelinesse. I made light and slender account, in respect heereof, of all the inestimable delights, riches, and great pompe which before I had behelde and seene, thinking their worthinesse nothing to speake of, in comparison of this. Oh happie hee that may enioy such and so great a treasure of loue; And not onely a happie possessor I account him, but most happie that shall possesse and obtaine her obedience, to hys desire and rule. But if *Zeues* had behelde this substance, hee would haue commended the same aboue all the *Agrigentine* maides, euery proportion would haue made vnto him an oportune shewe of the absolutest perfection in the whole world.

Which fayre and heauenly Nymph nowe comming neere vnto me, with a cheerefull countenance, incontinently her most rare beautie, before somewhat a farre of looked vppon with mine eyes, but nowe by them more neere and narrowly behelde, I was rauished and amased.

And her amorous aspect and louely presence, was no sooner brought by the message of mine eyes to my inward partes, but my recording and watchfull remembrance, stirring and waking vppe my heart, presenting and offering her vnto the same: it is become her shoppe; the quiuer for her piercing arrowes and wounding regardes, and the dwelling place and conseruable mansion house, of her sweete picture. Knowing that this was shee which had tædiously consumed my tender yeeres, in her hotte and prime loue, not to be resisted. For I felt the same leaping and beating against my breast, without ceasing, like as one that striketh vpon a hoarse Taber. And still me thought by her louely and delightfull countenance, by her fayre tresses, and the curling and wauing haire, playing vp and downe vppon her forheade, that it should be *Polia*, whome so greatly I had loued and desired, and for whom I had sustained so many & sundry griefes, without intermission, sending out scalding sighes, the outward reporters of my inwarde flames. But her rich and Nymphish habite, vnaccustomed, and the place vnknowne and strange, made mee still doubtfull and suspicious.

Shee (as beforesaide) carried in her snowe white left arme, close to her body, a kindled and burning Torch, somewhat higher then her heade a good deale, and the lower ende growing smaller and smaller shee helde in her hande: and stretching foorth that which was at libertie, more white then euer had *Pelopea*, wherein appeared the thinne smoothnes of the skynne, and the blewnesse of the veynes lyke Azure streames, vppon the faire and whitest paper. Shee tooke me by the left hande with a sweete and louing countenance and smiling grace, and with an eloquent speech, shee pleasantly saide in this manner.

Poliphilus, I thinke my selfe to come in saftie, but it seemeth that you stand doubtfull. Heereat I was more amazed, and my sences in a manner gone to imagine howe shee should knowe my name; and all my inward parts vanquished, and hemmed in with burning amorous flames, my speech was taken from mee with feare and reuerent bashfulnesse.

In this sort remayning, I knewe not vppon the suddaine what good aunswere I might make, or otherwise doe her reuerence, but to offer her my vnworthy and vnfit hande; which when it was streined in hers, me thought that it was in hot snowe and curded milke, and me thought indeede, that I touched and handled something which was more then humaine; which when I had so done, I remained moued in minde, troubled and doubtfull, vnaccustomed to such a companion, not knowing what to say, or whether to followe her, in my simple apparell and homely bringing vp, not agreeable with hers, and as a foole, vnworthy and vnfit for her fellowship, perswading my selfe, that it was not lawfull for a mortall and earthly creature to enioy such pleasures. For which cause my collour red and blushing, with reuerent admiration, being f. 81.
grieued at my basenesse, I setled my selfe to followe her.

At length, and yet not with a perfect recalled minde, I beganne to reduce and sommon together, my fearefull and distempered spirites: perswading my selfe, that I must needes haue good successe, being neere so faire and diuine an obiect, and in such a place; And so followed her on with a panting heart, more shaking than the birde *Sisura*, or a Lambe carryed in the mouth of a Wolfe.

And thus touched most feruently with pleasant heates, growing & encreasing more & more, they began to boyle & kindle my colde feare, and dispositiuely to adopt my altered heate to sincere loue. Which being thus brought to thys passe, by a prouoked inward desire, yet inwardly as I reasoned with my selfe, it was wonderfully

variable and doubtfull. Oh most happye Louer of all Louers, that in requitall of hys, might bee sure to participate of hers.

On the other side, I perswaded my selfe, that if I shoulde offer vnto her my amorous heart and loue, hauing no better thing to bestow vpon her, or present vnto her, it might be that she would not refuse it: like *Artaxerxes,* the King of the Percians; who hauing water presented to hys handes, accepted of it bowing downe himselfe. Heerewithall, me thought yet that a fearefull and chill trembling inuaded mee, infusing it selfe ouer all my body and breast, renewing the force of the extreame fire, euen like dry reede: which being once kindled, is enflamed and nourished with the fresh ayre, vntill at length it is increased so mightily, that it consumeth all to ashes.

And in like sorte, I fully founde in my selfe, an increase and flashing abroade of my inwarde flames, in their prepared subiect, so effectually, that her amorous regardes gaue me mortall and deadly woundes: euen as lightning and thunder, among the stronge and mightie oakes, suddainely with a great force, scorching & tearing them. And therefore I durst not looke vpon her bright eyes, because that dooing so, (being ouercome with the incredible beauty of her gracious aspect) if peraduenture her radious beames did reincounter mutually with myne, for a little while euery thinge seemed two vnto mee, vntill I had closed the lyddes together, and restored them to theyr former light.

Wherevpon, and by reason of these thinges captiuated, f. 81b.
spoyled and ouercome, I determined at that instant to plucke vp some fresh flowers, and in all humble sort to offer them vnto her, and it came to passe, that whilst my secret thoughts consented thervnto, consygning a free meane and large entrance for the discouery of my desire. But my burning heart humbly hauing opened the same, euen as a rype Apple being eyther bitten or shaken, so it fell and fayled me. And receiuing into his wounded and familiar estuation, in some interposition of time, immediatly his accustomed heat and feruor increased, piercing the inward parts with her virgineall aspects, exceedingly

beautified with a comely grace and vnexcogitable elegancie; Because that into this sweete introduction into my minde, of these first amorous flames, (lyke the Troian horse, full of weapons and deceite) the enterance was made for an euerlasting, vnknown, and vncessant plague, deeply festering in my tender and poore heart, perpetually remayning: which easily ouercome with one sweete looke, inconsiderately without delay, hasteneth his owne hurt and wholly layeth it selfe open to amorous incursions, and burneth it selfe with sweet conceits, going into the flames of his owne accord.

To all which burning desires, her present company did greatly inforce mee, which I esteemed to yeelde mee more comfort, then the North starre in a tempestuous night to the troubled Marriner: more acceptable then that of *Melicta* to *Adonis*, or to *Phrodites*, the obsequious Nymph *Peristera:* and more delightfull then *Dittander* to the daughter of *Dydo*, with the Purple flowre for the wounde of *Pius Æneas:* And finding my heart strooken and inwardly pricking, secretly filled and compressiuely stuft; recording and gathering together into it, varyable thoughts and working of Loue, my immedicable wounde grewe greater and greater. But gathering vp the remaynder of my sences, as one that durst, I assured my selfe to manifest and lay open before her, my intended desires and amorous conceites. And thus loosing my selfe in a blinde folly, I could not choose but giue place to my inuading desires, feruently boyling and inforcing me to say thus.

Oh delycate and heauenly Damosell, whosoeuer thou art, thy forcyble loue hath set me on fire, and consumeth my grieued heart; I finde my selfe all ouer, burning in an vncessant flame, and a sharpe dart cast into the middest of
82. my breast, where it sticketh fast, hauing made a mortall

wounde vncurable. And hauing spoken thus, to the ende I might discouer vnto her my hidden desire, and moderate by that meanes the extreamitie of my bitter passions: which I felt the more they were concealed, the more to augment and increase, I patiently helde my peace: and by this meanes all those feruent and greeuous agitations, doubtfull thoughtes, wanton and vyolent desires, were somewhat supprest; with my ill fauoured Gowne, that had still some of the Bramble leaues and prickes of the Wood hanging vpon it, and euen as a Peacocke in the pride of his feathers, beholding the fowlenesse of his feete, pulleth downe hys traine: so I considering the inequallitie of my selfe, with such a heauenly obiect, appaled the prouocations of my contumacious and high desires, looking into the vanities of my thoughtes.

And then I earnestly endeuoured by all the meanes that I might, to subdue, encloyster, and keepe in, my vnbridled gadding appetite, wandring minde, and immodest desire, intending nowe that it should neuer be vttered againe.

At length I beganne to thinke in the secret depth of my wounded heart, that vndoubtedly this my present continued griefe, was equall with that of wicked *Tantalus*, to whose hotte and thirsting lyppes, the coole and cleere water did offer it selfe, and to his hungry appetite, the sweete fruites honge ouer hys gaping mouth appresenting, but he neuer tasted any of either.

Ah woe is mee euen in like sort, a most fayre Nymph of an excellent shape, of a florishing age, of Angel-like behauiour vnspeakable, and of rare honour and exceeding curtesie as mine eies coulde beholde, whose company exceeded any exquesite humaine content; and I, iust by her, full of all whatsoeuer prouocation, forcing sollaciously loue and desire, heaping vppe in her selfe the whole perfections of delight, and yet my yauning and voluptuous desire, neuer the more thereby satisfied.

Well, on this sorte my burning concupiscence nothing allayed, as much as I might, I comforted my languishing hart, vnmeasurably tormented, in putting of it in minde, of solacious and amorous hope: and with that there was neuer a coale so neere put out, but it was presently renued and set on fire, with the company of the next. And my vnbridled eyes, the more they were vnarmed to resist her power, the more they were inflamed with the insolent de-
82b. sire and liking of her wonderfull and heauenly beautie; Still seeming more faire, more excellent, more louely, more to be desired, extreamly apt and præpared for loue: euedently shewing foorth in her selfe, a wonderfull increase of sweete pleasure.

Afterwards I thought with my selfe, it may be that she is some creature which I may not desire, and it may bee the place is not fitte for such thoughtes, and then it may bee I haue made a wise worke, and spunne a fayre thred, if I should bee punished for my impudencie, like *Ixion*. In like sort, the Thracian had neuer founde the deepe seate of *Neptune*, if he had not medled with *Thetis*: and *Gallantide*, the mayde of *Lucina*, shoulde not haue brought foorth in her mouth, if hee had not deceiued. It may [be] that thys Nymph is spowsed to some high and mightie Prince, and I to offer her this dishonour, what am I worthy of?

And thus resoning with my selfe, I thought that those thinges which had but slender assurance, woulde lightly slyppe away, and that it would not be hard to deceiue, where was no watchfull regarde: and to bolde spirites Fortune was not altogether fayling: and besides, that it was harde to knowe a mans thought. Where-vpon, euen as *Calistone*, being ashamed at her swelling belly, shronke aside from the presence of *Diana;* so I withdrewe my selfe, blushing at my attempt, and bridling my inconuenient desires. Yet with a lincious eye, I neuer left to examine, with great delight, the extreame beautie of the excellent Nymph, disposing my selfe to her sweete loue, with an vnfallyble, obstinate, and firme resolution.

THE THIRTEENTH CHAPTER.

f. 83. **Polia, as yet vnknowne to her Louer Poliphilus, shee gratiously assureth him: who for her extreame beautie, hee indeuoreth his minde to loue. And both of them going to the triumphes, they see innumerable youths and Damosels, sporting with great delight.**

HE ARCHER CUPID, IN MY wounding heart hauing his residence, like a Lord and king, holding me tyed in the bands of Loue, I found my selfe pricked and grieuously tormented, in his tyrannous and yet pleasant regiment. And abounding in doubtfull delight, vnmeasurably sighing, I watered my plaints; And then the surmounting Nymph, with a pleasing grace, incontinently gaue me comfort, and with her ruddy and fayre spoken lyppes, framing violent and attractiue wordes, she gaue me assurance; abandoning and remouing from my heart, all fearefull thoughts, with her Olymphicall aspects, and cooling with her eloquent speeches, my burning heart; and with an amorous and friendly regarde, and cast of her eyes, and smiling grace, she saide thus vnto mee.

Poliphilus, I woulde thou shouldest vnderstand and know thys, that true and vertuous loue hath no respect of outward things, and therefore let not the basenes of thy apparell, diminish or lessen thy minde, if perhaps noble and gentle, and worthy of these places, and fitte to beholde these maruellous tryumphes ; Therefore let not thy minde be dismayed with feare, but dilligently behold what Kingdomes they possesse, that are crowned by *Venus*. I meane, such as bee strongly agonished and yet perseuere still, seruing and attending vpon her amorous Aultars and sacred flames, vntill they obtaine her lawfull fauour. And then making an ende of her short and sweet speech, both of vs making forward, our pace neither too fast nor too slowe, but in a measure ; I thought thus, and thus discoursing with my selfe.

Oh most valiant *Perseus*, thou wouldest more feirsly haue fought with cruell Dragon, for the fauour of this, then for the loue of thy fayre *Andromada*. And after.

Oh *Iason*, if the marriage of this had beene offered vnto thee, with a more greater and more daungerous aduenture, then the obtayning of the golden fleece, thou wouldest haue let goe that, and vndertaken this, with a greater courage, esteeming it aboue al the iewelles and precious treasures of the whole worlde ; I, more then those of the ritch and mightie Queene *Eleutherillida*. Continually seeming more fayre, more beautifull and more louely, *Hippodamia* and all the greedy scraping and doubtfull Vsurers, neuer tooke suche delight in getting of gold. A quyet Harbour was neuer so welcome to a destressed Marryner, in a stormy, darke, and tempesteous winter night : nor the wished and oportune fall of rayne, at the prayer of *Crœsus* as the louing consent of this daintie Nymph : more welcome to mee then bloody broyles to warlike *Mars*, or the first fruites of *Creta* to *Dionisius* : or the warbling Harpe to *Apollo* : and yet more gratefull, then fertill grounde, full eares, and plentifull yeelding, to the labouring Husbandman.

And thus in most contented sort, passing on and pressing down the thicke, greene, and coole grasse: sometime my searching and busie eyes woulde haue a cast with her pretty & small feete, passing well fitted with shooes of Red leather, growing broader from the instepe, narrowe at the toe, and close about the heele; and somtimes her fine and moueable legges, (her vesture of silke beeing blowne about with the winde, vppon her virgineall partes) discouered themselues. If I might haue seene them, I do imagine that they did looke like the finest flower of *Peloponesus* or like the purest milke coagulated with Muske.

By all which most delectable thinges, tyed and bounde in the harde and inextricable knots of vehement loue, more vneasie to vndoe then that of *Hercules*, or that which *Alexander* the great did cut in sunder with hys sworde: and amorously masked in rowled nettes, and my subdued heart, helde downe with grieued cogitations and burning desires, leading mee whether they would, I founde in it more pricking torments then faythfull *Regulus* in Aphrica. So that my sorrowing spirites exasperated with an amorous desire and extreame vexation, continually burning in my panting breast, coulde by no meanes bee asswaged, but with supping vp of continuall sobbings, and breathing out of their flying losse. And thus drowned in a mist of doubts, and seeing me vyolently taken in her loue, I saide thus to my selfe.

f. 84. O *Poliphilus*, howe canst thou leaue at any tyme thy inseperable loue, kindled towardes thy sweete *Polia*, for any other? And therewithall, from this Nymph, thus close and fast bounde, more strongly then in the clawes of a Creuise or Lobstar, endeuouring to vntie my selfe, I found it no easie peece of worke, so that I coulde not choose but greeuously binde my troubled hart, to the loue and affecting of this; by all likelihoodes, hauing the true shape, sweete resemblance, and gratious behauiour of my most beloued *Polia*. But aboue all thinges, this came more neere vnto mee and grieued me worst, howe I should bee assured that shee was *Polia*. Wherevppon, from my watry eyes, the salt teares immediatly tryckling downe, it seemed vnto me a hard & contemptuous matter, to banish from my forlorne and poore heart, his olde soueraigne Lady and Mistresse, and to entertaine a newe, strange, and vnknowne Tyrannyzer.

Afterwards, I comforted my selfe again, with thinking that peraduenture this was shee, according to the sacred Oracle and true speech, of the mighty Queene *Eleutherillida:* and therefore, that I should not shrinke or stoope vnder my burthen; for if I were not greatly deceiued this was shee indeede. And hauing made thys amorous and discoursiue thought and swasiue præsuppose, abandoning all other desires whatsoeuer, I onely determined with my heart and minde, to come backe againe to this noble and excellent Nymph; in whose great loue I beeing thus taken, with extreame compulsion, I was bolde with an vnaccustomed admyration dilligently to looke vppon her rare shape, and louely features, my eyes making themselues the swallowing whirlpooles of her incomparable beautie: and they were no sooner opened, hotly to take in the sweete pleasure of her so benigne and conspicuous presence, but they were strengthened for euer, to hold with them solaciously agreeing, the assembly of all my other captiued sences, that from her and no other, I did seeke the mittegation and quenching of my amorous flames. And in this sort we came, whilst I was thus cruelly wounded by exasperating Loue, somewhat vppon the right side of the spacious fielde.

In which place, were set greene trees, thicke with

leaues, and full of flowers, bearing fruite, rounde about the place and seate of such variable and diuers sorts, neuer fading but still greene, giuing great content to the delightfull beholder.

84b. The gallant and pleasant Nymphe there stayed; and I also stood still: Where looking about, by the benignitie of

the fruitfull playne, with halfe my sight, because I coulde not altogether withdrawe the same from the amorous obiect. I behelde very neere vnto vs a certaine shewe of an inuyroning company, tryumphing and dauncing about vs, of most braue and fine youthes, without beardes and vnshorne heares, but that of their heads bushing, curling, and wrything, without any art as effæminate crysping: crowned and dressed, with garlands and wreathes of diuers flowers, and red Roses, with leauye Myrtle, with purple Amaranth or flower gentle, and Melliot: and with them a great company of yonge maydes, more fayre and delicate then bee to bee founde in Sparta; Both kindes apparelled very richly, in silkes of changable collours, hyding the perfect collour; some in Purple & Murry, and some in white curled Sendall, such as Ægipt neuer affoorded, and of dyuers other collours: some Tawney, some Crymosen, others in Greene, some in Vyolet, some in Blewe, Peach collour, Peacocke collour, perfectly engrayned, as euer Corica coulde yeelde: and powdered and wouen with golde, and edged and hemmed about with orient Pearle and stones set in pure golde; some in gownes, and others in hunting sutes.

And the most of the beautifull Nymphes, had their fayre haire smoothly bounde vppe together, and thrise rowled about, with an excellent finishing knot; Others had their vnstable & wauing tresses, spreading downe ouer their fayre neckes. Some, with aboundance of haire, cast vp ouer their forheades, and the endes turning into curles, & shaddowing ouer the fayrenes of the same: so as Nature and not Arte, shewed her selfe therein a beautifull mistresse; With fillets and laces of golde, edged with orient Pearle, and others in Caules of golde, wearing about theyr slender neckes, rich and precious Carkenets and necklaces, of Pearles and stone, and depending iewelles. And vppon theyr small eares, did hange dyuers precious stones, and ouer the variable dressings of theyr heades, before in two Hemycicles, were set shoddowes of oryent Pearle and stone, in flowers of hayre.

All which excellent ornaments, together with they most elegant personages, were easily able to alter any churlish, vile or obstinate heart.

85. Theyr fayre breastes, in a voluptuous and wanton sort, were bare to the middest of them: and vppon their prettie feete, some wore sandalles, after the auncient manner, beeing soles, and the foote bare fastened to the same, with a small chaine of golde, comming vp betwixt the great toe and the middle, and the little toe and the next, about the heele ouer the instep, and fastening vppon the vpper part, betwixt the toes and the instep, in a flower. Others hauing straight shooes, claspt vppon the instep with flowers of golde. Their stockings of silke; some of Purple, some of Carnation, some of parted collours: such as *Caius Galicola* neuer first brought vp. Others wearing Buskins, vppon the white swelling calfes of their legges, and laced with silke, some butned wyth golde and precious stone.

Their fore-heades most fayre, and beautified with the moueable wauinges of theyr crysping hayre, couered ouer with a thinne vayle, lyke a Spiders webbe, Theyr eyes byting and alluring, more bright than the twinkling starres in a cleere ayre, vnder theyr circulate trees: with a small nose betwixt their rounde and cherry cheekes: their teeth orderly disposed, small and euen set, of the collour of refyned siluer: vppon the test, betwixt their sweet and soft lyppes: of the collour of Corrall.

Many of them carrying instruments of Musique, such as neuer were seene in *Ausonia*, nor in the handes of *Orpheus:* yeelding in the flowring Meadowe & smoth playne, most delightfull sounds, with sweete voyces and noyces of ioye and tryumphing: and to increase the glory, amorously stryuing and contending one with an other, with solacious and pleasant acts, accompanied with faire speeches, and friendly aspects, And in this place, with a most delectable applause, I behelde foure Tryumphes, so precious and sumptuously set foorth, as neuer any mortall eye hath seene.

THE FOURTEENTH CHAPTER.

85b. Poliphilus in this prescribed place, did beholde foure tryumphing Chariots, all set with precious stones and iewelles, by a great number of youthes, in the honour of Iupiter.

HE FIRST OF THE FOURE maruceilous tryumphant Chariots had foure rounde wheeles, of Perfect greene Emeralds of Scythia; the rest of the Chariot did amase mee to beholde, beeing made all of table Dyamonds: not of Arabia or Cyprus, of the newe Myne, as our Lapidaries call them: but of India, resisting the harde stroakes of yron and steele, abyding the hote fire & striuing therwith mollified onely with the warme bloode of Goates, gratefull in the Magicall arte; which stones were wonderfully cut of a Cataglyphic explicature, and set very curiously in fine golde.

Vppon the right side of the Chariot, I sawe expressed, the representation of a Noble Nymph, with many accompanying her in a Meddowe, crowning of victorious Bulles with garlands of flowers, and one abyding by her very tamely.

The same Nymph, vppon the other side was also represented, who hauing mounted vp vppon the backe of the Bull, which was gentle and white, he carryed her ouer the sea.

Vppon the fore-ende I behelde *Cupid*, with a great number of wounded people and Nations, marueiling to see him shoote into the ayre. And in the hinder part, *Mars* standing before *Iupiter*, mourning because the boy had shotte through his impenetrable Brest-plate, and shewing the wounde; and with the other hande, holding out his arme, he helde this worde *Nemo*.

The fashion of this Chariot was a quadrangulat, of two

perfect squares, longe wayes, of sixe foote in length and three foote in height, with a bearing out coronice aboue and vnder the plynth: and about the same a plaine, in breadth two foote and a halfe, and in length fiue foot and a halfe, bearing towards the Coronice, all ouer scally, with precious stones, with an altered congresse and order of collours, variably disposed. And vppon the foure corners were fastned foure coppies, inuersed, and the mouth lying vpward vpon the proiect corner of the Coronice, full of f. 86.

fruites and flowers cut of precious stones, as it were growing out of a foliature of golde. The hornes were chased neere their mouth, with the leaues of Poppy, and wrythen in the belly: the gracylament & outward bending, ioyning fast to the ende of the plaine, and breaking of in an olde fashioned iagged leaf-worke, lying a long vnder the backe of the Coppisse, and of the same mettall. Vpon euery corner of the Plynth, from the Coronice downeward, there was a foote lyke a Harpies, with an excellent conuersion and turning vppon eyther sides of the leaues of Acanthus.

The wheeles, aboue the naues and axeltrees, were closed within the Chariot, and the sides thereof vnder the Harpies feete, bent somewhat vpward and growing lesser, turned rounde downward, wherevnto the furniture or trace to drawe it by, were fastned: and where the axeltree was, there vpon the side of the bottom of the Charriot, ouer the naue of the wheele, there came downe a prepention ioyning to the Plynth, twise so long as deepe, of two foliatures, one extending one way, and the other an other way: and vpon the middle thereof and lowest part, was a Rose of fiue leaues, in the seede whereof, the ende of the axeltree did lye.

Vppon the aforesaide Playne, I beheld the ymage of a fayre white and tame Bull, trymmed and dressed with flowers, in manner like an Oxe for Sacrifice. And vppon his large and broade backe, did sit a princely virgine, with long and slender armes, halfe naked; with her handes she helde by his hornes. Her apparell was exquesite of greene silke and golde, maruelously wouen, and of a Nymphish fashion, couering her body and girded about her wast, edged about with Pearle and stone, and a crowne of glittering golde vpon her fayre heade.

This Triumph, was drawne by sixe lasciuious Centaures, which came of the fallen seede of the sausy and presumpteous *Ixion:* with a furniture of gold vpon them, and a long their strong sides, like horses, excellently framed and illaqueated in a manner of a flagon chayne, whereby they drewe the Tryumph; such as *Ericthonius* neuer inuented for swiftnesse.

Vpon euery one of them did ride a goodly Nymph, with theyr shoulders one towards an other: three with their beautifull faces towards the right side of the Tryumyhes, and three to the left, with Instruments of Musique, making together a heauenly harmonie and consort. Their hayres yellowe; and falling ouer their fayre neckes, with Pancarpiall garlands of all manner of flowers, vpon their heades. The two next the Tryumph, were apparelled in blewe silke, like the collour of a Peacockes necke. f. 86v.

The middlemost in bright Crymosen: and the two formost in an Emerald greene, not wanting any ornamentes to sette them foorth, singing so sweetly with little rounde mouthes, and playing vppon their instruments, within so celestiall a manner, as woulde keepe a man from euer dying.

The Centaures were crowned with yuie, that is called *Dendrocyssos*. The two next the tryumph did beare in their handes, two vesselles of an olde fashion, of the Topas of Arabia, of a bright golden collour, gratefull to *Lucina*, and to the which, the waues will be calme: slender at the bottom, bigge swelling in the belly, and lessening small vp towardes the Orifice; In height two foote, without eares: out of the which, did ascend a thicke smoake or fume, of an inestimable fragrancie. The middlemost, did sounde Trumpets of golde, with banners of silke and golde, fastned to the Trumpets in three places.

The other two formost, with olde fashioned Cornets, agreeing in consort with the Instruments of the Nymph.

Vnder the which triumphant Chariot, were the Axeltrees conueniently placed, wherevppon the wheeles turned, and of a balustic lyneament, waxing small towarde the ende and rounde: Which Axeltrees were of fine pure golde and massiue, neuer cankering or fretting, which is the deadly poyson and destroyer of vertue and peaceable quyet.

This tryumph was solemnly celebrated, with moderate leaping and dauncing about, and great applause: their habites were girded with skarfes, the endes flying abroade.

And in like sort, those which did sit vpon the Centaures, commending in their song, the occasion and mistery of the Tryumph, in voyces consonant and cantionell verse; more pleasant than I am able to expresse, but let this suffice.

The second Tryumph.

The next Tryumph, was not lesse worthy to be beholden then the first. The foure wheeles, the spokes, and naues, were all of Fulkish Agate, and in dyuers f. 87.
places white veines, such as King *Pyrrhus* could not shewe, with the representation of the nine Muses, and *Apollo* playing in the middest of them vppon his Lute.

The Axeltrees and fashion of the same like the other: but the Tables were of orient blewe Saphire, hauing in them, as small as motes in the Sunne, certaine glinces of golde, gratefull to the Magicke Arte, and of *Cupid* beloued in the left hande.

Vpon the Table on the right side, I beheld engrauen, a goodly Matron lying in a princely bed, beeing deliuered of two egges in a stately Pallace: her Midwyues and other Matrons and Yonge women, beeing greatly astonished at the sight. Out of one of the which, sprung a flame of fire, and out of the other egge two bright starres.

Vppon the other side were engrauen, the curious Parents, ignorant of thys strange byrth, in the Temple of *Apollo*, before hys image, asking by Oracle the cause and ende heereof, hauing this darke aunswere. *Vni gratum Mare. Alterum gratum mari.* And for thys ambiguous aunswere they were reserued by their Parents.

Vppon the fore-ende of the Charyot, there was represented most liuely the figure of *Cupid*, aloft in the skyes, with the sharpe heades of his golden arrowes, wounding and making bleede the bodyes of dyuers foure footed

beastes, creeping Serpents, and flying Foules. And vppon the earth, stoode dyuers persons wondering at the force of such a little slaue, and the effect of suche a weake and slender Arrowe.

In the hynder ende, *Iupiter* appoynting in hys steade, a prudent and subtill Sheepehearde as a Iudge, awakened by hym, as hee lay sleeping neere a most fayre Fountaine, whether of the three most fayre Goddesses, hee esteemed best worthie. And hee beeing seduced by deuising *Cupid*, gaue the Apple to the pleasant working *Venus*.

This tryumphant Charyot, was drawen by sixe white Elephants, coupled two and two together, such as will hardly be found in Agesinua, nor among the Gandars of India. *Pompei* neuer had the like in his Tryumphes in f. 87v.
Affricke: neither were the like scene in the Tryumphes of the conquest of India; their tronckes armed with deadly teeth of yuory, passing on theyr way and drawing together, making a pleasant braying or noyse. Their furniture & traces of pure blewe silke, twisted with threds of

golde and siluer; the fastnings in the furniture, all made vp with square or true loue knots, lyke square eares of corne of the Mountaine Garganus. Their Poyterelles of golde, set with Pearle and stone different in collours; the beautie of the one striuing to excell the beautie of the other. And thus was all their furniture or armings to the traces, of silke as aforesayde.

Vppon them also, did ride (as before) sixe younge and tender Nymphes, in like sort, but theyr Instruments different from the former, but agreeing in consort: and what soeuer the first did, the same did these.

The first two were apparelled in Crymosen: the middle most two in fine hayre collour: and the foremost in vyolet. The Caparisons of the Eliphants were of cloth of golde, edged with great Pearles and precious stones: And about their neckes were ornaments of great round iewelles, and vpon their faces, great balles of Pearles, tasled with silke and golde, vnstable and turning.

Ouer this stately Chariot tryumphant, I behelde a most white Swanne, in the amorous imbracing of a noble Nymph, the daughter of *Theseus*, of an incredible beautie: and vpon her lappe, sitting the same Swanne, ouer her white thighes. She sate vppon two cushines of cloth of golde, finely and softely wouen, with all the ornaments necessary for them.

Her selfe apparelled in a Nimphish sort, in cloth of siluer, heere and there powdered with golde, ouer one and vnder three, without defect or want of any thing, requisite to the adorning of so honorable a representation, which to the beholder, may occasion a pleasurable delight. In euery sort performed with as great applause as the first.

The third Trynmph.

Then followed the thyrd Tryumph, with foure wheles of Æthyopian Chrysolite, sparkling out golde: that which hath beene helde in the same, in olde time hath beene thought good to dryue away malignant spirits. The wheeles vpwardly couered, as aforesaide, and the naues and spokes of the same fashion, of greene Helitropia of Cyprus: whose vertue is, to keepe secret in the day light, to diuine giftes, full of drops of blood. f. 88.

This Historie was engrauen vppon the right side of the

Table thereof, as followeth. *A man of great Maiestie, requesting to knowe what should happen to his fayre daughter: her Father vnderstanding, that by her meanes he should be dispossessed of his Crowne and dignitie; and to the ende she shoulde not be carried away or stollen of any, he built a mightie stronge Tower, and there, with a watchfull garde caused her to bee kept: and shee remayning there in this sort with great content, had falling into her virgineall lap, drops of Golde.*

Vppon the other side was chased out a valiant youth, who with great reuerence did receiue a protection of a Christall shielde, and with his sworde afterward cutting off the heade of a terryble woman, and afterwardes proudly bearing her heade in signe of victorie; Out of the hotte blood of whome, did rise vp a flying horse: who striking vppon a Mountaine with one of hys houes, made a strange springe of water to gush out.

Vpon the fore ende I behelde the mightie *Cupid*, drawing hys golden Arrowe, and shooting the same vp into the heauens, causing them to raine bloode: whereat a number stoode wonderfully amazed, of all sortes of people. Vpon the other ende, I did see *Venus* in a wonderfull displeasure, hauing taken her son by a Knight in a Net, and getting him by the winges, she was about to plucke of his fethers; hauing plucked of one handfull, that flewe about, the little elph crying out pitteously; and an other sent from *Iupiter*, tooke him awaye and saued him from his mother, and presented him to *Iupiter:* against whose diuine mouth, were in Attic Letter these wordes written, ΣΥΜΟΙΓΛΥΚΥΣΤΕ-ΚΑΙΠΙΚΡΟΣ and hee couered him in the lap of his celestiall gowne.

This tryumphant Charriot, was pompously drawne

with sixe fierce Vnicornes: their heades like Harts, reuerencing the chaste *Diana*. The poyterelles and furniture about their stronge breasts, was of golde set with precious stone, and fringed with siluer and hayre colloured silke, tyed into knots, in manner of a net worke, and tasseled at euery prependent point, their caparisons like the other before spoken of.

Vpon these did sit, six fayre virgines, in such pompe and manner as before, apparelled in cloth of golde, f. 88b.
wouen with blewe silke into diuers leaues & flowers; these had a consort of liuncyers winde Instruments, full of spirite. And vppon the toppe of the Chariot, was placed a stoole of green Iasper, set in siluer, needfull in byrth, and medicinable for chastitie; at the foote it was sixe square, and growing smaller towarde the seate, and from the middle to the foote, champhered and furrowed, and vpward wrought with nextrulles: the seate whereof

was somewhat hollowed, for the more easily sitting vppon it. The Lyneaments thereof most excellent.

A loft vppon the same did sit a most singuler fayre Nymph, richly apparelled in cloth of golde and blewe silke, dressed lyke a virgine, and adorned with innumerable sortes of Pearles, and stone; she shewed an affectious delight, to beholde droppes of golde fall from heauen

into her lappe. She sate in solemne pompe like the other, and with great applause, with her fayre and plentifull haire spreading downe ouer her backe, crowned with a Dyademe of golde, set with sundry precious stones.

The fourth Tryumph.

The fourth Tryumph was borne vppon foure wheeles, with Iron strakes, forcibly beaten out without fire; All the rest of the Charyot, in fashion like the former, was of burning Carbuncle, shewing light in the darkest places, of an expolite cutting: past any reason, to thinke howe or where it was possible to be made, or by what workeman.

The right side whereof, helde this History: *An honourable woman with childe, vnto whome Iupiter shewed himselfe (as he was wont with Iuno) in thunder and lightning: insomuch, as shee fell all to ashes, out of the which was taken vp a younge infant.*

Vpon the other side, I behelde *Iupiter*, hauing the saide Infant in his hands, & delyuering him to a yonge man, with winged buskyns, and a staffe with two serpents winding about it: who deliuered the Infant to certaine Nymphes in a Caue, to be fostered.

In the fore-ende, I might see howe *Cupid* hauing shot vp into heauen with hys mischeeuous Arrowe, had caused *Iupiter* to beholde a mortall Nymph: and a great number of wounded people woondering at it.

In the hinder end was *Iupiter* sitting in a tribunall seate as iudge, and *Cupide* appeering limping before him, and making grieuous complaints against his louing mother, bicause that by hir means he had wounded himselfe extreemly with the loue of a faire damsell, and that his leg was burnt with a drop of a lampe, presenting also the yoong Nymph and the lampe in hir hand. And *Iupiter* with a smiling countenance speaking to Cupid,

Perfer scintillam qui cælum accendis & omnes. This *Monosticon* was grauen in Latine letters in a square table before the faces of their supreame maiesties, the rest as is described.

This mysticall triumph was drawen by sixe spotted beasts of yealow shining colour, and swift as the tygers of *Hyrcania* called Leopards, coupled togither with withes of twined vines, full of tender greene leaues, and stalkes full of greene clusters. This chariot was drawen very leisurely.

Vpon the middle of which plaine there was placed a base of golde by the lowest diameter, one foote and three handfuls high, the lataster or lowest verdge round and hollowed, in the middle vnder the vpper sime or brimme in forme of a pullie with nextrubs, rules and cordicels; the vpper plaine of this base was euacuated wherein rested the traines of the fower eagles standing vpon the plaine, smooth superficies of the base, which were of pretious Ætite of Persia, of the colour of a sakers plume. And these stood with their shoulders one opposite against another, and their pounces of gold fastened and sticking in the said base, euery one serueying with their wings, and the flowering tips of their sarcellets touching one another. Ouer these, as vpon a nest, was placed this maruellous vessell of Æthiopian Hyacints cleere and bright, *Celso inimicus, Comiti gratiosus.* This vessell was crusted with emeralds and vaines of diuers other pretious stones, a worke incredible. The height thereof two foote and a halfe, the fashion in maner round, the breadth by diameter one foote and a halfe, and the circumference consisted of three diameters. From the heads of the eagles the bottome or foote of the vessell did ascend vp one triens, and a border going about the thicknes of a
89b. hand, from which border to the beginning of the belly of the vessel, and to the bottome of the foote with this hand breadth, was a foote and a halfe. Vpon this stood the forme of the vessell aforesaid one handfull and a halfe broader, which halfe handfull was distributed to the border, about the brimme of foulding leaues and flowers standing out from the hyacinth. The diameter two

quarters & a halfe. Vnder this border there did stick out round about certaine proportions like walnut shels, or the keele of a ship, somwhat thicke and broade at the vpper end, and lessing themselues to nothing belowe. From thence to the orifice it did rise vp two quarters and a halfe, furrowed with turning champhers, and an excellent sime: and in steed of eares to take vp the vessell by, it had two lips standing out and turning in round like the head of a base viall.

Vnder and aboue the borders, the vessel was wrought with turned gululs, vnduls, and imbossings, and with such lineaments were the borders wrought, both vnder and aboue.

Vppon the border in the necke of the couer, were two halfe rings, suppressed in the border by transuersion, one of them iust against another, which were holden in the biting teeth of two Lysarts, or byting Dragons of greene emerauld, bearing out from the couer. They stoode with their serpentlike feete vpon the lower part of the couer vnder the necke, betwixt the which and the lower vessell was one quantitie, and from his vpper gracilament descending, he ioyned with the turned in sime of the circumferent lymbus or verdge, where they did closely byte togither. This couer to the necke was made in skalie worke of *Hyacinth*, except the vaynes of smaragd, for the little dragons, their bellies and feetes fastening to the skalie couer. These little dragons one against an other, their brests and throtes hollowing out from the border and the couer, and their tayles turning vpwards againe, did serue for the eares of the couer, iust ouer them of the lower vessell.

The lower turning about, where the couer did close with the vessell being of two parts, ioyned togither with an excellent foliature, halfe a foote broad, as if they had bin inseparable.

The bodie of this vessell was all run ouer with a Vine, the stringes and vaines whereof, and small curling twists, were of Topas, farre better then is founde in the Ilande Ophiadis, the leaues of fine smaragd, and the braunches of Amethist, to the sight most beautifull, and to the vnderstanding a woonderfull contemplable. The subiect vessell appearing thorough the same of Hiacinth so round and polished, as any wheele can send foorth : except, vnder the leaues there was a substaunce left, which helde the foliature to the vessell of Hiacinth, passing ouer and separated from the subiect. The hollowed and bending leaues with all the other lapicidariall lineaments, were performed with such an emulation of nature as was woonderfull.

Let vs nowe returne to the circumferent brim of the pretious vessell. In the smooth partes whereof, vppon eyther sides of the tayles of the Lysarts, I behelde two hystorials woorthy of regard, ingrauen in this sort. Vpon the foreside of the vessell, the representation of *Iupiter*, holding in his right hande a glistering sword, of the vayne of the Æthiopian Chrysolits : and in the other hande a thunder bolt of shining Rubie. His countenance sauour of the vaine of Gallatits, and crowned with stars like lightening, he stoode vpon an aultar of Saphyre. Before his fearefull maiestie, were a beuie of Nymphs, seauen in number, apparrelled in white, proffering with their sweete voices to sing, and after transforming themselues into greene trees like emeralds full of azure flowers, and bowing themselues downe with deuotion to his power : Not that they were all transformed into leaues, but the first into a tree, hir feete to rootes, their armes and heads into braunches, some more then other, but in a shewe that they must followe all alike, as appeared by their heads.

Vpon the other Anaglyph, I did behold a merrie pleasant maiesticall personage, like a yoong fat boye, crowned with two folding serpents, one white, and the other blacke, tied into a knot. Hee rested delightfullie vnder a plentifull vine tree full of ripe grapes, and vpon the top of the frame there were little naked boies, climing vp and sitting aloft gathering the ripe clusters: others offering them in a basket to the God, who pleasantly receiued them: other

some lay fast a sleepe vpon the ground, being drunke with the sweet iuice of the grape. Others applying themselues to the worke of mustulent autumne: others singing and piping; all which expression was perfected by the workman in pretious stones, of such colour as the naturall liuelinesse of euery vaine, leafe, flower, berrie, body, proportion, shape, and representation required. And in this imagerie, although it was very small, yet there was no defect to be found in the least part belonging thereunto, but perfectly to be discerned.

Out of this former described vessell did spring vp a

greene flourishing vine, the twisting branches thereof full set with clusters of grapes, the tawny berries of Indian Amethyst, and the leaues of greene Silenitis of Persia: Not subiect to the change of the moone, delighted of *Cupid*. This tree shadowed the chariot: At euery corner of this triumphant chariot vpon the plaine where the vessell stood, was placed a candlesticke, of excellent workmanship, vpon three feet of red corrall, well liked of the ruder sort, resist-

ing lightening and tempests, fauourable and preseruatiue to the bearer: The like were not found vnder the head of *Gorgon* of Persia, nor in the Ocean *Erythreum*. The steale of one of the candlesticks was of white corrall, beloued of *Diana*, of a conuenient length, with round knobs and ioints, in height two foote. Another was of most fine stone *Dionisias*, hauing spots growing from a blackish to a pure red, the same pounded smelleth sweetly. The third was of perfect *Medea* of the colour of darke gold, and hauing the smell of Nectar. The fourth of pretious *Nebritis* from a blacke growing to a white and greene. Out of the hollowed steales whereof, there ascended vp a pyramidall flame of euerlasting fire, continually burning. The brightness of the works expressed through the reflexion of

the lights, and the sparkling of the pretious stones were such, as my eies dazeled to behold them.

About which heauenly triumph, with a maruellous and solemne pompe, infinite troups of Nymphs, their faire and plentifull tresses falling loose ouer their shoulders, some naked with aprons of goates skins and kids, others with tymbrels and flutes, making a most pleasaunt noise, as in the daunce called Thiasus, in the trieteric of *Bacchus*,

with green leaffie sprigs and vine branches, instrophyated
91. about their heads and wasts, leaping and dauncing before the triumphs : immediately after the triumphs followed an olde man vpon an asse, and after him was led a goate adorned for a sacrifice: And one that followed after carrieng vpon hir head a fanne, making an vnmeasurable laughter, and vsing furious and outragious gestures.

This was the order of these *Mimallons*, *Satirs*, and seruants to Bacchus, bawds, *Tyades*, *Naiades* and such as followed after.

THE FIFTEENTH CHAPTER.

The Nymph doth shew to Poliphilus the multitude of yoong Louers, and their Loues, what they were, and in what sort beloued.

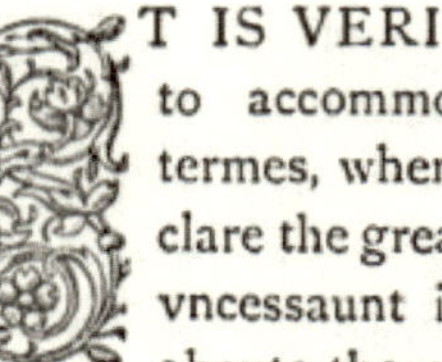

T IS VERIE HARD FOR A MAN to accommodate his speech to apte termes, whereby he may expresslie declare the great pompe, indefinite triumph, vncessaunt ioie and delightfull iettings aboute these rare and vnseene chariots, and being once vndertaken, it is as vneasie to leaue off: besides the notable companie of yoong youths, and the increasing troups of innumerable faire and pleasant Nymphs, more sharpe witted, wise, modest, and discreet, then is ordinarily seene in so tender yeeres, with their beardles Louers, scarce hauing downy cheekes, pleasantly deuising with them matters of Loue. Manie of them hauing their torches burning, others pastophorall, some with ancient spoiles vppon the endes of streight staues, and others with diuers sorts of Trophes vpon launces, curiouslie hanging, caried before the mystical triumphs, with shouting resounds aboue in the aire. Some with windeinstruments of diuers fashions and maner of windings, sagbuts and flutes. Others with heauenly voices singing with ineffable delights, and exceeding solace, past man's reason to imagine : within them passed about the glorious triumphs, turning vpon the florulent ground, and green swoord, a place dedicated to the happie, without anie stub or tree, but the fielde was as a plaine coequate medowe of sweete hearbes and pleasaunt flowers, of all sorts of colours, and sundry varieng fashions, yeelding so fragrant a smell as is possible to speake of, not burnt with the extreeme heat of the sunne, but moderate, the ground moystened with sweete ryuers, the aire pure and cleane, the daies all alike, the earth continually greene, the spring neuer decaieng but renuing, the coole grasse with variable flowers like a painting, remaining alwaies vnhurt, with their deawie freshnesse, reseruing and holding their colours without interdict of time. There grewe the fower sortes of Violets, Cowslops, Melilots, Rose Parsley, or Passeflower, Blew bottles, Gyth, Ladies seale, Vatrachium, Aquilegia, Lillie conually, Amaranth, Flower gentle, Ideosmus, all sorts of sweete pinks, and small flowring hearbs of odoriferous fragrancie and smell, Roses of Persia, hauing the smel of muske and Amber, and innumerable sorts of others without setting, but naturally growing in a woonderfull distribution, peeping out from their greene leaues, and barbs very delightfull to behold.

In this place I might see goodly braue women as the Archadian *Calisto* the daughter of *Lycaon*, with the vnknowen *Diana*. The Lesbian *Antiopa* daughter to *Nycteus*, and mother to *Amphion* and *Zeteus* that built Thebes, with hir satyre. *Issa* the daughter of *Machareus* with hir shepheard. *Antichia* the daughter of *Aceus* and yoong *Danaë*. *Asterie* the daughter to *Cœus*, and *Alchmena* with hir fained husband. Afterward I beheld the pleasant *Ægina* solacing hir selfe with the cleere flood and diuine fire. The daughter of *Fullus* and that of *Menemphus*, with hir counterfeit father, and that other of

Diodes with hir lap full of flowers and a writhing serpent, and the faire yoong gyrle no more sorrowing for the growing of hir hornes. *Astiochia* and *Antigone* the daughter of *Laomedon* solaciously delighting hir selfe in hir storkish plumes, and *Lurisile* the first inuentrix of wheeles. *Garamentide* the dauncing Nymph holding by hir little finger, and washing hir delicate pretie feete from sweate in the riuer Bagrada. After that I beheld a quaile flying, and a faulcon pursuing hir: *Erigone* hauing hir faire shining brest stickt full of sweete grapes, and the f. 92.
daughter of king *Chollus* with hir bull, *Eriphile* and hir changed husband: The daughter of *Alpes* and the virgin *Melantho* with hir dolphin, *Phyllira* the daughter of old *Oceanus* with the father of Chiron. Next hir *Ceres* with hir head instrophyated with ripe eares of corne imbracing the scalie *Hydra:* And the faire Nymph *Lara* sorting with *Argiphon:* and the sweete *Futurna* of the riuer *Numicus.*

And whilest I stood with excessiue delight beholding onely as an ignorant this rare companie and mysticall triumphes, circumsept with these and such like sorts, and so also the delicious fields, but that me thought it was a louely sight to behold, and so I should haue continued: then the gratious Nymph associating and leading me, seeing my simplicitie and carelesnes, with a ready countenance and sweete and pleasant words, without asking, she said thus vnto me: My *Poliphilus*, doest thou see these? (shewing me those of the olde world) these were beloued of *Iupiter*, and this, and this was such a one, and these were in loue with him, by this meanes shewing vnto me their high and mighty linage, and not knowing their names, she in great curtesie told me. Afterward she shewed me a great number of little virgins, vnder the gouernment of three sober and discreete matrones the leaders to so great delight: Adding thereunto very pleasantly (changing hir angellike countenaunce) My *Poliphilus*, thou shalt vnderstand, that no earthly creature can enter in heere without a burning torch as thou seest me, either with extreeme loue and great paines, or for the fauour and company of those three matrones. And from hir hart fetting a deepe sigh, she said: This torch haue I brought hither for thy sake, minding to put it out in yonder temple.

These speeches pearced my hart, they were so delightfull and desired, and so much the more, bicause she called me hir *Poliphilus*. Whereupon I assured my selfe, that she was *Polia*, and from top to the toe I found an extreeme alteration into a supreame delight, my hart flying onely to hir. Which thoughts were bewraied by my countenance, and whispering small sighes.

Which she cunningly perceiuing, brake off this new accident with these words: Oh how many be there which would most gladly behold these triumphes, and therefore *Poliphilus*, addresse thy thoughts to other matters, and behold what noble and woorthy Nymphs shew themselues deseruedly consorted with their amorous louers, curteous and affable: who with sweete and pleasant notes in measured verse, praise and commend one another without wearines, incessantly celebrating their turnes with excessiue delight, and extolling the triumphs, the aire also full of the chirpings of diuers pretie birds, yeelding a diffused charme.

About the first triumph among the reioising companie, the nine Muses did sing, with their leader the diuine Luter *Apollo*.

This verse consisted of *Strophe*, *Antistrophe*, and *Epodus*.

After the triumph followed the faire Parthenopeian

Homer. *Leria*, with a lawrell crowne, accompanied with *Melanthia*, whose habites and voices represented the pride of Greece, whereupon the great Macedon rested his head: She bare a splendent lampe, communicating the light thereof with hir companion; then the rest more excellent both in voice and song.

There the faire Nymph shewed me the auncient *Iphianassa*, and after the old father *Himerinus* his daughters and their drinke, and one betwixt the two Theban brothers: These with pleasant noises, sweete musicke and fine agilities, paste on about the first triumph.

About the second triumph was the noble *Nemesis* with the *Lesbian Corina*, *Delia* and *Neæra*, with diuers others amorous Nymphs, making pleasaunt soundes vppon stringed instruments of yealow wood.

About the thirde triumph, the glorious Nymphs shewed me *Quintilia* and *Cynthea Nauta*, with others, in great solace, making sweete harmonies, and singing pleasant verses: there also I beholde the virgin *Violantilla* with hir Doue, and the other sorrowing for hir Sparrow.

About the fourth triumph, before it went the *Lidian Cloe*, *Lide*, *Neobole*, sweete *Phillis*, and the faire *Lyce Tyburts*, & *Pyra*, with their harps singing and making a most pleasant noyse. After this fourth triumph among the Mænades and sacrificers to *Bacchus*, there folowed an amorous damosell singing in the commendation of the head of hir Louer *Plaon*, she desired hornes. And after them all she shewed me two women, one of them appa- f. 93.
relled in white, and the other in greene, which came hindermost singing togither.

And thus they marched about in a most pleasant and delightfull maner vpon the fresh greene and flourishing plaine : Some instrophiated with laurel, some with myrtle, and others with other sorts of flowers and garlands, incessantly without any wearines or intermission in a perfection of the felicitie of this world, mutually enioying one another's aspect and companie.

THE SIXTEENTH CHAPTER.

The Nymph hauing at large declared vnto Poliphilus the mysticall triumphs and extreeme loue, afterwards she desired him to go on further, where also with great delight he beheld innumerable other Nymphs, with their desired louers, in a thousand sorts of pleasures solacing themselues vpon the greene grasse, fresh shadowes, and by the coole riuers and cleere fountaines. And how Poliphilus there had with madnes almost forgotten himselfe in the passions of desire, but hope did asswage his furie, quieting himselfe in the beholding of the sweete fauour of the faire Nymph.

NOT ONELY HAPPIE BUT ABOUE all other most happie were he, to whom it should be granted continually by speciall fauour to beholde the glorious pompe, high triumphs, beautiful places sweet scituations, togither with the goddesses, halfe goddesses, faire Nymphes of incredible delight and pleasure, but especially to be seconded and accompanied with so honorable a Nymph of so rare and excellent beautie And this I thought not to be the least and smallest point of my felicitie. Now hauing looked vpon these sights, I remained a great space recording of the same, being therewith beyonde measure abundantly contented.

Afterwards, the faire and sweet damsell my guide said thus vnto me: *Poliphilus*, let vs now go a little further. And then immediately we tended our walke toward the f. 93b.

ſresh ſountains and shady riuers, compassing about the flourishing fields with chrystalline currents and gratious streames.

In which cleare water, grew the purple flowering sonne of the Nymph *Liriope*, looking vp from his tender stringes and leaues. And al the ſaire riuers were ſul of other

flowers sweetlie growing among their greene and ſresh leaues. This delightfull place was of a spatious and large circuit, compassed about and inuironed with wood-die mountaines, of a moderate height of greene lawrell, ſruitefull memerels; hearie, & high pine trees, and within the cleere channels, with graueled banks, and in some places the bottom was faire soft yealow sande, where the water ran swifte, and the three leaued driope grew.

There were a great companie of delicate faire Nymphs of tender age, with a redolent flower of bashfulnes, and beyond all credite beautifull, with their beardles louers continuallie accompanied. Among which Nymphs, some verie pleasantly with wanton countenaunces in the cleere streams shewed themselues sportefull and gamesome, hauing taken vppe finelie their thin garments of silke of diuers colours, and holding them in the bouts of their white armes, the forme of their rounde thighs were seene vnder the plytes, and their faire legges were reuealed to the naked knees, the current streames comming vp so high: it was a sight which woulde haue prepared one to that which were vnfit, and if himselfe had been vnable thereunto. And there where the water was most still, turning downe their faire faces of exceeding beautie, and bending their bodies of rare proportion, as in a large goodly glasse they might behould their heauenly shapes, breaking off the same with the motion of their pretie feete, making a noyse with the contrast of the circulating water. Some solaciouslie striuing to go by the tame swimming swans, and sportingly casting water one at another, with the hollownes of their palms: others standing without the water vpon the soft coole grasse, making vp of nosegaies and garlands of sundrie sweete flowers, & giuing the same to their louers as tokens of their fauorable remembraunce, not denieng their sweete kisses, & louing imbracings, with f. 94.
the amorous regardes of their star-like eyes.

And some were set vpon the greene banks not ouergrown with reed and sedge, but finely beautified with sweete hearbs and flowers, among the which the tender Nymphs comming wet out of the water more cleere then *Axius* in

Mygdonia, vnder the vmbragious trees, did sit sporting and deuising one with another in delightfull imbracings, with their reuerencing louers, not cruelly scorning & reiecting them, but with a sociable loue and benigne affablenesse, disposing themselues to the like shew of true affection, their sweete gestures and pleasant behauiours far more gratious to the eie, then flowing teares be to the frowarde and vnmercifull *Cupid*, the sweete fountaines and moist dewes to the green fieldes, and desired forme to vnfashioned matter.

Some did sing amorous sonnets, and verses of loue, breathing out in the same from their inflamed breasts, scalding sighs ful of sweete accents, able to enamorate harts of stone: And to make smooth the ruggednesse of the vnpassageable mountaine *Caucasus*, to staie whatsoeuer furie the harpe of *Orpheus* woulde prouoke, and the fowle and euill fauoured face of *Medusa*, to make any horrible monster tame and tractable, and to stop the continuall prouocation of the deuouring *Scylla*. Some rested their heads in the chaste laps of their faire loues, recounting the pleasaunt deuises of *Iupiter*, and they instrophyating their curled locks with sweete smelling flowers.

Others of them fained that they were forsaken, and seemed to flie and go awaie from them, whom dearely they did affect, and then was there running one after another with loud laughters, and effeminate criengs out, their faire tresses spredding downe ouer their snowie shoulders like threeds of gold, bound in laces of greene silke: Some loose after a Nymphish maner, others bounde vp in attyres of golde set with pearle. Afterwards comming neere togither, they would stowpe downe, and twiching vp the sweete flowers with their faire and tender fingers, fling the same in the faces of their pursuing louers with great pleasure and solace, maintaining their fained disgracings.

Others with great curtesie were putting of Rose leaues one after another into their laced brests, adding after them sweete kisses, some giuing their louers (if ouer-bold) vpon the cheekes with their harmles palmes pretie ticks, making them red like the wheeles of *Phœbus* in a faire and cleere morning: with other new and vnthought contentions, such as loue could deuise. They all being pleasant, merrie, and disposed to delight: Their gestures and motions girlish, and of a virgineall simplicitie, putting on sincere loue without the offence of honorable virtue: Free and exempt from the occursion of griefe or emulation of aduers fortune: Sitting under the shade of the weeping sister of the whited *Phaeton*, and of the immortall *Daphne* and hairie pineapple with small and sharpe leaues, streight Cyprus, greene Orenge trees, and tall Cedars, and others most excellent, abounding with greene leaues, sweete flowers, and pleasant fruits still flourishing in such sort as is inestimable, euenly disposed vpon the gratious banks, & orderly growing in a moderat distance vpon thee grassie ground, inuested with green Vinca peruince or laurel. What hart is so cold and chilling, that would not be stirred vp to heate, manifestly beholding the delightfull duties of reciprocall loue, such as I was perswaded would haue kindled *Diana* hir selfe?

Whereupon I was bold to shew that folly which tormented my inward spirits, enuying to see what others possessed, that was a continuall delight in pleasure and solace without any wearines in full cloying, and thus diuers times my hart being set on fire by my eies, and extreemely burning, my minde still fixed vpon delightfull pleasures and their smacking kisses, and regarding with a curious eie the abounding guerdons of the fethered god, me thought at that instant, that I did beholde the extreeme perfection of pleasure. And by this meanes I stood wauering and out of measure amazed, and as one which had droonke an amorous potion, calling into remembrance the ointments of the mischeeuous *Circes*, the forcible hearbs of *Medea*, the hurtfull songs of *Byrrena*, and the deadly verses of *Pamphile*, I stood doubtfull that my eies had seene somthing more than humane, and that a base, dishonorable, and fraile bodie should not be where immortall creatures did abide.

After that I was brought from these long and doubtfull thoughts and phantasticall imaginations, and remembring all those maruellous diuine shapes and bodies which I had personally seene with mine eies, I then knew that they were not deceitfull shadowes, nor magicall illusions, but that I had not rightly conceiued of them.

And now with earnest consideration among these beholding the most excellent Nymph fast by me, my eies filled with amorous darts ceased not to wound my passionate hart, by means wherof incontinently all my wandering thoughts were stirred vp, compact, and fixed vpon hir their desired obiect, recalling my mortified soule afresh to be tormented in his first flames, which most cruelly I suffered, in that I durst not be bold to aske if she were my desired *Polia*, for she had put me in some doubt thereof before, and now fearing to offend hir with my being ouer bolde, and ore troublesome with my rude and vntilled toong, diuers times when my voice was breaking out betwixt my lips, vpon that occasion I suppressed the same. But what she should be, it was beyond my compasse to imagine, and I stood as suspicious thereof, as the deceiued *Socia* with the fained *Altantiades*. Thus with diligent regards and cordiall searches examining hir heauenly features inuaded with a burning desire beyond measure, I said to my self: O that I might be, if it were possible, a freeman in such a place, for no sorrow shoulde greeue me, nor imminent danger should make me afraid: although that frowarde fortune shoulde oppose hir selfe against me, I woulde spende my life without any regard therof, not refusing to vndertake the laborsome and great enterprise of the two gates shewed to the sonne of *Amphitrio*.

To spend the prime of my youth and pleasure of my yeers in the mortall daungers of the merciles seas, and in the fearfull places of *Trinacria*, with the excessive trauels and terrors of *Vlysses*, in the darke caue of the horrible *Polyphem*, the son of *Neptune*, to be transformed in the companie of *Calypso*, although I lost my life, or indured the most hard & long seruitude of *Androdus*, for all wearines is forgotten where loue is vehement. To vndertake with the amorous *Minalion* and *Ileus* to runne with f. 95b.
Atalanta, or to com but in such sort as the strong and mightie *Hercules* for his loue *Deianira*, did with the huge *Achelous*, so as I might atchieue so gratious a fauor, and attaine to so high delight, as the remaining in these solacious places, and aboue all to enioy the precious loue and inestimable good wil of hir, more faire without comparison then *Cassiopeia*, of better fauour then *Castiamira*. Ah me, my life and death is in hir power! And if so be that I seeme vnwoorthie of hir fellowshippe and amorous commers, yet would God it might be granted me as a speciall rewarde and priuiledge to looke vpon hir: and then I saide to my selfe, oh *Poliphilus*, if these heauie and burthenous weights of amarous conceits do oppresse thee;

the sweetenes of the fruite doth allure thee thereunto, and if the peremptorie dangers strike thee into a terror, the hope of the supportation and helpe of so faire a Nymph will animate thee to be resolute. Thus my thought being diuers, I said, Oh God, if this be that desired *Polia* which I see at this present, and whose precious impression without intermission. I haue stil born in my burning and wounded hart fro[m] the first yeers of my loue vntil this present, I am contented with all sorrows, & besides hir, I desire no other request but only this, that she may be drawne to my feruent loue, that it may be with vs alike, or that I may be at liberty, for I am no longer able to desemble my griefe, or hide the extremity of my smart, I die liuing, & liuing am as dead: I delight in that which is my griefe: I go mourning: I consume my self in the flame, & yet the flame doth norish me, & burning like gold in the strong cement, yet I find my self like cold yce. Ah wo is me, that loue should be more greeuous vnto me then the weight of *Inarime* to *Typhon*. It disperseth me more, then the rauenous vulturs the glomerated bowels of *Tityus:* It holdeth me in more, then the labirinth crooking: It tosseth me more, then the northeast winds the calme seas: It teareth me woorse then *Acteons* dogges their flieng master: It troubleth my spirits more then horrible death doth them who desire to liue: It is more direfull to my vext hart, then the crocidils bowels to *Ichneumon*. And so much the more is my greefe, that with all the wit I haue, I knowe not to thinke in what part of the worlde I shoulde be, but streight before the sweete fire of this halfe goddesse, which without any corporall substance consumeth me: hir aboundant and faire yealow haire, a snare and net for my hart to be masked in: hir large and phlegmatique forehead, like white lillies, bynd me in as with a withe: hir pearcing regards take away my life as sweete prouocations to afflict me: hir roseall cheekes do exasperate my desire, hir ruddie lips continue the same, and hir delicious breasts like the winter snow vpon the hyperboreall mountaines, are the sharp spurs and byting whip to my amorous passions: hir louely gestures and pleasant countenance do draw my desire to an imaginatiue delight, heaping vp my sorrow. And to all these insulting martyrdoms and greeuous vexations of that impious and deceitfull *Cupid* I laie open, mightilie striuing to beare them, and no waie able to resist them, but to suffer my selfe to be ouercome: neither coulde I shun the same, but remained still as one vnawares lost in the Babylonian fen.

Oh *Titius*, thou canst not perswade me that thy paine is equall with mine, although that the vultures teare open thy breast, and taking out thy smoking warm hart, do pluck it in peeces with their crooked beaks, and pinch the same in their sharpe tallents, eating vp also the rest of thy flesh, vntill they haue ingorged themselues, & within a while after thou renewed againe, they begin afresh to prey vpon thee. Thou hast a time to be reuiued againe, and made sound as euer thou wert: but two eies without all pitie or intermission haue wounded me, deuour or consume me, leauing me no time of rest, or space to be comforted.

And hauing had these discourses with my selfe, I began secretly to mourne and weepe, and desire a way that I might die, fetching deepe sighes as if my hart had torne in sunder with euery one of them. And diuers times I had purposed with a lamentable voice to desire hir helpe, for that I was at the point of death: but as one drowned and ouerwhelmed, I deemed that way to be vaine, and to no purpose, and therfore furiously, and as one of a raging spirit I thought thus: Why doest thou doubt, *Poliphilus*? Death for loue is laudable, and therefore my greeuous and malignant fortune, my sorrowful accident and hard hap in the loue of so beautifull a Nymph will be writ and reported when I shall lie interred. The same will be sung in doleful tunes vpon sweete instruments of musicke, manifesting the force of hurtfull loue.

And thus continuing the follie of my thoughts, I said: It may be that this Nymph, by al likehoods, is some reuerend goddesse, and therefore my speeches will be but as the crackling reedes of Archadia in the moist and fennie sides of the riuer Labdone, shaken with the sharpe east wind, with the boisterous north, cloudy south & rainie south west wind. Besides this, the gods will be seuere reuengers of such an insolencie, for the companions of *Vlysses* had been preserued from drowning and shipwracke, if they had not stolne *Apollos* cattell kept by *Phaetusa* and hir sister *Lampetia*. *Orion* had not beene slaine by a scorpion, if he had not attempted the cold & chast *Diana*, and therefore if I should vse any indecencie against the honor of this Nymph in any sort, such like reuenge or woorse woulde be vsed vpon me. At last getting foorth of these changeable thoughts, I did greatly comfort my selfe in beholding and contemplating the excellent proportion and sweete sauour of this ingenuous and most rare Nymph, containing in hir al whatsoeuer that may prouoke amorous conceits and sweete loue, giuing from hir faire eies so gratious and fauorable regards as thereby I somewhat tempered my troublesome and vnbrideled thoughts. And my resounding sighes reflexed with a flattering hope (oh the amorous foode of louers and sauce of salt teares) by these and no other rains I did manage my vehement thoughts, and made them stop in a conceiued hope, fixing mine eies with excessiue delight vpon hir faire bodie and well disposed members, by all which, my discontented desires were gently mitigated and redeemed from that furie and amorous fire, which so neere had bred the extremitie of my passions.

THE SEVENTEENTH CHAPTER.

The Nymph leadeth the inamored Poliphilus to other pleasant places, where he beheld innumerable Nymphs solacing them, and also the triumph of Vertumnus and Pomona.

BY NO MEANES I WAS ABLE TO resist the violent force of *Cupids* artillerie, and therefore the elegant Nymph hauing amorously gotten an irreuocable dominion ouer me a miserable louer, I was inforced to follow still after hir moderate steps, which led me into a spatious and large plaine, the conterminate bound of the flowered greene & sweet smelling vallie, where also ended the adorned mountaines and fruitfull hils, shutting vp the entrance into this golden countrie, full of incredible delight with their ioining togither: couered ouer with green trees of a conspicuous thicknes & distance, as if they had been set by hand, as Yew trees, wild Pynes, vnfruitfull but dropping Resin, tall pineapple, straight Firre, burning Pitch trees, the spungie Larix, the aierie Teda beloued of the mountains, celebrated and preserued for the festiuall Oreades. There both of vs walked in the greene and flowering plaine, shee being my guide through the high cypres trees, the broad leaued beech, coole shadie okes full of maste, and other hornebeames, pricking iuniper, weake hasell, spalt ash, greene lawrell, and humbryferous esculies, knottie plane trees & lyndens moouing by the sweet breath of the

Larix, is a tree hauing leaues like the pine, & good for building, it will neither rot, woorm-eate nor burne to coales.

Teda, is a tree out of the which issueth a liquor more thinne than pitch.

Oreades, be countrie Nymphs.

Lyndens, or teile trees, in Latin *Tiliæ*, they beare a fruit as big as a bean, hauing within seedes like anyse seedes.

Dryades, be Nymphs of the woods.

pleasant Zephirus, whistling through their tender branches, with a benigne and fauorable impulsion.

All which greene trees were not thickly twisted togither, but of a conuenient distaunce one from another, and all of them so aptly distributed as to the eie the sight thereof bred great delight.

This place was frequented with countrie Nymphs and *Dryades*, their small and slender wastes being girded with a brayding of tender corules of sprigs, leaues, and flowers, and vpon their heads their rising vp haires, were compassed about as with garlands. Amongst them were the horned faunes, and lasciuious satyres, solemnising their faunall feasts, being assembled togither out of diuers places, within this fertile & pleasant cuntrie: bearing in their hands so tender green and strange boughs, as are not to be found in the wood of the goddes *Feronia*, when the inhabitants carrie hir image to the fire.

Feronia a goddesse of the woods. *Dabulam*, a fertile place in Arabia. *Scænits*, be a people in Arabia, that dwell altogither in tents. *Sauromatans*, be people of Sarmatia, which is a large cuntry, reaching from Germany & the riuer Vistula to Hycænia, and is deuided into two parts Europea and Asiatica. *Lynx* is a beast spotted, but in shape like a wolph, being quicke of sight. *Hamadryades* were nymphs of the wood

From thence we entered into a large square inclosure compassed about with broade walkes, straight from one corner to another, with a quick-set vpon either sides, in height one pace, of pricking iuniper thicke yet togither, and mixt with box, compassing about the square greene mead. In the rowes of which quick-set there were symmetrially planted the victorious palme-trees, whose branches were laden with fruite, appearing out of their husks, some blacke, some crymosen, and many yealow, the like are not to be found in the land of Ægypt, nor in Dabulam among the Arabian Scænits, or in Hieraconta beyond the Sauromatans. All which were intermedled with greene Cytrons, Orenges, Hippomelides, Pistack trees, Pomegranats, Meligotons, Dendromirts, Mespils, and Sorbis, with diuers other fruitfull trees.

In this place vppon the greene swoord of the flowering

mead, and vnder the fresh and coole shadowes, I might behold a great assemblie met togither of strange people, & such as I had neuer before seene, full of ioyes and pastimes, but basely apparrelled, some in fauns skins, painted with white spots, some in lynx skins, others in leopards : and manie had fastened togither diuers broad leaues,

and *Symenides* *Vertumnus* the God of fruits.

instrophiating them with sundrie flowers, therewithall couering their nakednes, singing, leaping, and dauncing with great applause.

These were the Nymphs Hamadryades, pleasantly compassing vppon either sides the flowered *Vertumnus*, hauing vppon his heade a garlande of roses, and his gowne lap full of faire flowers, louing the station of the woollie ramme. He sate in an ancient fashioned carre, drawne by fower horned fauns or satyrs, with his louing and faire wife *Pomona*, crowned with delicate fruits, hir haire hanging downe ouer hir shoulders, of a flaxen colour, and thus she sate participating of hir husbands pleasure and quiet, and at hir feete laie a vessell called Clepsydra. In hir right hand she held a copie full of flowers, fruits, and greene leaues, and in hir left hande a branch of flowers, fruits and leaues. f. 98.

Clepsydra is sometime taken for a diall measuring time by the running of water, but here for a pot to water a garden and yoong sectlings in a nourcery for an orchyard.

Before the carre and the fower drawing satyrs, there marched two faire Nymphs, the one of them bare a trophæ with a præpendant table, whereupon was written this title,

Integerrimam corporis valetudenem & stabile robur castasque mensarum delitias, & beatam animi securitatem cultoribus me offero.

And the other bare a trophæ of certaine greene sprigges bound togither, and among them diuers rurall instruments fastened. These passed on thus after the ancient maner, with great ceremonies, and much solemnitie, compassing about a great square stone like an aulter, standing in the middest of this faire mead, sufficiently moystened with current streames from beautifull fountaines.

This square stone or aulter was of pure white marble, curiouslie cut by a cunning lapicidarie, vpon euery front wherof was a woonderfull goodly expression, of an elegant image, so exact, as the like else-where is hardly to be found.

This first was a faire goddesse, hir treces flieng abroad, girded with roses and other flowers, vpon a thin vpper garment couering hir beautifull and pleasant proportion. She helde hir right hand ouer an ancient vessell, in maner of a chafing-dish, called Chytropodus, sending foorth a flame of fire, into the which shee did cast roses and flowers, and in the other hand she held a branch of sweete myrtle, full of berries. By hir side stoode a little winged boy smiling, with his bowe and arrowes. Ouer hir head were two pigeons. And vnder the foote of this figure was written

Florido veri S.

Vpon the other side I beheld in an excellent caruing, the representation of a damosell of a maidenly countenaunce, whose stately maiestie gaue great commendation to the curious deuise of the workeman. She was crowned
f. 98v. with a garland of wheat eares, hir haire flingering abroade, and hir habyte Nymphish. In hir right hand she held a copie full of rype graine, and in the other hand three eares of corne, vpon their strawie stalks. At hir feete lay a wheat sheaue bound vp, and a little boy with gleanings of corne in either hands. The subscription was this.

Flauæ Messi S.

Vpon the third side was the likenes in a deuine aspect naked of a yoong boy, crowned with vine leaues, and of a wanton countenance, holding in his left hand certaine clusters of ripe grapes, and in the other, a copie full of grapes which did hang ouer the mouth thereof. At his feete laie a hayrie goate and this writing vnder.

Mustulento Autumno S.

The last square did beare vpon it a kingly image passing well cut, his countenance displeasant and austere, in his left hand he held a scepter vp into the heauens, the aire cloudie, troublesome and stormie, and with the other hand reaching into the clouds full of haile. Behinde him also the aire was rainie and tempestuous. He was couered with beasts skins, and vpon his feete he ware sandals, where vnder was written,

Hiemi Æoliæ S.

From thence the most faire and pleasant Nymph brought me towards the sea side and sandie shore, where we came to an olde decaied temple, before the which vpon the fresh and coole hearbs, vnder sweete shadie trees we sate downe and rested our selues, my eies very narrowly beholding, with an vnsatiable desire, in one sole perfection and virgineall bodie, the accumulation and assembly of all beauties; an obiect interdicting my eies to behold any gracious, that except, or of so great content.

Where refreshing in a secret ioy with new budding conceits my burning hart, and leauing off vulgar and common follies, I began to consider of the intelligible effect of f. 99.
honest loue, and withall of the cleerenes of the skies, the sweete and milde aire, the delightfull site, the pleasant countrie, the green grasse decked with diuersity of flowers, the faire hils adorned with thicke woods, the quiet time, fresh windes, and fruitfull place, beautifully enriched with diffluent streames, sliding downe the moist vallies betwixt the crooked hils in their grauelled channels, and into the next seas with a continued course softly vnlading themselues.

Thessalie is a region of Greece, hauing vpon the one side Macedonia, and on the other Bœotia, reaching

A ground most healthfull, the grasse coole and sweet: and from the trees resounded the sweete consents of small chirping birds. The flouds and fields of Thessalie must giue place to this.

And there sitting thus togither among the sweete

flowers and redolent roses, I fastened mine eies vpon this heauenly shape of so faire and rare a proportion, whereunto my sences were so applied, drawen and addicted, that my hart was ouerwhelmed with extreeme delights, so as I remained senceles, and yet cast into a curious desire to vnderstand and knowe what should be the reason and cause that the purple humiditie in the touch of hir bodie, in the smoothnes of hir hand should be as white as pure milke: and by what meanes that nature had bestowed in hir faire bodie the fragrant sweetnes of Arabia. And by what industrie in hir starrie forehead pampynulated with threds of gold aptly disposed, she had infixed the fairest part of the heauens, or the splendyeant Heraclea.

betweene Thermopylæ, and the riuer Pineus, euen to the sea side, it is the garden of Grecia. *Heraclea*, is the name of diuers faire cities, one in the confines of Europe, another in Italie & in Pontus by the riuer Licus, also in Narbon by Rodanus, also in Caria, Crete & Lydia, whereof the Lodestone taketh his name.

Afterward letting fall mine eies towards hir prety feete, I beheld them inclosed in red leather cut vpon white, fastened vpon the instep with buttons of gold in loopes of blew silke. And from thence I returned vpward my wanton regard to hir straight necke compassed about with a carkenet of orient pearle, striuing but not able to match with the whitenes of the sweet skin. From thence descending down to hir shining breast and delitious bosome, from whence grew two round apples, such as *Hercules* neuer stole out of the garden of *Hesperides*. Neither did euer *Pomona* behold the like to these two standing vnmoueable in hir roseall breast, more white than hils of snowe in the going downe of the sunne. Betwixt the which there
f. 99b. passed downe a delicious vallie, wherein was the delicate sepulcher of my wounded hart exceeding the famous *Mausolea*.

Hesperides, were the 3 daughters of Atlas, Ægle, Aretusa and Hesperetusa, who had an orchard of golden apples, kept by a dragon whom Hercules slew & tooke away the apples.

A sepulcher built by Artemisia in the honor of hir husbande Mausolus king of Cania.

I then being content with a wounded hart full well vnderstanding that mine eies had drawen it dying into all these elegant parts. Yet neuertheles I could not so bridle and suppresse my amorous inflamed sighes, or so closely couer them, but that they would needs expresse my inward desire.

By meanes whereof she was changed from contagious loue, and striking with hir stolen regards (enuying the same) she turned it vpon me, so as I perceiued an incensing fire pruriently diffusing it selfe through my inward parts and hollow veines: and during the contemplate beholding of hir most rare and excellent beautie, a mellifluous delight and sweete solace constrained me thereunto. Thus discordinately beaten with the importune spur of vnsatiable desire, I found my selfe to be set vpon with the mother of loue, inuironed round about with hir flamigerous sonne, and inuaded with so faire a shape, that I was with these and others so excellent circumstances brought into such an agonie of minde and sicknes of bodie, and in such sort infeebled, that the least haire of hir head was a band forcible ynough to hold me fast, and euery rowled tramell a chaine and shackle to fetter me, being fed with the sweetnes of hir beautie, and hooked with the pleasant baits of hir amorous delights, that I was not able with whatsoeuer cunning deuise to resist the inuading heates and prouoking desires still comming vpon me, that I determined rather to die than longer to endure the same, or in this solitarie place to offer hir any dishonor.

Then againe I was determined with humble requests and submissiue intreaties to say thus:

Alas most delighted *Polia*, at this present to die by thee is a thing that I desire, and my death if it were effected by these thy small, slender and faire hands, the ende thereof should be more tolerable, sweete and glorious vnto me, bicause my hart is compassed about with such tormenting flames, still more and more cruelly increasing and burning the same without pitie or intermission, so as by meanes thereof I am bereft of all rest.

And heerewithall intending to put in execution another
100. determinate purpose, behold my hart was tormented with more sharpe flames, that me thought I was all of a light fire. Ah wo is me, what wert thou aduised to do *Poliphilus?* Remember the violence done to *Deianira* and

the chaste Roman lady. Consider what followed them for a reward, and diuers others.

Call to minde that mighty princes haue beene reiected of their inferiors, how much more then a base and abiect person, but tract of times giueth place to them which except the bountie thereof. Time causeth the fierce lions to be tame, and whatsoeuer furious beast: the small ant by long trauell laieth vp hir winter foode in the hard tree, and shall not a diuine shape lying hid in a humane bodie take the impression of feruent loue, and then holding the same, shake off all annoyous and vexing passions, hoping to enioy amorous fruits, desired effects, and triumphing agonismes.

The Nymph *Polia* perceiuing well the change of my colour and blood comming in more stranger sort than *Tripolion*, or *Teucrion*, thrise a day changing the colour of his flowers, and my indeuoring to sende out scalding sighes deeply set from the bottome of my hart, she did temper and mitigate the same with hir sweete and friendly regards, pacifieng the rage of my oppressing passions, so as notwithstanding my burning minde in these continuall flames and sharpe prouocations of loue, I was aduised patiently to hope euen with the bird of Arabia in hir sweet nest of small sprigs, kindled by the heate of the sunne to be renewed.

FINIS.

CHISWICK PRESS:—C. WHITTINGHAM AND CO.,
TOOKS COURT, CHANCERY LANE.

www.ingramcontent.com/pod-product-compliance
Lightning Source LLC
Chambersburg PA
CBHW030634030726
47497CB00006B/1780

* 9 7 8 3 3 3 7 4 3 8 8 5 2 *